Outsider

BOOK 3
SECRET OF ALBA

Lindsey Winsemius

Did you enjoy the Secret of Alba series? Don't forget to leave a review!

You can also join my mailing list to find out first about promotions and new releases.
Lindseywinsemius.com

Want to name a character, or tell me what book you'd like to read next? Check out my Reader Exclusives!

Get a glimpse of my upcoming Contemporary Romantic Suspense *Just to Keep You.*

All on www.lindseywinsemius.com!

Published by ApogeeINVENT
www.apogeeinvent.com

ISBN-13: 978-0692749623
ISBN-10: 0692749624
BISAC: Fiction / Romance / Science Fiction

First Edition September 2016

To my children; you are my biggest adventure.

And to my girlfriends, who are absolutely essential to my survival.

Maggie H-G, this book would never have happened without you. Thanks for being my cheerleader, beta reader, booth babe, and fellow SAHM in the trenches, fighting beside me for our sanity.

SASSy ladies, Kelsey, Mikhila, Maryann, Natasha, and everyone not mentioned who has helped and supported me through this publishing process.

This series is about love between couples and for family, but it is also very much about friendship. I can't tell you what your support means to me. XOXO

And Joe and Dwight, thanks for humoring this side passion of mine. I blame you, Joe, for getting me started on this journey.

Chapter 1

"This is our new reality. Embrace it and flourish." - Recorded Speech by Consul Cecilia Delacroix

The steady drip, drip, drip of the alley overwhelmed his senses as he stood, listening. His arm was around the petite woman beside him, her face dark in the shadows so he was unable to make out her features.

But he knew he needed to protect her. He would do anything to keep her safe.

The shadows around him began shifting slightly, making his heart freeze in his chest. The drip, drip, drip was so loud, he couldn't hear himself think. Growling with frustration, he stepped forward, straining to see in the dark. He had no weapon besides his fists.

The shadows exploded around him, blow after blow reigning down on his head, shoulders, back... the pain was nothing compared to the fear nearly paralyzing him as he watched blood spill onto the pavement.

Drip. Drip. Drip.

Not his blood.

Hers.

*   *   *

Vicktor March awoke with a rush, sitting up so fast his head hit the bunk above him, his ElectroMagnetic Weapon gripped in his fist.

He cursed as reality swiftly returned. He wasn't in an alley of New Glory, but in the recruit lodgings of Alba's Training Grounds.

Drip. Drip. Drip.

The steady drip of water down the stone walls enraged him further. Goddamn Trent, why couldn't he have decent sleeping quarters for his men? This was fucking medieval.

He ran his hands over his face, trying to wipe away the remnants of the disturbing dream he hadn't had in years. Glancing at the bright digital clock above the door, he swung his legs over the side of the bed. It was almost time to get up, anyhow.

Tying his hair back in a short ponytail at the nape of his neck, he splashed water on his face, eyeing it in the small mirror above the sink.

His hazel eyes were dark and shadowy, the lines of his face taut with tension that still lingered from his restless sleep. His square jaw was hidden beneath a trimmed beard, the face that had been nationally recognizable in the Southern Empire as a young man now covered.

He'd successfully remained hidden for nearly a decade, believed dead by everyone he'd left behind in the nation on the east side of old America.

Until now. To help his nemesis-turned-friend, Marcus Trent, Vick had made a little trip to the Empire for the first time in ten years. Had seen the people who had thought him dead, and become more than the dead son of the President. He'd become a traitor, helping Marcus and his team escape the city with captured Alban Lina Rhodes and the coveted Technology that had caused the world's downfall once before. And now might again.

Turning away from the haunted gaze in the mirror, Vick dressed in his worn t-shirt and jeans. Today they would decide the fate of his younger brother, a former Southern Empire spy.

Guess he'd better show a little brotherly support and at least show up.

*   *   *

Vick slouched against the cold stone wall of the Alban Training Grounds. His watchful hazel eyes belied the casualness of his stance. He'd been spending way too much time lately in this city. He missed his isolated existence in the tiny outpost town of Vicksburg.

The other inhabitants of the room leaned in around a small metal table, discussing the future of the Southern Empire after its former President was forcibly deposed and incarcerated.

The President, who was also his psychotic mother who'd killed his father and tried to kill him.

But hell, whose family wasn't dysfunctional?

Qui asi sea. His father's favorite phrase.

So be it.

Marcus grilled Vick's younger brother, Jayden March, about the current Empire leaders that had taken over with Jay's help.

Jay answered each question, but it was apparent that he just wanted out of the whole political mess.

Vick couldn't blame him. It was the reason he'd faked his own death and settled here on the old California coast.

He tried to ignore the cold trickles of fear and desperation that arose each time he thought of his past; of the dysfunctional family and dangerous existence he'd barely escaped.

Shifting his muscular form again on the uncomfortable stool, Vick reigned in his meandering thoughts and tried to focus on the men's discussion.

"It will be months if not years before they reorganize enough to even think about returning for the Technology," Jay assured Marcus. He cast a quick look at Vick, doing his own uncomfortable shifting. The chairs in the interrogation rooms weren't built for comfort. "They remember how easily you almost destroyed New Glory with it last time. As long as they feel safe from your nation, they'll keep to themselves. The Southern Empire is a mess right now without the fear of President March's retaliation to keep the regions in line. I don't envy the current leaders. They might have a fight on their hands before this is all over to avoid secessions."

"What about *her*," Vick finally spoke. "She can't be completely without support, and she'll never give up. Not as long as she's alive."

"I know the team guarding her. They'll notify me of any changes." Jay looked again briefly at his brother. Both men had been treading carefully around one another. They'd never been close, and now they were practically strangers. Had until recently been enemies.

"I would have killed her," Vick said softly, his eyes hard.

Jay leaned back, his own gaze guarded. "I considered it. But it seemed like an unnecessary move that would completely alienate her supporters and create more chaos. This way, the people are given a rational reason, and the law is upheld."

Vick said nothing, but his disapproval was obvious.

Marcus intervened. "My men in the Empire have confirmed your claims. I am still a little unclear about your motives, however. Why do it? And why come here to tell us?"

Jay grinned, a look Vick had seen in the mirror many times. It was eerie how much alike he and his brother were, even after all these years apart.

"You've never done anything crazy for a woman?"

Marcus paused for a long moment, then nodded abruptly. Vick grinned, too, thinking of Marcus' dramatic changes recently all because of one small yet opinionated lady.

"What will you do now?" Marcus asked.

"Hell if I know," Jay answered. "I found I have a talent for gardening—"

"Forget it," Marcus interrupted bluntly. "We won't kill you, but you will not be welcome here in Alba."

Jay was silent for a moment and then nodded. "I understand that. I wouldn't trust me, either. If you don't mind, I'd like to say goodbye to Lina."

Marcus nodded. "Make it quick. Vick will escort you to the gate. He was leaving himself." Marcus glanced over at him, and Vick raised one brow.

Yeah, it was past time for him to return home. He just had one stop to make first...

*   *   *

Jay fought the frustration threatening to overcome him. He'd come to find a future here with Lina on the west coast, but he'd only been here for two weeks and they were already kicking him out.

He slouched in the passenger seat of Vick's restored Bronco. His brother had always shared their father's love of the antiquated culture from the pre-war era.

So did he, for that matter. He'd just had to hide it from his sociopath mother.

He couldn't blame Vick for trying to escape their life in the Empire. From the corner of his eye, he studied the brother who was practically a stranger to him. Slightly shorter than Jay, but with a broader chest, Vick had been the tinker of the two, and Jay the athlete. As children, everyone had thought they were twins, with barely over a year between their ages and such a close resemblance. Now, however, while Jay wore his hair buzzed short, Vick had let his tawny-brown hair grow long, and sported a full beard trimmed close to his face. He looked every inch the rugged frontiersman he was trying to be.

"You did a nice job on the truck," Jay finally said to break the awkward silence. Vick glanced over.

"Thanks, it took me forever to find the right transmission. And then to convert it to use a powercell instead of gasoline ... that was a bitch of a job."

"The Empire still has plenty of petroleum preserves, so I didn't have to convert my LaFerrai. Runs on high octane."

"No shit," Vick said in awe. "I bet the engine sounds magnificent. The powercells are great, but don't have quite the same punch as old world fuel."

A month ago, Jay would have laughed his ass off at anyone who would suggest he'd be talking antique cars with his presumed-dead brother in Alba. But a lot had changed in a short time.

And he was pretty damn glad of it.

"I think you missed the turn—" Jay began, seeing Lina's mother's road pass by.

"Lina's staying at her brother Stephen's old place," Vick informed him.

"Great," Jay muttered. Stephen's death at the hands of the Southern Empire would always be between them, since he had been part of the Empire's top intelligence team. An enemy spy. If she was living in her brother's house, he wasn't sure if she'd ever get past it.

But then, they'd been doomed since before they started.

Good thing he wasn't afraid of a challenge. He'd given up wealth and power to come to Alba on the chance they wouldn't kill him, and he could be with Lina.

He was still alive, but that didn't mean Lina was going to give him another chance after everything he'd done to her. He'd kidnapped her, stabbed her, threatened her, and dragged her across the entire continent against her will. He couldn't really blame her if she did tell him to go to hell. She had a good thing going here, even if she did claim to care about him. Could she forgive everything he'd done—the man he was—to have some kind of future together?

Vick slowed in front of the stately villa. Slim columns framed the front door of the white stone two-story, the flat roof perfect for viewing the stunning vistas of ocean and city far below.

"I'll pick you up in a few hours. Good luck."

Jay nodded, exiting the vehicle with a strange reluctance mingled with anticipation. Vick disappeared down the cobbled street, leaving Jay standing alone on the walk, feeling like a fool.

What was he doing? Yeah, she'd said that she might love him. And he knew how he felt about her. But what future did they have? He was never going to live in Alba. And how could she, a Patrician to the core, ever leave? Particularly now that she'd found her place.

Could he ask that of her?

Stop pussy-footing around out here and get in there, he told himself, striding forward purposefully.

He knocked, not having an ID to swipe on the door scanner.

After several long moments, the door opened. Lina stood there, her dark hair mussed and eyes red-rimmed.

She looked a mess. A beautiful mess.

"Were you crying?" he asked fearfully. Dammit, what now? He felt so helpless around emotional women. He'd just seen her at the Training Grounds the day prior, and she'd been fine. Happy, even.

Lina laughed, her voice sounding muffled. "No, I'm sick." She paused, sneezing loudly into a tissue she held in her hand.

Jay breathed with relief, his shoulders loosening slightly.

"Well, I could ... make you some soup. Or something."

Lina smiled again, making her puffy eyes look even more swollen.

"I won't turn you down. But I will warn you. I gave this to Helen, so don't blame me if you get sick, too."

"Some things are worth the risk."

Vick pulled up before Helen's villa, sitting in the car for a long moment, thinking. It was highly unlikely anything would ever come from his visits to the prickly but extremely fascinating woman. Since his "death" nearly a decade before, he'd never thought much about the future, just riding the wave to where life took him. He'd avoided attachments, and lived for the moment. He wasn't sure what about Helen made him keep coming back; she certainly had never encouraged him. But he found her appealing to something within him he'd kept on ice for a long time. She was witty, beautiful, and he sensed vulnerability beneath the aloof exterior that made him want to delve deeper.

I must be a masochist. Otherwise I wouldn't be so excited to see a woman who despises me. He was sure it was all an act. A very convincing act.

Pushing himself out, he loped up the walk, pounding on the door. Anticipation built as he waited for a response.

Nothing.

Frowning, he knocked loudly again. He was sure she was home; he'd checked Marcus' locator grid before coming here.

Finally after a third knock, he tried the handle.

Locked.

"Helen, I know you're home. It'll be easier to get rid of me if you just open the door."

Still nothing.

What the hell? She wasn't the type to hide behind a closed door; she'd be more likely to open it and tell him to jump off the cliff.

Concern replaced irritation and he rattled the knob again. Heading around back, he pushed open the unlocked gate that led into her Serenity Garden. It was empty and quiet, the only sound the gentle lapping of the waters of the Serenity Pool in the center.

"Helen?" he called again as he approached the glass sliding door that led inside. Without an ID to scan, the doors wouldn't automatically open for him. He didn't pause, concern leading him straight to the paned door, slamming an elbow through the glass. As the shattered fragments clattered around his feet, he forced the slider open.

A quiet beeping alerted the inhabitants to forced entry, and Vick paused to listen for the sound of Helen's approach.

When no indignant footsteps sounded anywhere in the house, Vick's unease grew to worry.

Something was wrong. Very wrong.

"Helen?" He rushed through the main floor, seeing no sign of the petite woman. Taking the stairs two at a time, he did a methodical search of the upstairs.

It didn't take long for him to find her in the second bedroom. She was under the covers, her body visibly shivering, her breaths coming hard and unevenly.

"Shit."

*   *   *

Helen opened her eyes, knowing she couldn't feign sleep forever. The middle-aged Medella was waiting, a look of disapproval clear on her rounded features.

"You're a trained Medella. You should have had a prenatal monitor inserted the day you suspected you were pregnant," the doctor chastised, checking the IV attached to Helen's arm.

It hadn't taken Vick more than a few minutes to carry Helen to his truck and drive her to the Patrician clinic. Helen was grateful he'd come when he did, but her pride had taken a hit to accept help from him. And now the Medella was lecturing her like a youth. "Your hormones have not fully balanced, since your anti-pregnancy shot was never neutralized. And your immune system—"

"My immune system is depressed, making me highly susceptible to common illnesses such as influenza," Helen interrupted impatiently. "Yes, I am aware. It was foolish of me. I suppose I was avoiding the issue."

The Medella carefully inserted a needle into Helen's IV, watching the blood fill the tube in her hand. "I've run some preliminary tests, and I must say this virus is a strange one. It is quite different from our normal Alban viruses that run through the population now and then. I'm sending more samples to the lab for additional testing."

The Medella's eyes went to Vick's large form, lounging indolently in the chair he'd confiscated.

"Would you like a paternity test when I run the others?"

Helen's light green eyes narrowed, following the health worker's disapproving gaze.

"No, I am fully aware of the paternity of my child."

"Of course. I was merely concerned. With an outsider parent, we can hardly be sure of vaccinations, disease exposure, and—"

"My child is the offspring of two Alban parents. Not that it is your business. And not that it should matter. All Medella are sworn to equal treatment of all classes, regardless of circumstances. If you're not capable of remaining impartial, please send someone who is." Helen's voice was frosty, putting the older woman in her place.

The woman flushed slightly, her voice defensive as she quickly removed the needle from Helen's arm, "He is hardly one of our classes. He's an outsider."

"Mr. March" —Helen's voice had dropped another degree— "was instrumental in the recent operation that rescued an Alban and averted further war with the Southern Empire. He is a valuable ally to our nation and deserves the respect that position demands."

The Medella flushed even darker. She nodded, unable to meet Helen's eyes, and excused herself, practically running from the room with the blood samples.

Helen dropped back against the pillow, putting a hand to her throbbing head.

"I can't remember the last time someone defended me. I don't know whether to be grateful or frightened," Vick spoke. A surprisingly serious note belied the flippancy of his words.

"I didn't do it for you. I just can't stand ignorant prejudice."

Vick raised one brow. "Aren't you part of the ruling class of a highly segregated society?"

Helen shook her head slowly, trying to clear the fuzz that seemed to be overtaking her. "Division isn't prejudice. Everyone is equally vital, we just have different roles to play. Balance is important … to preserve peace." She could feel herself fading, the rote words she'd been taught coming to her lips of their own accord. Did she believe them? She wasn't even sure what she believed right now.

The weight was too much, dragging her body down into the grey awaiting her. Through the hazy tunnel of her vision, she met the concerned hazel eyes of the man she was trying desperately to remain distanced from.

It was becoming more and more difficult. And now she owed him. This kind of complication was the last thing she needed right now.

"Vick. Thank you. I owe you."

Vick grinned, the sardonic twinkle returning to his eyes. "Don't worry, sweetheart, I always collect on my debts."

"That's what I was afraid of," Helen murmured weakly as darkness overcame her.

Chapter 2

"Balance and serenity bring peace." - Alban relaxation mantra

The former President March stepped over the fallen bodies of two guards without a second look. She smiled, the elegant lines of her face creasing slightly.

She needed a treatment. The wrinkles were re-appearing, and she couldn't look less than her best for the lovely family reunion she had planned.

Glancing to the side, she gave the slender, dark-skinned man a nod of approval.

"Very good, Royce. I know field work is not your strength, and you have far surpassed my expectations.

Royce's serious features lightened with pleasure. Ah, people were so easy to manipulate, she thought as she watched him type in the code to leave the high security mental institution. Find their insecurities, and it was a simple matter to control them.

Except her own children. A frown skittered across her face before she carefully schooled her features, not wanting the wrinkles to continue forming.

Thinking of her offspring often brought on mixed feelings of rage and disgust. Jayden was her biggest disappointment. She had thought him to be under her thumb; her loyal and powerful supporter. The people had loved him, and even Congress had respected him.

And he'd betrayed her. Rage filled her again, making her long fingers tremble as she followed Royce down the long hallway. She wanted to lash out; to watch someone writhe in agony. She imagined herself taking the knife Royce had used on the guards to cut the young man; imagined his screams of agony as the blade sawed through flesh, tendon, and stuck in bone…

Her breathing increased as pleasure began to overtake the rage, and Royce glanced back at her.

"Are you alright, President March?"

"I'm fine." She controlled herself with effort, banishing the fantasy. She could revisit it later. And when she no longer needed Royce… It could become more than just a fantasy.

But Vicktor, her first born… he'd been a disappointment from the start. He'd worshipped his father, shadowing her foolish husband's every footstep. And just like her husband, she'd never been able to read her oldest son, although she'd found ways to control him.

The two men had spent more time in Texico than the Empire until their deaths. Killing them had been necessary to gaining the Presidency.

Only now Vicktor wasn't dead. That meant she'd need to have him killed a second time. And what better way to end him than by using the Texican warlord who'd been like a brother.

How she loved the irony. When her traitorous children were dealt with, she'd take over Alba and use their Technology as the launching pad for her new empire.

The world needed a ruler like her.

"Well?" Marcus stood beside Simon, the new Head of Research and Development. He was the first Virmortus in a position of authority that hadn't gone through the years of brutal training required of the security agents. Times were certainly changing quickly, Marcus thought. He still wasn't sure if he was relieved or concerned.

He didn't really have time to be either, trying to lead both the elite group of assassins, the Virmortus—nicknamed Reapers by the people—and the increasingly unhappy Senators whose votes ran their city-state.

The new Senators from different classes he'd recently appointed helped to take pressure off from the Patrician

Senators. Those self-righteous, over-privileged men and women could go to hell for all he cared. They were nothing but a proverbial albatross around his neck.

Too bad one of those damn albatrosses was Aerina's father.

He'd never had to worry about playing nice as a Reaper. As the current interim Consul, he had to be political.

He hated being political.

"It is amazing," Simon answered his question, bringing his thoughts back to the issue at hand: The Technology that was destined to destroy the world for a second time. "Some of the subjects, like Lina Rhodes and young Jamia, show amazing aptitude for the injection. It seems to bind better with some, giving them a vast advantage over other Users."

Simon paused to cough into his elbow, then running a lean hand over his tired face. Marcus noted the dark shadows under the other man's eyes, and the gauntness of his already lean form.

"Something wrong?"

Simon glanced over in surprise. "Nah, just came down with something and can't seem to shake it."

Marcus studied him for another long moment. "Go home and rest. If our new friend Jayden March is correct, we shouldn't have to worry about the Southern Empire for a little while."

Simon stiffened slightly as if offended. He still didn't take well to being ordered around, and Marcus was hardly the diplomatic type. Too damn bad. He'd better get used to it.

"Yes sir," the other man finally replied wryly, saluting. Marcus ignored the insubordination that in another recruit he'd punish harshly.

He was getting soft. He wasn't sure if it was the political mess or spending so much time with Aerina, but he had certainly mellowed.

"Go home, Simon," he ordered a final time as he walked towards the lift that would take him up to his office.

He didn't bother to look back and see the other man's expression, but the cough that followed him didn't sound good.

Damn, he hoped he wouldn't catch whatever it was. The last thing he needed now was some virus slowing him down.

*   *   *

Jay's eyes were concerned as he watched Lina settle weakly onto her lounge. All his thoughts of discussing their future, or lack thereof, were forgotten. This seemed like more than just a little cold.

Even though the villa was warm, she shivered uncontrollably. He glanced around, grabbing a blanket thrown over a nearby chair.

"Damn, Lina, you should be in bed."

She cast him a wry look from reddened eyes. "I *was* in bed."

Jay scooped her up, ignoring her protests as he carried her to the bedroom in the back. It was the same unrelenting white as the rest of the house, and the villas all over the Capitol Terrace.

Settling her on the rumpled covers, he began briskly tucking her in.

"Jay, I'm not going to bed. You just got here…"

"I'll sit with you," he said, settling beside her on top of the coverlet. Lina rested her head on his chest and he pulled her closer, stroking dark strands of hair back from her flushed face.

She felt warm. Overly warm.

"Have you taken anything for the fever?"

Lina nodded sleepily. "A few hours ago, I'll take another pill soon. The Medella said to come back if it doesn't get better by tomorrow."

Jay said nothing, continuing to stroke her head gently. Inside, concern began to rise. He couldn't leave her here, sick. But there was no way that cold bastard, Marcus, was going to let him hang around.

A slow fear was born as her breathing slowed. He settled deeper onto the bed, his eyes on the distant horizon outside the large window. It was early evening, and the setting sun cast its lackluster glow over the dark waters of the Pacific. A light fog was slowly forming in the low areas, and low clouds cast an eerie light over the landscape.

He'd sit here with Lina until Vick returned. Then they would need to talk. He hoped to hell he was wrong. Intentionally or not, the Southern Empire may not be done wreaking havoc on Alba.

*   *   *

Helen woke slowly, her head still fuzzy and her mouth feeling as if she had licked a chalkboard. Coughing, she cracked eyes that felt swollen, focusing on the figure still lounging indolently beside her bed.

"You're still here?" she asked, gratefully taking the water he handed her. She tried to still the trembling of her hand as she took a careful sip, attempting to hide the weakness from his watchful eyes.

"Are you sure you're pregnant?" he asked suddenly.

Helen raised one elegant brow at the question. "I'm certain."

"You just don't look pregnant," he responded, his eyes going over her prone form slowly, causing an unexpected warmth that had nothing to with fever to follow his perusal. She resisted the urge to cross her arms defensively over herself. Since she had become pregnant, she felt as if her body had turned against her. The queasiness she could deal with, but the hormonal moodiness was awful. She'd never felt so out of control of her emotions.

"I assure you, I *feel* pregnant."

Vick grinned at her acerbic response, raising his hands as if in surrender. "I'm sorry, you just look so tiny, I couldn't imagine a baby in there."

Helen leaned back tiredly, the tiny bit of strength she'd

had when waking already used up. Normally she enjoyed their sparring, probably a little too much, but today she couldn't seem to work up the energy for an appropriate riposte.

Vick leaned over, adjusting her pillow gently, tucking a blanket back over her. It felt strange to have someone caring for her. Normally she would never allow herself to be in this position; she'd worked too hard to be seen as strong and independent. But the difficult first months of pregnancy and now this virus were a double punch that was threatening to take over her completely.

She fought the sleep that hovered, waiting to claim her.

"You never answered. Why are you still here?"

"I didn't realize it was a question. Don't get too excited. I just didn't think it would be very chivalrous to dump you here and take off…"

Helen smiled slightly, letting her eyes fall closed. This felt better. She could handle the light-hearted, sarcastic Vick. Concerned, gentle Vick was alarming.

"Don't worry, I'd never mistake you for a knight in shining armor. Lone Ranger, maybe. But mostly, you remind me of a James Bond character. Sarcastic, closed off, doing the job forced upon you but never really giving a damn…"

"I didn't realize you were a fan of pre-war film." His amused voice sounded distant as the heaviness of sleep waited in the wings to descend.

"I'm not. But all your references made me curious, so I've been watching some holofiles, doing a little research." The words came out before she realized what they disclosed. She was more interested in Vick than she wanted to admit.

And naturally, he couldn't just let the ramblings of a sick woman slide like any other gentlemen. Oh no, not that son of a bitch.

"I'm flattered. I didn't know you cared." The amusement was still evident in his tone, a gentle drawl entering when he was relaxed.

"Don't be. It was mild curiosity that has already abated."

He made a non-committal sound, and she felt his cool hand touch her brow. She wanted to throw it off to prove her point, but it felt so good against her burning skin.

She'd leave it for just a moment longer.

Just another moment...

*   *   *

Vick frowned with concern as Helen again drifted to sleep, the medicine doing little to bring down her high temperature. The facsimile of humor he'd held during their bantering disappeared as quickly as his false grin, the blunt lines of his face going taut with concern.

The doctor's words echoed in his mind. *This virus is a strange one. It is quite different from our normal Alban viruses...* This wasn't an ordinary sickness that one could treat with fluids and rest. This seemed like something more sinister.

Hours had passed. He should notify Jay, who was expecting him to return and drive him from the city as Marcus had decreed. But he was not about to leave Helen here alone, even if she was surrounded by her colleagues and friends. An irrational fear had begun building that if he didn't watch out for her, something terrible was going to happen.

Since when did you start caring about anyone besides yourself? He ignored the inner voice that sounded remarkably similar to his mother's clipped accent.

Picking up his holoreader, he saw Jay had already messaged him.

Lina is ill. I'm not leaving until she's better. We need to talk.

Damn. Lina and Helen were best friends, so one must have passed it to the other.

His mind began working quickly. Who else was ill? No one, as far as he was aware, before Jay had arrived two weeks ago. And Jay had been kept in confinement during that entire time.

Except Lina had been allowed to visit him.

It didn't take Vick long to put a scenario together. He immediately commanded his holoreader to contact Marcus. Perhaps he was being overly cautious, but if he was right, this needed to be dealt with immediately. He watched Helen's fragile chest rising and falling gently, forcing down the fear that rose in his own broad chest.

Chapter 3

"Just because a person creates a child, it doesn't make them a parent..." - Letters from Matias Emmanuel March

Marcus arrived at the clinic less than an hour later. His forbidding expression told Vick the other man did not like being summoned.

"We might have a situation," Vick told him without preamble.

"We always have a situation."

Vick raised his brow in surprise at the weariness he detected in Marcus' normally unflappable demeanor.

"Yeah, well, sorry my friend. I'm about to be the bringer of bad news."

Marcus' eyes flicked past Vick to Helen's still-sleeping form in the room behind him. "Did Helen lose her baby? I'm sure that's something you can tell Aerina—"

"No," Vick interrupted, horror washing through him at the words. He had been so concerned about Helen, he hadn't even thought about the toll a grave illness could take on a fetus. "No, the baby is fine. I think. At least for now. But Helen's illness... I don't think it came from some harmless Alban germ. We won't know for sure until the test results come back, but... I think this is something else."

Marcus' face went blank but his jaw began to flex.

"Your goddamn brother. I'm going to kill him."

Vick's smile didn't reach his eyes.

"While I won't stop you, I don't think that's going to solve our problem. The damage has already been done, if he is the one who brought the illness here. We can't know for sure if this is intentional, or just the result of Alba's long isolation from other groups. Either way, your vaccines aren't going to protect from it; it's a foreign germ already wreaking havoc on the few infected."

Marcus said nothing, his dark eyes hard as he ran through options.

"If you are correct—"

"Have I ever been wrong?"

"—then the virus has already been spreading, with both Lina and Helen as victims. We're talking about a possible epidemic. We haven't had to deal with this in at least two generations with our strict isolation policy. Damn."

"We can't afford to wait and find out for sure. By then, the illness will have spread even further. It is best to err on the side of caution."

"That is what I planned to do."

Marcus was already leaving, snapping orders into his holoreader. He paused at the doorway. "You can't leave the city. We might need your Confederate blood. And I'm going to lock your brother back up."

"That's going to go over well," Vick commented drily.

"Until we know the depth of his involvement, I don't give a damn how he feels."

Vick saluted. He hadn't intended on leaving, anyway. In fact, Marcus would probably have had to incapacitate him before they would have been able to drag him away from Helen's side.

As for Jay, his brother could take care of himself. He was more concerned about his unexpected attachment to a certain Patrician. And the unpredictable illness ravaging her over-thin body.

He'd let Marcus deal with the epidemic threat. He had a sick patient to check on.

*   *   *

"Yes, that's right, shut down the Ferry at once. And the Patrician tram. No one is allowed to leave the Capitol Terrace. Anyone who has left the Capitol Terrace in the last two days must return at once."

Marcus closed his holoreader and turned to face the

gathered men and women who made up his team of trained enforcers. Before Aerina, this group was the closest thing to family he'd ever had. He had always kept his distance as their leader, but he admitted to himself he cared about these people.

"Listen carefully. We have a possible epidemic that may have been brought from the Southern Empire by our recent prisoner. It seems to be some kind of influenza, but so far it has been resistant to any attempts at treating it.

"The Medellas will begin creating a vaccination. Until one has been developed, no one enters or leaves the Capitol Terrace. The Armati will be notified to patrol the other terraces. Anyone showing signs of illness will be quarantined immediately to stem the spread."

Marcus met the eyes of his Reapers. "Anyone who attempts to disobey our edict, or hide the illness, will be dealt with immediately."

He waited until each man and woman had nodded their understanding. Death to a fellow Alban was never easy, but if this illness was allowed to spread, it could mean many more deaths.

"Titus, Rachel, Isaak… you will secure the Confederate Jayden March. Keep him alive for questioning."

The three experienced assassins nodded, leaving the room.

"Sir."

Marcus turned to see Nemo, a young recruit nearly at the end of his training who worked as his assistent, standing in the doorway.

"What is it?"

"The patrols reported back just a few moments ago. Two Senators are ill already; both have been seen by Medellas."

"Who?"

Nemo cleared his throat, the only sign he was hesitant to continue. "Senators Caius and Delacroix, sir."

Damn. Aerina's father was ill. The unfamiliar sensation of fear turned his blood cold. If Delacroix was ill, that meant Aerina had been exposed. She'd been fine when he checked in with her just an hour before, but that meant nothing. They knew little about this illness; how long the incubation period was, how long it lasted.

How deadly it could be.

He hoped they were being overly cautious, and it would turn out to be just a bad case of influenza that would run its course without any fatalities.

But he'd learned as a young child that hope was often the pastime of fools and dreamers.

Of which he was neither.

"Thank you, Nemo," he said curtly, his mind already going through the next steps in his quarantine.

"Er, sir?" Nemo spoke up as Marcus began to walk away.

"Yes?" Marcus replied impatiently.

"Ramus did not report in today, sir. Shall I send someone to his villa?"

A few beats passed as Marcus' mind whirled with the implications. Ramus had never missed work. He had to be deathly ill, or dead. Was it possible this illness was so infectious? He was going through the motions to handle a possible epidemic, and now each moment was making him more convinced that was what he was dealing with. And he couldn't afford to lose Ramus.

"I'll go myself."

*　　　*　　　*

Jay looked up from reading Vick's message on his Com device just in time to see a familiar black e-car speed past Lina's villa. When he'd been working undercover in Alba, he'd always been aware of its location.

Marcus' vehicle.

Marcus is dealing with the situation. Don't leave Lina's house, someone will come get you. He re-read the message again.

Short and to the point. Even after all these years of playing the easy-going mayor, his older brother hadn't lost his ability to command.

It was in their blood. Their very tainted blood.

Jay gathered up the cold cloth he'd gotten from the sink and the glass of electrolyte juice from the Dispensare. He hadn't planned on leaving, anyway. Not with Lina being so sick. The only place he would be taking her was the clinic. He'd let her rest a few hours first, but he didn't dare wait too long. She was already getting dangerously dehydrated.

He stepped into her bedroom, the unrelenting white already wearing on him. It was the smaller of the two bedrooms, and he determined she hadn't been ready to take over the master suite which had belonged to Stephen.

She might be improving, but he knew she'd never get over her brother's death completely.

The sound of heavy, uneven breathing brought him back to the present. He studied her pale features, and fresh fear passed over him in waves.

This is all my fault. I'm still doing nothing but causing her pain. Shaking off the useless self-disgust, he set the cool cloth on her forehead. He couldn't wait any longer. He needed to bring her in.

Grabbing a bag, he opened her closet. So much goddamn white. Shoving clothes into the bag, some instinct had him pausing. Stepping out of the room, he listened.

A knock.

No polite announcement of the visitor from the automated doorbell.

That meant a Virmortus, or several, were at the door. And he knew why they had come.

For him.

The Confederate. The infector. The outsider in their midst.

Dropping the bag, he strode back to Lina's room, scooping her into his arms. They could take him, but first, he was taking her to the clinic.

*   *   *

Aerina stepped into her childhood home. Her parents' villa was neat and tidy, the understated elegance visible in each perfect column and carefully placed statuary.

Hesitantly, her eyes raised to meet her mother's. Raina Delacroix also embodied the elegance Aerina had grown up knowing; not a hair was out of place, and her white pencil skirt and blouse were perfectly pressed.

"How is he?" Aerina asked.

"He seems to be doing better," Raina answered coolly. They hadn't spoken in months; not since Aerina had chosen to move in with Marcus. In her mother's eyes, Aerina had turned her back on the family name by aligning herself with a man from another caste.

Aerina had long ago given up trying to please her mother, finally accepting that nothing she did could make up for what her mother considered her fault: the death of her little brother.

I tried to save him, she wanted to scream. But, as always, she kept the words buried where they would never be voiced.

"May I see him?" she asked instead, pleased at her polite restraint. Spending time with Marcus was good for her; she must be picking up on his talent for self-control.

Raina nodded, leading the way through the climate-controlled villa to the master suit in back overlooking the ocean. Aerina's old bedroom was directly above on the second floor.

Her worried blue eyes fell on the sleeping figure of her father. He had the typical build of Patrician males, lean and carefully toned, his hair trimmed short and utilitarian in style. The Patrician's careful attention to diet and exercise made them all age well, only a few wrinkles appearing on his handsome features.

Her father's normal vitality had been dimmed, the illness stealing the tan from his face, and making his body look gaunt.

Aerina turned shocked eyes to her mother.

"How long has he been ill?"

"Only two days. But it seems to have hit him hard. All that worry recently made him weak." Her mother's words were accusatory, and Aerina immediately knew her mother blamed her for her father's condition.

A new cross to bear. Aerina nodded her head, accepting her mother's blame.

She moved closer to the bed, sitting carefully on the edge beside her father. She reached a hesitant hand to touch his brow. It was hot, but his eyes opened slowly.

"Aerina."

Aerina smiled, fighting back the tears that sprang to her eyes.

"Father, I came as soon as I heard you were ill. Have you gone in to see a Medella?"

Anthony Delcroix shook his head. "Of course not. This is just a little cold; it will pass. I just need some rest, some fluids, and a little less fussing." His blue eyes, so much like Aerina's, flicked to where her mother stood in the doorway.

"Oh Father, you know you like when Mother fusses," Aerina chided gently. "Promise me you'll go in if this continues another day?"

"I'll promise that when you promise to leave that Reaper's villa and return to your family," her father returned with a hint of his old spirit.

Aerina sighed. "I love him, Father. And I certainly cannot abandon him now. As much as he would deny it, he needs me. And I need him."

"He needs no one!" her mother burst out from the doorway. "He is just using you to take control of the Senate, to sway the people in his favor! It is shameful, you living with him instead of your own family. You could have had so much—"

"I have everything I ever wanted, Mother," Aerina

interrupted quietly. "Everything except your approval. But I gave up on that long ago—"

"Enough!" her father interrupted, subsiding into a fit of coughing. Aerina bit her lip, her hand hovering over her father's heaving chest.

Raina had come around the other side of the bed, offering her husband a glass of water. He sipped it, nodding his thanks to his wife.

"I'm sorry," Aerina said once the room was again silent. "I'm sorry about everything." She stood, knowing her presence would only cause more harm than good at this point. "I'll come back tomorrow," she told her father gently, pointedly ignoring her mother's face. Anthony nodded slightly, laying back against the pillows, his eyes closing.

"Please let me know if anything changes," she asked of her mother as the two women faced off in the hallway. "He's still my father."

"If he were really your concern, Aerina, I would think you'd be supporting him instead of your Virmortus lover."

Aerina nodded, again accepting her mother's angry accusations. She knew the anger came from the hurt her mother kept buried; hurt over the loss of little Max, and fear over her husband's health.

"Please, Mother."

Raina finally nodded stiffly. "I will let you know if anything changes."

Aerina turned, walking herself back towards the door. At the end of the hall, she turned.

"I love you, Mother."

Her mother glanced at her, the older woman's eyes looking tortured; conflicted.

"I love you too, Aerina."

While worry and sorrow still weighed heavily on Aerina's heart, she left feeling like something had changed for the better.

Chapter 4

"Emotion is a weapon you hand to the enemy before the battle begins." - Virmortus Training Manual

Vick looked up at the commotion in the hallway. They were bringing in another patient, the third one since he'd brought in Helen.

The others had been an older man—the Senator of Law, Vick thought—and a younger child.

When he saw the newest patient, he was glad Helen was asleep.

Lina.

He met the familiar blue-green gaze of his younger brother. The two men nodded, acknowledging the other, before Jay carried a half-conscious Lina into an adjoining room. Three figures suited in biosuits followed close behind. From the way they moved, Vick knew it was Marcus' men beneath the red suits.

The staff had taken to wearing masks and suits that covered their bodies to prevent the spread of the infection. The Medella that had worked on Helen initially had disappeared, no doubt in her own quarantine room.

Vick was just waiting for the doors to be locked. He knew it was only a matter of time until Marcus tightened the barricade he was placing around the sick.

It was the same thing he would have done.

He'd had a similar situation, on a much smaller scale, happen in his own little town of Vicksburg only a few years earlier. Some drifter had come into town looking for shelter; turned out the young man had some kind of illness like smallpox. Vick had immediately quarantined the young man and the few townspeople who had come into contact with him. Thanks to his relationship with Marcus, all his people were vaccinated for smallpox and other diseases. Only the young man had perished, but Vick remembered the fear that had spread quickly through his town.

The unknown was the biggest fear. Education was the only cure for that kind of debilitating panic.

He sat back down beside Helen, his eyes moving slowly over her sleeping form. The past few hours had given him too much time to contemplate why he was so captivated by this woman. He'd never been one to crave companionship of any person, male or female. While he had many acquaintances, and considered the people of his small town family, he'd never gotten close to any of them. Marcus was probably his closest confidante, but it was hard to use the word "close" to describe his relationship with that cold son-of-a-bitch. They understood and respected one another, but that was as deep their relationship went.

Since his father, he could say with certainty he'd never loved anyone.

He didn't want to start now. But as he looked down at the feisty spitfire laying helpless before him, he couldn't stop the strange rush of feelings he was afraid to name. Protective, yes. Affection, perhaps. Love?

Hell no.

Shaking his head at his own ridiculous, fanciful thoughts, he pulled the cover up higher on Helen. She murmured something, rolling to her side.

The Medella had just given her some medicine in her drip that would help her sleep and keep the fever down. Vick rose, heading into the hallway to find a restroom and then to hunt down his brother.

He came face-to-face with his younger counterpart, still flanked by his red-suited entourage.

"Back to lock up, eh?"

Jay matched his brother's grin. "Yeah, guess they missed me too much to let me go."

Vick's grin became slightly feral and he pulled his brother close, his hand behind the younger man's neck. "I hope you don't have a part in this illness. Because if this illness was a gift from you and that bitch who ran the Empire, I'll kill you myself."

Jay's own smile went up a watt or two. "Glad the ties of blood remain strong as ever. I'm no more of a killer than you are, brother. And I don't kill innocent people. Not even for our mother."

"Just because someone has a child, it doesn't make them a parent. That bitch was no mother."

"Still have mommy issues, hmm?"

Vick clenched his hands into fists, then forced himself to relax, running his hand absently over his beard, feeling the familiar grooves beneath the thin layer of hair.

"Don't we all? Enjoy your time back in Interrogation, dear brother."

Jay rolled his shoulders. "I always do."

Vick watched his brother stride towards the lobby of the clinic, followed closely by the Virmortus who would no doubt bring him back to the Training Grounds to be questioned. Possibly tortured.

He felt a twinge of guilt. It was his little brother. But he'd also been the right-hand agent to the sociopathic President of the Southern Empire. Perhaps deposing her had been part of a twisted plot.

And perhaps his brother was innocent, and the illness was just a coincidence.

He admitted, if only to himself, that he hoped his brother was innocent. Because dammit, he kinda liked the arrogant pretty boy.

*   *   *

"Ramus?" Marcus entered his second-in-command's small villa. Like his own, this villa was built for safety, and it wasn't white. Ramus had chosen blues and browns, giving the surroundings an aura of a calm.

Striding almost silently through the entrance, Marcus crossed the living space to the bedroom in back. He found what he'd been afraid of.

Ramus' large body was sprawled across the bed, his breathing heavy and his dark skin feverish.

"Ramus." Marcus gently shook his friend. Getting no response, he turned back to the kitchen, getting a glass of electrolyte water from the Dispensare.

"Drink this," he commanded, pulling his friend up into a reclining position. He poured the liquid into Ramus' mouth, and the other man sputtered, swallowing reflexively.

Ramus' dark eyes finally opened, meeting Marcus' own nearly black gaze.

He looked around, disorientated for a moment. "I'm pretty sick. I tried to get my holoreader to call you...I don't really remember how I got back in bed."

"I'm going to bring you in to the clinic. I need someone keeping an eye on you." Marcus ran a critical eye over his friend. "And from the looks of it, you need an IV and constant monitoring."

Marcus raised his friend up to sitting position. "Can you walk, or do I need to carry you?"

"Like hell you're gonna carry me." His large, ebony hand curled around Marcus' shoulder and the men stood together. They shuffle-walked to the door, nearly tumbling down the single front step, and made their way slowly to Marcus' e-car waiting in the drive.

Marcus lowered his friend carefully in the passenger side before taking his own spot behind the wheel.

He glanced over at his long-time friend and second-in-command. The large man was slumped in his seat, his eyes closed.

"Goddamnit Ramus, you better pull it together." Marcus was rewarded by a weak flash of white teeth against dark skin.

"Sorry to inconvenience you, boss."

"Just get better, Ramus. I can't run this place without you."

*   *   *

Helen felt so much happier than she remembered being in a long time. But she was tired. So tired. And it felt as if someone had tied her eyelids closed.

Swearing in frustration, she shoved the wet cloth off her eyes. Someone was laughing, making her even angrier. Cursing again, she forced open her eyes.

"Stephen?"

The dark figure beside her stilled, a large hand touching her forehead. She swatted it away angrily. It was a man in her bedroom, but it didn't really look like Stephen... He was too large, too unkempt.

Perhaps he'd been caring for her. Was she ill?

She tried to concentrate, to think about where she was, but the effort made her head hurt too much and she gave up.

"Dammit Stephen, I told you I don't like it when you hover," she muttered. Her tongue felt thick and uncomfortable in her mouth, forcing her to swallow several times.

A glass of water appeared at her lips, and she took an eager sip. It reminded her of the time she'd let Stephen talk her into joining him in drinking some of the Aggie-brewed whiskey. Wanting to appear unfazed, she'd swallowed down the entire tumbler of liquor and taken a second. For someone who'd never had a sip before in her life, the liquor had hit her hard, and the rest of the evening had been a blur. The following morning, however, had been absolutely awful.

Kind of like this.

She frowned, squinting blurry eyes at the man who still *hovered.*

"Did you give me more liquor? I told you I was never touching the stuff again after last time."

The voice that responded sounded different than Stephen's, a little raspier with a hint of a drawl. She frowned even harder at the strangely familiar sound, trying to place it. "Unfortunately you've never accepted my offer of a drink, my dear."

She shook her head. That wasn't true. Unless this wasn't Stephen...

"Take one more sip for me, sweetheart."

Stephen would never have dared call her sweetheart.

"Vick, why are you still here? I thought I told you to leave."

His large, callused hand gently slid behind her neck, blessedly cool on her overheated skin. He raised her slightly, putting the glass to her lips. She obediently swallowed the cold liquid.

"I don't need you to care for me," she said sharply, ruining the effect with a hacking cough.

"I know you don't. You don't need anyone, right?"

"That's right. And furthermore...furthermore..." she couldn't seem to remember what she wanted to say to put him in his place.

Sleep was again sweeping over her in waves. She fought against it, knowing there was something she needed to do. Something she needed to say...

"Stephen, don't leave while I'm asleep."

A long silence came from the man beside her and Helen felt panic rising. She didn't know why it mattered, but she didn't want this man to leave. Somehow, she knew that if he weren't here, something very bad was going to happen. To her. To her baby.

The baby. Stephen's baby.

Stephen was dead, but his baby was growing even now inside her.

And she needed Vick to help her protect it.

"Please." She didn't have the strength to explain to Vick, to explain how she felt.

"I'll be here."

Satisfied for the moment that things would be ok,

Helen let sleep pull her into its grasp.

*   *   *

"My darling daughter."

Chelsea March gasped as the voice of her nightmares brought her from her restless dozing. She'd come to this little beach south of New Glory to escape the constant assault of sounds and smells that were inevitable with so many people living so close together.

She valued her privacy, even more so now. And this tiny stretch of beach, which her father had sometimes taken her to as a small child, gave her the quiet she needed. It had been her escape. Her secret place.

But no longer.

Turning, she looked up into the calculating grey eyes of her mother. Her stomach rolled, bile burning in the back of her throat.

"How did you escape?"

Her mother smiled, the stretching of her lips not matched by the coldness of her gaze.

"You didn't think they'd keep me there forever, did you?"

God, I had hoped so.

"What do you want?" Chelsea glanced over at her bag. Her Com was in there, just a few feet out of reach. If she could just get closer, she could get it and call Stix…

Her mother noted the direction of her gaze, stooping to pick up the small black bag.

"I need your help with a little mission, darling." Her mother opened the bag, slowly pulling out items and inspecting them. Chelsea's stomach continued to twist, and she focused on keeping her breathing steady and even. If the monster knew of her fear, it would use it against her.

Chelsea remained silent, waiting.

Her mother raised a thin brow, looking impressed. "You've grown up, my dear. You remind me of your father more and more every day."

Chelsea still said nothing, knowing that was more of an insult than anything. Her mother had hated her father. Had ordered his death, Chelsea was sure.

A mosquito buzzed around her ear, and Chelsea resisted the urge to swat at it. She was afraid if she took her eyes from her mother for a moment, the monster would attack.

The older woman sighed as she pocketed Chelsea's phone. "We're going to take a little trip. I want you to reunite with your brothers. Jay, at least, has always had a soft spot where you're concerned. I just want to know what they're up to. Maybe have a nice family reunion when the time is right."

"Fuck you."

The former President's eyebrows went up. "I see that your less than savory lifestyle has had a detrimental effect on your temperament. You might benefit from a little more time at the rehabilitation clinic. What do you think?"

Chelsea's control over her fear was swept away at the sight of the man who had been waiting further back on the trail. Jeremy MacDonald walked slowly into view, his thinning black hair and blunt features sending waves of horror through Chelsea.

"I see you remember Dr. MacDonald." Satisfaction dripped from her mother's light accent, but Chelsea was barely aware. Another monster had emerged, one that Chelsea feared even more.

Flashes of memory flickered before her eyes; his cruel sneer as he grunted over her restrained body. The burning pain, the desperate, consuming fear. The helplessness…

Her breath was now coming in gasps, and she involuntarily took a step back, her body telling her to run; to flee the monsters waiting to devour her soul.

"Unless you agree to come with me, Dr. MacDonald is going to take you back to the clinic with him. Indefinitely. What's it to be, daughter?"

Chelsea managed to tear her gaze from MacDonald, knowing her fear and hatred were obvious but unable to disguise them.

"I've always wanted to see the continent," she said with heavy sarcasm.

"Excellent. We leave at once. I have a plane waiting to take us to Texico."

Chapter 5

"The family structure is crucial to societal balance. Divorce and unsanctioned pregnancies are a threat to our society and will be dealt with accordingly." Law of Population, Alban Charter of Government

Aerina arrived at the clinic, unable to banish the rising fear overtaking her.

What was going on?

Helen, Lina, her father, Ramus—all victims of this strange illness.

Guarding the door was a Virmortus she knew well from her recent journey to the Southern Empire. Lucien nodded to her, motioning for her to follow him inside. In the open, airy lobby, Aerina was met by a Medella, dressed from head-to-toe in a red canvas suit. All that showed were the health worker's eyes.

His voice was muffled as he spoke. "Welcome, Madame Emissary. If you'll follow me, I'll get you suited up."

Aerina followed, glancing back only once as Lucien remained at his post near the door. Keeping people out, or keeping patients in?

She pulled on the suit, following the Medella's instructions carefully. The suit was thin but strong, hooking under her shoes to cover her from heels to neck. A second portion fit over her head, overlapping to her shoulders. The front of the head-covering was open, allowing her to see and speak easily. The Medella showed her the face piece that could fit onto the head-covering. Taking a step back, he looked her over one last time, nodding in satisfaction.

"This way. Mr. Trent is with his colleague."

They walked down the tiled hallway, every room with

a closed door.

Helen and Lina were in those rooms. She'd ask to see them after. Right now, she needed to see Marcus; to find out what was going on.

"Sir, Ms. Delacroix is here to see you."

Marcus' dark gaze met hers, and Aerina was shocked to see the evidence of pain on his stark features.

"Thank you," she murmured to the doctor, who nodded and left the room.

She walked forward slowly, taking in the sleeping form of Ramus, his strong body ravaged by illness. Marcus faced his friend, stiff and silent. Aerina slid her arms around his waist, resting her head against his hard back, offering him comfort as best she could.

"It's not your fault."

Instead of comforting him, the words seemed to draw forth the emotions he'd been keeping bottled up.

"Of course it's my fault," he growled, whirling to face her. His fist came down heavily on the desk behind her, scattering its contents and a loud crack resounding through the sterile room.

Aerina stood silently, waiting for him to bring himself back under control.

He clenched his hands, then forcing them open and placing them carefully on her shoulders. His voice was even, nearly emotionless, as he continued.

"I am the ruler of this nation, so everything that happens is my responsibility. I let that outsider in, and he brought the goddamn plague with him."

"You couldn't have known. We all traveled to the Southern Empire; were all exposed. Lina was there for weeks and came back healthy. This isn't anyone's fault, Marcus. This is just life. Just an isolated society suddenly exposed to the world. This was inevitable."

Marcus said nothing, squeezing her shoulders gently before lowering his hands. Her red biosuit crinkled in the quiet room.

"Why aren't you suited?" Aerina asked suddenly.

"I wasn't wearing one when I brought Ramus in. The damage is already done."

Aerina felt fresh fear flooding in, filling her with foreboding.

What would they do without Marcus? What would *she* do?

"You should go home and rest," she ordered, fear making her voice sharp.

Marcus looked at her. "I need to complete the quarantine plans."

Aerina absently tucked the blanket tighter around Ramus' sleeping form, again surprised at the condition he was in after only a few days of sickness.

"I'll stay here with the sick. You go."

"How is your father?"

Aerina bit her lip to fight back the tears that unexpectedly sprang to her eyes. "He's sick, but I think improving."

"We'll need to bring him and your mother in. No one who is ill can be in the general population."

Aerina opened her mouth to argue, but then shut it, nodding.

"Any word from the other terraces?"

Aerina started, turning towards the new voice from the doorway.

Vick lounged there, his intent gaze belying the casualness of his stance. His beard looked a little more unkempt than normal, and strands of his long, tawny hair had escaped the leather tie that secured them at the base of his neck.

"No evidence of sickness so far, but the Armati have just started looking. Most Plebs wouldn't know to go in to the clinic; hopefully our announcement will help."

"'Announcement'? That's what you're calling your

orders these days? How very political of you."

Aerina opened her mouth to chastise Vick for his flippancy, but closed it again, noting his obvious exhaustion. And carefully concealed worry.

His white cotton t-shirt and faded jeans were as rumpled as his hair, and lines of strain were evident on his tanned skin.

"I'll run home and get you a change of Marcus' clothes," she offered instead. "Unless you'd like to come with me and get some rest in our villa?"

Vick was already shaking his head. "I might be contaminated. I should stay."

Aerina glanced down at her red suit, protecting her from the microorganisms wreaking such havoc on their city. Technically, she'd already been exposed numerous times herself. It would be a miracle if she didn't get ill.

Noise in the hallway had Vick stepping further into the room to allow the red-suited Medellas to pass with a new patient.

Aerina recognized Antony Caius, the elderly Senator's oldest son. He had been friends with Stephen. His normally swarthy features were pale beneath his surfer tan, his dark hair stringy and standing on end. She met his bloodshot eyes as he passed, and he looked away without recognizing her in the encompassing biohazard suit.

"Have you talked to Jay yet?"

Aerina's attention was drawn back to the new tension in the room.

"Not yet," Marcus replied.

"I'd like to be there when you do."

Marcus and Vick stared at one another. "I don't think that is a good idea," Marcus finally said.

Vick shrugged. "I know him. I'll be able to tell if he's lying. Or hiding something."

"Fine. I'll tell you when."

Aerina cleared her throat to break the tension. "I guess

I'll be back soon. Anything else you need besides clothes?" She directed the question at Vick, but her eyes remained fixed on Marcus.

Vick shook his head, his gaze also on Marcus. Then he shoved off from the doorframe and headed back down the hall, no doubt towards Helen's room.

"Are you going to stay for a bit or...?"

Marcus turned away from the window overlooking a small Serenity Garden.

"No, I'm going back to the Training Grounds to check in with the Virmortus patrolling the Capitol Terrace, and see if there is any news from the other Terraces. I'm going to have the Armati patrolling door-to-door once the biohazard suits have been distributed. Then I am going to interrogate Jayden March."

Aerina sighed. So much for getting him to rest. Her blue eyes scanned his harsh features, noting each line and scar that marred their surface with aching affection.

"Alright. Just please don't be up all night again." He nodded absently, checking Ramus' display one last time. "And Marcus?"

He turned, raising one dark brow in the familiar way that always accelerated her heartrate.

"I love you."

He nodded curtly. Her lips curved, knowing he was returning the sentiment in his own way.

*   *   *

"I've delivered the package. The virus has taken hold. Inform the Council that the first step is successfully completed." The dark-clothed man stood in the shadows, his face hidden from the single light in the underground tunnel.

"They will be pleased. I'll let them know at once. They've requested constant updates as the situation develops. I believe they want to be sure the product isn't damaged during your coup."

The man in shadow made a slicing motion with his

hand. "That killer running this nation has no clue. That's the problem with a soldier in charge rather than a politician; they are too focused on the present. They don't know how to see the big picture."

"Very good, sir. I'll report back the success you've had so far."

The steady drip, drip, drip deep in the old tunnel mingled with the quiet steps of the retreating agent. The shadow man watched until his counterpart disappeared to report back to the Council.

This entire situation was unfortunate. He hated to do this to the Alban people. Good people. But he had no choice. It was his duty. And he'd see it through, regardless of how difficult it was for him or those around him.

Chapter 6

"Fear of death is your biggest enemy. When you let go of this fear, you will be unstoppable." - Virmortus Training Manual

Two days had passed since Vick had brought Helen in, and she'd spent much of the time sleeping from the medicine or out of her mind with the fever they couldn't seem to get under control.

He'd changed into the clothes brought in by Aerina. They fit surprisingly well; although Marcus was a little taller, both men were built on the brawny side. He showered in the small bath adjoining Helen's room, afraid to be too far from her side.

The only time he'd left her side these entire two days was the few hours at the Training Grounds, interrogating Jay.

They'd run tests on the recent ex-patriot of the Southern Empire, checking him for any kind of device or unusual markings.

They questioned him, going over his last contact with former President March, having him recount his journey from the Empire to Alba, including anyone he'd come into contact with.

He became reacquainted with the Nerve Stimulator, a fancy little toy that could be used to simulate any kind of sensation in the victim attached to it. Anything from broken limbs, crawling insects, to the sensation of being on fire were possible.

Vick had to admit, as he observed through the camera, that his brother was amazingly resilient. Jay answered the same question for the third or fourth time through gritted teeth, his face twisted in agony.

His story never changed or wavered. Either he was one

of the best agents to ever live, or he was telling the truth.

Vick was inclined to believe the latter.

Then Marcus began asking again about the Technology. Jay answered each question, again and again, but Vick noticed he rolled his shoulders once, in between questions. It looked like he was just working out the pain, but Vick had seen that action throughout the years from his brother. A tell.

Was he lying about something?

Marcus asked the questions again, his low voice muted through the camera, "Do you know of any Alban Technology in the Empire?"

Jay answered in the negative again, his words ending in a shout as he tried to reach his eyes with his manacled hands, shaking his head desperately.

Vick watched closely. No tell.

Perhaps it had just been his imagination. He watched the rest of the interrogation closely, not seeing again any signs of deceit from his younger brother.

It seemed that Marcus agreed, finally leaving the room to speak with Vick. Jay lay slumped over the heavy metal table in the barren room, his hands still bound before him on the table, his body strapped to the metal chair anchored to the stone floor.

"Your thoughts?"

Vick watched his brother on the camera screen, resting the same tawny head he himself sported on the table.

"I don't think he's part of any plot. At least not with the virus. If he did infect us, it was unintentional."

Marcus nodded, also watching the screen. "I agree. He's more concerned about Lina than himself. Just a fool who let emotional attachment get the better of him."

Vick's brows raised in surprise. "A fool? I know another man who's mellowed quite a bit recently, and you can't tell me it isn't because of a certain 'emotional attachment' he has with one feisty woman."

Marcus' face darkened slightly, proof Vick's words had

found their mark.

"Love makes fools of many men."

"So you're saying you love Aerina?"

Marcus said nothing, stiff and straight as he watched Jay's exhausted form on the camera.

"Give him an hour and cut him loose. But monitor him closely." His order was directed to the Virmortus standing near the heavy metal door of the interrogation room. The man nodded.

"A wise man once told me to embrace love, and not to run from it," Vick said quietly as Marcus turned to leave.

Marcus paused, not turning back. "Where is this man now?"

"Dead."

"Precisely." He continued out. Vick grinned, shaking his head. The idiot obviously loved Aerina. He wondered how long he would make himself suffer by denying it.

He's not the only idiot here, a voice in his head taunted.

I don't love Helen. I barely know her. I just need to see this through before I head back to Vicksburg.

Somehow, the words didn't ring true.

*   *   *

Vick's world had shrunk to the size of Helen's twelve-by-twelve-foot room.

Sometimes Helen awoke, seeming to be aware of him and her surroundings. But mostly she rambled about things from her childhood, or talked to Stephen, whom she often confused him with.

He'd be a liar to say it didn't rankle a little to be mistaken for her dead lover. How the hell did one compete with a ghost? But he was also willing to do whatever it took to calm her and get her through this.

And her baby. His eyes moved again to her very-flat stomach covered by the light cotton blanket. He should be wary of caring for someone with baggage like Helen. He'd been so careful to avoid any kind of commitment after what had happened to the first woman he'd loved. Even before faking his own death to escape his mother, he'd kept his distance from his dysfunctional family, and from any woman who'd come across his path that he might want more than just a night with.

He couldn't risk the life of another person he cared for.

Now he found himself strangely attracted to a punctilious pregnant woman. And he already cared about the tiny life tucked inside her more than he should.

Shit.

Standing quickly, the walls in the room closing in, he burst into the hall like a drowning man escaping the water. He took several deep breaths to calm the rising panic.

Once this is over, Helen will go back to her life of importance and prestige, and I'll return to Vicksburg. Everything will return to normal. Helen would be safe from the bad luck that surrounded him, and his heart would be hardened against these debilitating *emotions*.

Carefully unclenching his fists, he made the familiar trek to the room just to the left, entering after a perfunctory knock.

Jay looked up from his own vigil beside Lina's bed. He'd returned there as soon as they'd released him, allowing an ID chip to be inserted in exchange for the privilege of sitting in this new prison. He must really be in love with the woman to go through all this for her.

The woman in question was sitting, carefully eating soup from a tray before her. Vick couldn't help the stab of resentment he felt at seeing her already up and recovering from her own bout with the tiny virus wreaking havoc on Helen's frail body.

"You're looking better," he said.

Lina wiped her mouth with a napkin.

"Thanks to your brother." She smiled over at Jay, and Vick again felt the bite of envy.

Damn, what the hell was wrong with him?

"Maybe this thing isn't as bad as we thought," Jay said, meeting Vick's eyes. Vick recognized the veiled expression; he'd seen it in the mirror many times over the years. Jay knew how severe the situation was.

Lina didn't. She was recovering, and Vick knew Jay didn't want her worrying about Helen; about the rest of the Patricians.

"I'm glad to see you're recovering, Lina. Jay, can I talk to you for a minute?" Vick indicated the hall, and Jay stood quickly, following him.

"What? Is it Helen?" Jay asked in a concerned undertone.

Vick shook his head. "The virus has claimed its first fatality. Senator Caius died this morning."

"Shit. The Senator of Technology? Lina works for him; hell, she probably gave it to him after she picked it up from me, just like she did Helen." Jay's voice had dropped to a stark whisper and he whirled away, clenching his fists.

Vick understood how he felt, wanting to protect the woman he cared about from the results of his mistake. Any lingering doubts about his brother's innocence dissipated in the face of Jay's obvious self-recrimination.

It was one of the many reasons Vick refused to enter a relationship; he didn't need to be responsible for wrecking another life.

Not again.

Comforting someone was new and strange territory, but Vick entered it cautiously.

"You've been cleared by Marcus, or you wouldn't be here. No one is blaming you. At least no one who matters," Vick added, thinking of the whispers he'd overheard from the Medellas about outsiders bringing the plague.

But outsiders included him, as well.

"Thanks," Jay said drily.

Vick shrugged. "If you need me, you know where to find me. There's more encouragement where that came from."

With a wave and a rude gesture, Vick headed back towards Helen's room. He heard Lina asking what their conversation was about, and wondered how much Jay would tell her.

All thoughts fled when he entered Helen's room to see her attempting to get out of bed.

"What are you doing?" He rushed forward to push her gently back down. She was so thin, fear clawed at his heart. Could she survive much more?

"I need to use the bathroom," she mumbled, pushing ineffectively at his hand.

"I'll help you," he said, lifting her gently from the bed.

"I don't think so. Put me down at once," she ordered, her dry throat making her cough. He set her down in the bathroom, bringing her a glass of water. She sipped it, then motioned for him to leave. He hesitated before reluctantly standing outside the door, waiting for her to finish.

He didn't wait long, going back in to help support her while she washed, watching her cup shaking hands and try to lift them to splash her sweat-drenched face with water.

She glared at him but said nothing as he grabbed a rag, dampening it and gently washing her face while supporting her.

"I need to shower," she croaked, clearing her throat. Vick was already shaking his head.

"Unless that's a shower for two, you'll have to make due with a sponge bath."

Helen opened her mouth to argue, then closed it, nodding her acquiescence.

He helped her back to the bed, lowering her gently. He covered her, brushing her blonde hair back with his hand. As he turned away, she caught his hand in a surprisingly tight grip.

"Vick."

He raised his brows questioningly.

"Thank you."

He grinned. "Was that so painful?"

"Agonizing," she confirmed. His smile widened, and he couldn't help but feel ridiculously excited at the bit of bantering that proved she was still hanging in there.

"How is the baby?" Fear was evident in her tone, but her light green eyes met his unwaveringly.

"I don't know," he admitted, afraid himself to find out what toll her illness might have had on the unborn life inside her. "I'll go find someone who can help us."

As Vick summoned assistance, Helen's hand went instinctively to the tiny life inside her that she'd only just begun to think of as a little person.

What would she do if something had happened to her baby? Sick fear rolled over her in waves, threatening to paralyze her.

Her baby.

It hadn't seemed real until this moment; that a life was growing inside her. A life she and Stephen had created; a life that would continue on even as its father had died.

If this illness didn't steal it from her.

Please no…

As the Medella entered the room, dressed in the red biohazard suit, Helen couldn't help the involuntary urge to push the woman away.

Her palms were sweating, her heart pounding in her ears as the woman pulled out the Doppler and began moving it gently around in her flat stomach. She almost didn't notice when Vick took her clenched fist in his, gently rubbing the white fingers with his callused ones.

Please oh please oh please…

Silence filled the room but for the quiet static from the Doppler. Helen felt panicky fear pressing down on her chest, making it difficult to breath. The Medella was frowning, pressing harder against Helen's stomach, trying different angles to locate the tiny heartbeat.

What if there wasn't one? What if the illness had stolen

the life she'd barely known about? That she'd barely had time to consider was real, but still loved with every part of her being...

I can't lose this baby, too.

"What's the goddamn problem?" Vick growled, his gentle grip on her hand belying the frustration in his tone. Helen was surprised at the note of genuine fear she detected. She'd only begun to accept and love this life herself, but Vick seemed just as attached.

Just as scared.

Their shared worry calmed her heart slightly, bringing tears to her eyes. She opened her fist, squeezing his hand. He glanced down at her, the normally relaxed lines of his face hard and flexed with his worry.

She found herself in the strange position of trying to comfort him.

"Infant heartbeats can sometimes be difficult to find," she said quietly. The Medella cast her a grateful look as she continued, a little less desperately this time. Helen realized the doctor had been somewhat intimidated by Vick.

A few more tense moments passed, and then the fast staccato of a developing heart came pounding through the Doppler.

Helen breathed a cry of relief, tears flowing down her gaunt cheeks. Vick let go of her hand abruptly, sitting back in his chair. His face had gone blank, but she thought his eyes looked a little watery.

Without a word, he stood and left the room. Helen was too happy to care, crying tears of joy at the beautiful sound of her child's heart.

Vick paced the hallway, desperately needing to get out of the clinic. Out of this city. Back to his safe haven where he could be as isolated as he wished. Away from the ruin that awaited him in that room.

The emotions in him swirled, a tsunami threatening to

drown him. This wasn't what he wanted. He couldn't get this close to anyone again. Relationships always ended up going to hell, no matter how well-intentioned. Or they became like his parents, a parasitic relationship that eventually drained one partner dry.

His breath hissed through his teeth as he struggled to bring himself back under control.

The Medella exited the room a few minutes later, stepping around him warily and leaving him to his thoughts. He was glad. The last thing he needed right now was some well-meaning—

"Want to talk about it, big brother?"

He glared at his younger brother, leaning nonchalantly against the hallway wall near Lina's door. Vick wanted to knock the mocking grin off his brother's pretty face.

He rubbed a hand absently over his own bearded jaw, feeling the uneven lines that ran below the carefully trimmed hair.

"Hell no."

Jay's smile spread even wider, amusement written clearly on his face. "I may not have seen you in nearly a decade, but you were always the cool player. And from what I saw in the Empire just a few weeks ago, you still are. But here is one tiny woman, ruffling your feathers like—"

Vick couldn't stop his fist from flying, but Jay was ready; had been goading him. He blocked the blow with his forearm, ducking to the side with a laugh.

"Shit, you're fast."

Vick didn't waste time with words, swinging again to put a dent in his brother's perfect face. Jay ducked again, but wasn't quite fast enough, and Vick clipped his chin, throwing Jay's head back.

Jay let loose a string of profanity, gingerly touching his jaw. He grinned again, this time with a harder glint in his eye. Then he made his own move, a quick twist and hit that put Vick against the wall with a crash that shook the hallway.

Helen's worried voice came from in the room, while a Medella appeared, followed immediately by the Virmortus on guard duty at the door.

Vick pushed away from the wall.

"Sorry, just letting off a little steam." He wacked Jay on the shoulder before turning back to the room that now didn't seem quite so terrifying.

Chapter 7

"Power always corrupts. Giving a ruler a lifetime of power is a deadly mistake." - Letters from Matias Emmanuel March

Marcus alighted from his low e-car, striding across the street towards the understated elegance of the Capitol clinic. The day seemed unexpectedly warm, and he resisted the urge to loosen his weapon vest, wishing for a drink of water. And a moment of rest.

But there would be no rest for him in the foreseeable future.

He'd noted the small gathering of people when he'd pulled up to the curb, but didn't slow his stride as he approached.

Surprisingly, while a few stepped back, most of the dozen white-clothed people remained firm. The spokesperson stepped forward. It was Senator Strauss, the woman responsible for the health of the city.

"Mr. Trent, you have been avoiding our calls and skipping our emergency meetings. We demand to know what is going on."

"You're in violation of curfew."

Senator Strauss looked taken aback, apparently not used to such disrespect. She straightened her trim form, boldly taking another step forward. "People are falling ill. Important people. We are dying, Mr. Trent. We need to know so we can reassure the people: What is going on?"

Suddenly Marcus' sica blade was in his hand, making the crowd gasp and fall back. He gripped the blade easily, a little surprised at his own action.

"There is a time for politics, Senator. And that time is not now. I won't tell you again. Stand down. I'll brief you when necessary."

The crowd around him was silent with shock. A Reaper had never threatened a Senator before. Not publicly.

"You're making a mistake," Senator Strauss hissed. But she turned, motioning to the crowd to disperse.

"We need to remain in our homes for our own safety; to avoid contamination. I will meet privately with our leader and brief you all later."

The Patricians obeyed, appearing eager to escape Marcus' presence.

A wave of dizziness overcame Marcus as he turned towards the clinic. Pushing through the door, he paused in the lobby. Darkness crept into his peripheral as a heavy weight tried to pull him into oblivion.

"Lucien," he heard himself rasp. The Virmortus rushed over as Marcus fought the encroaching darkness with sheer force of will. Deep breath in, deep breath out.

A worker came up with a glass of water, and he gulped it. "Get Aerina," he ordered as the weight pressing on him became too great even for his indomitable will.

He was barely aware of his surroundings as Lucien helped him to a chair.

"He's burning up," he heard distantly. Then Aerina was kneeling before him, her smooth hand cool on his cheek.

"Marcus? When did you start feeling ill?" she asked, her sapphire eyes shadowed with worry. He shook his head, trying to clear the lingering fuzz. Someone appeared suddenly at his elbow and instinctively he moved defensively to push them away.

"It's ok, Marcus. It is the Medella. She has something for the fever. You're on fire, love." Her voice was soothing, and he knew she was patronizing him.

"I'm sick, not a goddamn infant," he muttered, struggling to form the words.

Aerina smiled at that, her hand moving from his face to cover his clenched fist. "Get better and I won't coddle you. Until then, you're just going to have to suffer."

"We don't have rooms available here," a Medella said distantly.

"The emergency clinic is ready at the University. We'll take him there."

The ride, combined with the torturous heat pounding in his head made Marcus nauseous, but he made it to the nearby University clinic without incident.

Aerina fussed until he demanded she stop. "I need you to get Vick."

"Vick?" She turned to look at him questioningly.

Marcus leaned back, knowing sleep was imminent. "Yes, Vick. Someone is going to need to run this city while I'm ill. Those damn Senators will take over otherwise. And then we'll all be dead."

"But *Vick*?" Aerina asked again. "He's not an Alban."

"Precisely." He needed her help in convincing his friend to run the city, so he felt compelled to explain further. "Whoever is going to get this city through an epidemic is going to need a heavy hand. Not someone political; a dictator. And that person is going to be hated. Vick will leave when this is all over."

"A scapegoat."

Marcus nodded, then regretted it as the pounding in his head increased at the movement.

"In a sense."

"But Vick is your friend. Why would you put that on him?"

"It doesn't matter what he is. This is necessary."

"He'll never agree to do it."

"He owes me. It'll just take a little arm-twisting. But he's a natural hero. He'll do it."

Aerina sighed, and Marcus knew she was going to help him. He let his eyes close, the grasp of sleep pulling him down.

"And then he actually read the clause, and saw he'd been

wrong the entire time," Helen finished her story about the Senator of Law, making Lina laugh outright.

"He needs to be replaced; he's getting senile." She leaned casually on Helen's bed, a pillow under her arms as the women talked. Both had improved remarkably in the last day, signaling that the worst of it had passed.

Helen still felt ridiculously weak, but she blamed that on her pregnancy as much as her illness. Her thoughts wandered to Vick again, as much as she tried to avoid it. He had been much more distant since the previous day when she'd been terrified the baby hadn't survived.

Perhaps he thought now that she was improving, his responsibility was over and he was eager to return to his town.

To be honest, she'd been surprised that he'd stayed as long as he had. He had always seemed a loner, a man who was not very quick to form attachments beyond casual friendships. Friendly with everyone, close to no one.

But he did take his commitments seriously, when he made them. And apparently he felt some kind of obligation towards her, and her unborn child.

It was a good thing this was almost at an end, and both could go back to their separate lives. It was best. Her place was here in Alba working to become the next Senator of Law, and he was obviously attached to his little town outside Alba. And as much as she hated the word, he *was* an outsider. They had no future, not that he'd even hinted at wanting one.

So stop thinking of him as anything other than a friend of Aerina's, she chided herself.

As if she'd conjured her, Aerina appeared in the door.

"Hi!" Lina called happily, pushing off the bed to give her friend a hug. She stopped suddenly, seeing the look of shock on Aerina's face, pale beneath her tan.

"What is it?"

"Marcus. Marcus is sick," she said, her voice breaking. She collapsed into Lina's arms, and Lina guided her gently to the chair beside the bed, settling her into it.

Aerina didn't look her normal vivacious self. Her red-streaked blonde hair was hanging in a messy ponytail, her face drawn and pale, eyes puffy.

"And my father is still ill, and now that Senator Caius has died..." Aerina shook her head, looking more lost than Helen had ever seen her.

Her heart ached for her friend, but she let Lina offer comfort. She'd never been able to relate well; to be expressive like her friends and her parents.

"Doctor says you are—" Vick entered the room, already relaying the good news of Helen's improvement, when he noticed Aerina.

"Aerina, what happened?"

"Marcus is sick."

Vick said nothing for a long moment, then crouched before Aerina, taking her hands in his. "He's strong; hell, he'd be the last guy I'd worry about. He'll be back to telling us all what to do soon enough."

Aerina nodded, swiping angrily at the tears that continued to trickle.

"Ramus is still sick, and two more Senators are ill. The new Senators from other Terraces aren't allowed to travel here." Aerina looked Vick in the eye, and Helen had a feeling she might know what her friend was getting at.

He will never do it, she thought.

Vick stood, turning away. He must have figured out where Aerina was going with her statements, too.

"You are closer to Marcus than anyone; you know his system, the politics here. You know how to handle the world outside, and to deal with these kinds of situations." Aerina stood, her voice becoming more persuasive as she saw the stiffening of Vick's back.

"We need an interim leader; someone who isn't afraid to deal with the crazy this epidemic is going to unleash."

"That's ludicrous," he said calmly. "I'm an outsider. No

outsider can run the Virmortus, much less the entire Republic."

"You're likely immune to this and won't get sick. You are a trained agent. And the Virmortus are familiar with you. If Marcus appoints you—"

"I'm not going to do it," Vick stated with quiet finality. "I already have enough responsibility in Vicksburg—"

Helen felt unexpected anger at his attempt to skirt any kind of real responsibility. "What, less than a thousand people who are living independently; living comfortably thanks to the technology Marcus has been sharing with you for years? Whose town has been kept safe in the shadow of Alba's military prowess? Yes, you must be crushed by the weight of responsibilities you carry. By all means, please hurry back before it's too late. And when Alba begins crumbling because you've turned your back—"

"Alright," Vick interrupted her tirade, his eyes gleaming with reluctant admiration. "You made your point. I do owe Marcus. If he asks me, I'll consider it."

Aerina smiled, relief lightening her features. She shot Helen a grateful glance.

"Come, Marcus is in the emergency clinic."

Vick followed Aerina down the University hallway, knowing that this was a turning point in his life. First staying to watch over Helen, and now... Damn, was he really about to run this place?

Entering the room at the end of the hall, he was brought up short. Marcus looked so different, laying on the bed, his body weak and cheeks streaked with the red of fever.

Aerina went straight to his side, sitting gently on the edge of the bed, her hand going to Marcus' brow. He swiped it away irritably.

"I'm not feeble. Don't fuss over me." His voice, though slightly hoarse, still carried with it the weight of authority.

Aerina just rolled her eyes as Vick sat on the chair

adjacent to the bed.

"You look quite capable of still running this place. I don't know what Aerina thinks you need me for," Vick said.

"It's going to be bad, Vick. I need someone willing to..." he glanced at Aerina "to be harsh. Someone like me. Politics isn't going to get Alba through this. A heavy hand and a tough bastard is what is needed."

"None of your Virmortus—"

"None that I trust enough. None that are immune to this disease. None like you."

"So I guess I'll get to play the heavy-handed dictator? You know that's not how I do things now."

"It will be when everyone's survival depends on it. And when they all turn on you. You owe me, Vick."

"I was afraid you were going to say that," Vick said wryly, looking out the window at the outline of the University just across the street, and the Capitol's dome gleaming beyond that.

Que asi sea.

"Alright, guess I'm your man."

The two men shook hands.

"I'll make an announcement. Aerina, you record it on my reader." Marcus raised himself to a sitting position. Vick resisted the urge to offer assistance as Marcus' arms shook slightly, knowing his friend would not appreciate any recognition of his weakened state.

He hoped he didn't live to regret this. If he lived through this at all.

Vick left the room several minutes later. The message they'd just created would soon be broadcast to the entire Republic and surrounding outposts.

"Congrats, brother." Jay met him in the hallway back at the clinic, a familiar smirk on his face.

"How did you know already?"

"Lina."

"Of course."

Jay grinned even wider at Vick's long-suffering tone. "It's kind of refreshing to be with someone who is so terrible at subterfuge."

"So you and Lina…?"

Jay shrugged. "She hasn't kicked me out yet. As soon as the doctor give the ok, we're abandoning this sinking ship—"

"I don't think so." Lina's calm voice interrupted. Jay turned to face her. Dressed in a crisp white pantsuit, her chocolate-colored hair clipped neatly back, and shoulders squared as if ready for battle, she looked every inch the Patrician. "We're not leaving our friends here to fend for themselves."

Jay opened his mouth to argue, but Lina had already turned to Vick.

"I can help create a system that identifies the infected through the ID chips, and it can send an Armati automatically to collect the sick."

Vick nodded, his mind already working on ways to organize with the quarantine restrictions in place.

"Great, meet me at the Training Grounds when you're discharged from here." He looked over at his brother's disgruntled face. "Bring your boyfriend. I'm gonna need him, too."

He entered Helen's room. She was watching the broadcast on her holoreader. He inwardly cringed as his own image popped up, and he began to speak about banding together and protecting neighbors by making sure the ill were brought to assigned clinic locations.

"You're leaving," Helen stated. Vick nodded, unable to read her expression.

"I'm heading to the Training Grounds. I'll come back to check on you—"

"My parents plan on visiting. I'll be fine. You have a new set of responsibilities now."

Her tone was cool and distant. Did she think this was it? She wasn't going to get rid of him this easily.

"I'll be by your room tonight, probably late. Don't wait up."

He headed out the door.

"Wait, what do you mean...?"

He ignored her indignant questioning, her voice fading as he exited the hall into the lobby. He nodded to the Virmortus guarding the door, who returned the greeting, adding respectfully, "Sir."

The transition of power was official. He was now the Alpha Virmortus and Interim Consul of Alba.

Holy hell, how much crazier was this going to get?

"Mom. Dad." Helen smiled to see her parents enter the room, but the red suits they wore made the severity of her situation hit home. The situation was bigger than her. Much bigger.

The visit with her parents did little to alleviate her concerns. They talked about things like the weather, and upcoming votes, overly careful to avoid the state of Alba's health. That surprised her. Her parents were not avoiders. They faced issues head on, and had taught her to do the same.

"How is everyone holding up?" she finally asked.

Her mother glanced at her father, shaking her head.

"Darling, let's not get into that. We want you to focus on recovering."

"Mother —"

"Helen, your mother is right. You'll find out details soon enough. Right now, just rest. Eat what you can. You don't need any extra stress. It's bad for my grandchild."

Helen set her teeth to keep from responding, knowing once her father played the "baby card", the argument was over. For now.

She'd wait up for Vick and get the information from him.

As it happened, she had to wait a full day before getting the answers she wanted. Vick spent the rest of that day and most of the evening at the Training Grounds. She knew he returned to the room, because the couch had blankets and a pillow neatly folded and stacked. Vick did that each morning, and the assistant Medella came and took them to launder, returning with fresh sets in the evening.

His tidiness was another quirk she found at odds with the persona he put forth, that of the unconcerned drifter. He was an enigma, and perhaps that was the reason for her fascination.

Determined not to miss him again, Helen napped most of the next day. She was struggling to keep her eyes open when the door opened quietly and the familiar broad form slipped through.

"I'm awake, don't bother being quiet," she informed him.

Vick dropped onto the thin couch, leaning his head against the back. "Shouldn't you be sleeping?" he asked. Helen swallowed the ire his comment caused. It was growing rather annoying how everyone seemed to have such an opinion about how she should take care of herself.

It is just because they are concerned, she reminded herself.

"I'm fine. I wanted to know how your day went. What is going on outside?"

Vick leaned forward, studying her in the low lamplight. "It isn't a great bedtime tale. Maybe we could talk about it in the morning."

"Vick, if you don't start talking, I'm getting out of this bed and driving myself home. I have two parents and a fairly competent doctor, I don't need you worrying and doing things 'for my own good'."

Vick put his hands up as if in surrender. "I got it. No worrying. No protecting. You want the truth? This virus is fucking scary. Two Patricians are dead already and its only been a week since we discovered it."

"Has it spread to the other Terraces?"

"Not yet. But it's only a matter of time." Vick rubbed his eyes, and Helen finally noticed in the low light how red they appeared. Vick was exhausted.

He needed rest.

Now who is worrying? A tiny voice taunted.

I'm only being courteous, she told herself.

"We can talk more in the morning. Where are you planning on staying?"

Vick shrugged. "Here, tonight."

"I should be able to go home in another day. If you need a place to stay..." The offer slipped out before she could stop it.

Vick's brows raised. "Are you inviting me to live with you? I'm shocked. We hardly know each other."

"It was hardly a solicitation. It just seemed practical under the circumstances. However—"

"I appreciate the offer. I'll borrow some of Marcus' things and plan to stay there once you're home. Not to look after you, of course," he added with a grin.

"Just while you are needed in Alba. As roommates." Helen felt even more foolish after attempting to clarify the situation. *Just shut your mouth before you stick your foot in any further.*

His smile told her he knew how awkward she felt. Then he intentionally made the situation worse by pulling off his shirt. She hastily averted her gaze, but not before she got an eyeful hair-covered pectorals, well-defined abdominals, and sculpted biceps, all well-bronzed by the sun.

You're sick and you're pregnant, she reminded herself. Her body wasn't listening. She couldn't help but steal one quick glance as they both settled down into their beds. He was stretched uncomfortably on the too-short couch, his legs dangling off the end. He'd undone the tie from his hair, and the thick, slightly wavy locks gleamed in the light, brushing the back of his neck. Rather than softening his features, the hair framed the squared line of his jaw. Seeing him half undressed with his hair mussed was strangely erotic, and Helen turned away, taking a few deep breaths to eradicate the unexpected heat.

For serenity's sake, get yourself together. You barely know this man, you almost died, and his motivations for helping you are suspect. You're not a silly girl; you're a mature, responsible woman. You don't have time for frivolous emotions like this.

The pep talk didn't help. Helen forced herself to close her eyes, growing irritable as she heard Vick's breathing even out as he dropped off to sleep. Apparently he wasn't having the same issue she was.

Vick's even breathing and exhaustion from her illness soon lulled her into a doze. She felt safe and protected, and for this moment, she would relish the feelings. Just for tonight. Sleep overcame her, deep and dreamless.

"Have you made contact with the Council?" the woman asked, smoothing her white suit with a slender hand.

The man in shadow nodded, keeping his back turned as he watched a holoscreen, tracking the creation that was his life. And his duty.

"Have they agreed to wait until after our takeover to act?"

"Yes. I doubt they have the resources at this time to take any major action, anyhow. They're tied up with their own rebellion."

"Excellent. We can't waste any time. He's becoming increasingly volatile."

"He may not be much of a danger for much longer. But the new order emerging needs to be completely crushed. I have no doubt this epidemic will create the fear we need."

The woman crinkled her nose at the heavy scent of mildew in the air around them. "Good. Then we'll no longer need to meet in these deplorable conditions."

"No. I expect soon the Capitol will be in our hands. And we will complete our deal with the Council."

"Are you leaving the city during the trouble?"

The shadow man shook his head. "No, I need to be seen

publicly. And I can't leave my partner while she is ill."

"Ahh, yes. Still have loyalties, do you? Be careful she doesn't get in the way of the ultimate goal."

"It won't," he snapped, standing stiff and tall. "I haven't come this far to let anything get in my path. Not even her."

The white-clothed woman was silent for a moment, before nodding in acceptance. "Soon now it will be all over. And things can be the way they were intended. And you will have the power you deserve, as will I."

Chapter 8

"The ability to adapt is a key survival skill. Make sure we're testing for that." - Recorded Conversations with Cecilia Delacroix

The next few days passed slowly. Helen was anxious to get out of the clinic and find a way to help the crisis taking over the city.

Vick was no longer around to help pass the time, waking up before her in the mornings and often arriving late.

Lina visited once, telling her of the restrictions being placed on the citizens. A strict curfew was implemented, travel between the Terraces had been halted, and Patricians were taking over the day-to-day tasks usually performed by Pleb and Aggie employees.

"My mother actually did the dishes when I visited. And emptied the robovac. I'm still in shock."

Helen shook her head, struggling to accept what Lina was telling her. How could things have changed so dramatically in a matter of weeks? Even after the attacks by the Southern Empire, things hadn't altered so drastically.

It wasn't that Patricians were doing menial chores; for the most part, they were a practical bunch that would do what was necessary to survive. It was how quickly things were changing that had her concerned. Change in itself wasn't bad, but quick change could be devastating to a society.

She just hoped Vick was capable of holding onto control, or things would fall apart quickly.

It was after two more seemingly endless days that the Medella finally deemed Helen safe to go home. They performed one last routine checkup, and then cleared her to leave. The Virmortus on duty scanned her wrist, making sure her ID read Uninfected.

When her father finally arrived around dinner time to pick her up, she couldn't wait to put the clinic behind her. Although, a small part of her would miss the quiet moments with Vick, she admitted. She felt a strange mixture of anticipation and anxiety, thinking of him invading her home. Did she dare let him? She could only imagine how it would look to other Patricians...

How it would look to her friends. Not that Lina or Aerina would care. They'd both formed their own strange attachments. In fact, Jay and Lina had left a few days earlier, returning together to Stephen's villa.

Lina's villa, she reminded herself.

She'd watched them leave together, the fierce stab of envy at their unashamed affection catching her off guard. But while they had an undeniable connection, they also had a long road ahead of them. A relationship for them would not come easy; not as long as they remained in Alba.

Not surprisingly, they had been arguing still about leaving the city. Jay wanted to find a safe place to wait out the plague that had descended, while Lina naturally wanted to stay.

Helen had known Lina would win that battle. From what she'd seen of Jay so far, he had a real soft spot where her friend was concerned. And he was working hard to make up for the rocky start of their relationship.

"Father." She forgot her musings in a moment of elation as her father entered the lobby where she waited impatiently.

They embraced, although Helen was still nervous about infecting him. It was irrational, being a trained Medella herself she was quite aware the contagious period was past, but fear was more powerful than logic.

Hagen Vanderbilt looked Helen over, tears in his pale green eyes. "I'm so glad you're getting better. And... and the child?"

Helen smiled, taking a small step back. She had always

been uncomfortable with displays of affection, even though her parents were both very tactile with each other and with her as a child.

They'd often joked she had been switched at birth, but her resemblance to her petite, light-haired, green-eyed father was unmistakable. Their personalities, however, were much different.

"Your grandbaby is fine, Father. Now let's get out of here before they change their minds," she joked, nodding to the receptionist and the Virmortus guarding the door.

"Your mother and I would like you to stay with us, until you're recovered," her father said as he pulled his e-car away from the clinic.

"I appreciate the offer, but I'd really like to be in my own home."

"Our home is your home, too, Helen—"

"No, Father. I do have a friend coming to stay with me. I'll be fine."

"Oh, I didn't realize… Is it Aerina?"

Helen sighed, feeling like a child admitting to wrongdoing. "No, a friend of Aerina's. Vicktor March."

A long silence came from her father's side of the vehicle, and Helen looked over, reading the displeasure on his face.

"He's just a friend, Father, and he needed a place to stay while he's running Alba. Surely if he is acceptable as the temporary Alpha and interim Consul, he is acceptable as a roommate for your daughter."

"Just because a man is the Consul, it doesn't make him good enough for my daughter," Hagen said darkly. Helen shook her head, a small smile on her lips.

"Everything will be fine, Father. Now, how is Mother?"

Her father's face went blank, causing her heart to sink. "She's not sick, is she? What—"

"No, no," her father was quick to reassure her. "It's your grandad. He's ill."

"How? I haven't seen him in weeks."

Hagen shook his head. "He wasn't infected by you. This illness is spreading quickly. Patricians are falling ill all over the Terrace. Deathly ill."

"I've heard. I suppose I didn't fully comprehend..." Helen's voice trailed off in horror, the reality of the situation settling in. She'd been wrapped in a cocoon of oblivion in the clinic, with Vick looking after her, Lina and Aerina close by.

Her hand settled on her stomach protectively.

This was going to be ugly. No wonder Vick had been so hesitant to take it on. When she had pressured him to take the position, she hadn't realized the gravity of the situation.

She owed him any help she could offer. More than just a place to stay, she would join the research team looking for a vaccine, and offer her public support of him as leader.

He deserved that much, at least.

Vick's days as Alpha passed quickly. He first met with the uninfected Senators who were demanding updates. He knew he was going to need their support to succeed. The Senators of Health, Population Control, and Law met him in the Capitol meeting room.

The beauty of the day belied the grave atmosphere of the room. The three Senators all wore masks and thin gloves to protect from the germs, adding to the portentous aura of the meeting.

Vick motioned for the Senators to sit, leaning forward in his own chair. He met the gaze of each Senator in turn, looking for signs of their true feelings about the current situation. All seemed wary but respectful. "Thank you for coming. I'm sure we'll all be glad when we can return to normal and put this behind us. I hope until then we can work together."

The three Senators nodded, saying nothing. Vick was certain this was unpleasant for them, but so far they seemed surprisingly accepting of the situation. He supposed the Virmortus had become so powerful that no one dared stand against the Alpha.

Or they were plotting behind his back and didn't want him to know.

He understood now why the previous Consul, Julius, had tried to do away with the Virmortus. The two groups were naturally at odds, and the balance of control was questionable.

They discussed the quarantine, and what Marcus had already implemented.

Food transfer from the Aggie Terrace was limited, so supplies were being carefully rationed. No travel was allowed between Terraces. Armati were patrolling to ensure no sick were avoiding the clinic. Every unessential business was closed, and citizens were being encouraged to remain at home.

A limited curfew was being enforced on the Capitol Terrace, and they discussed the possibility of expanding it if an outbreak occurred on other terraces.

"I want a full report in the morning of the progress the University lab has made on a vaccine, and the entomology of this illness."

"Yes, sir," the Health Senator answered, her voice muffled behind her mask.

Vick absently rubbed his beard, his fingers finding the familiar raised lines beneath the groomed hair along his jaw.

"That's all for now," he completed. "Please meet me here again tomorrow at the same time. If anything new arises, you can contact me anytime on my reader." Once each Senator had nodded, he turned to go.

"Mr. March." The Senator of Law approached as the others gathered their things to leave.

"Call me Vick," he offered, turning to face the older man who was Helen's boss. The slight man had well-groomed silver hair, and his skin hung loosely around the mask he wore.

The Senator nodded. "Vick, can you tell me how Helen is

doing?"

Vick raised an eyebrow in surprise. He'd thought the man was going to have an issue with the severity of law and punishment put in place to avoid spreading the sickness or the inevitable breakdown of authority. At the very least, he thought the man of law would take issue with his authority, being an outsider.

But apparently no one wanted to be in his shoes right now. He couldn't blame them. He really didn't want to be, either.

"Helen is recovering. She has been discharged from the clinic today and should be returning home."

"Good; good news," the Senator said, hesitating for a moment as if there was more he wanted to say. Finally, he cleared his throat before asking, "And her…the pregnancy?"

"The fetus is fine," Vick answered shortly, wondering at the man's curiosity.

He nodded, his mask making it difficult for Vick to see his expression.

"I'm glad, for her," the man continued, his voice thinning nervously at Vick's increasingly foreboding expression. "It just makes it difficult for me, you understand. I had given her quite a position of authority, due to her high marks and obvious ambition. But now… well, it just isn't acceptable for an unmarried mother to be in such a position. But of course I'll have to speak with her about this once she's fully recovered and this situation has passed," the older man finished quickly, meeting Vick's eyes with effort.

Vick wanted to say something harsh in the face of such obvious prejudice, but now wasn't the time. He knew Alba's laws; knew unsanctioned pregnancies were taboo. It was Helen's problem to deal with. He was already enmeshed enough in her life. So he said nothing, turning away and leaving the Senator of Law standing awkwardly in the Meeting Room overlooking the gleaming ocean far below.

It was already late afternoon, and the sun was lowering

in the sky, bright and warm. Vick slid into his converted Bronco, the low roar of the engine calming his uncertain temper.

He'd love nothing more than to be driving over the rocky terrain, wind blowing his hair, the smell of the ocean whipping through his truck.

Instead, he was driving sedately towards the Training Grounds to take on Marcus' thankless task of trying to save Alba.

The large metal and stone building loomed before him as he climbed the narrow road up the mountainside. He didn't have access to the underground garage, so he parked and walked to the unimpressive entrance, pressing the call button and waiting patiently.

"Buzzing you in, sir," came the almost immediate response through the tiny speaker, and the door beeped long and loud.

Vick entered into the familiar long white hallway leading to a second door that was being quickly opened by a young Virmortus recruit, probably about fourteen or fifteen years of age. He nodded to the kid, not entirely certain if the close-cropped hair belonged to a boy or girl.

"I need to speak with Simon, is he in today?"

"No, sir, Simon has fallen ill."

Vick breathed an expletive. "Is he back on the Pleb Terrace?" The young recruit nodded, drawing more profanity from Vick.

"Has an Armati been to check on him; to bring him to a clinic?"

"I'll check, sir."

Dammit, Simon was sick, which meant the Technology Project would need to be put on hold. He would need to call on the other tech agents to get a system built quickly that would track the sick, and also some way to deal with resource allocation.

It also meant someone on the Pleb Terrace was infected.

If the disease began spreading...

He'd need to watch and make sure people didn't start fleeing the city. The last thing they needed was this illness to begin infecting the surrounding outposts. The small towns and settlements all around the area were not equipped to deal with this kind of illness. They'd be decimated.

Towns like Vicksburg.

He picked up the plan Marcus had created, going over the fine points, seeing which ones had been implemented, which ones were in process, and what still needed to be done.

Summoning the Virmortus assigned to lead each task, he watched the millions of blinking lights on the grid that tracked each citizen through tiny ID chips. He couldn't stop his mind from picturing each light slowly blinking out until the grid was black. An entire nation extinct.

That wasn't going to happen. They'd caught it early and were taking swift steps to contain the virus. Some people might die, but the young, the strong, would survive.

It was his job to make sure of it.

"Lina, things are going to go to hell fast. And it is only going to get worse. It will be safer —"

"I'm not leaving."

Jay's jaw clenched at her response, and he whirled away from her, stalking to the window of the study overlooking the ocean. His tall frame was taut with frustration.

"I can't have something happen to you. I've already caused you enough harm."

She had to strain to hear him. The self-derision in his voice made her heart soften. Walking up behind him, she put a hand on his arm.

"This isn't your fault, Jay."

He muttered something under his breath before saying more clearly, "Tell that to the rest of Alba. I'm lucky to have escaped that interrogation room the second time." He rolled his shoulders as if the manacles were still binding him. "I left everything behind to come here. I don't know what I expected... hell, forget it." He continued looking out over the city, letting out a bitter laugh. "And here I am, standing in the office of the war hero who died fighting against me. I'm never going to be able to escape my past."

Lina wasn't sure what to say, surprised at the depth of emotion. Jay always seemed so certain; so sure of himself and unapologetic of his actions.

He turned to face her, his blue-green eyes stormy. "You have a place here; an important role. I can't compete with that. I want to steal you away again, have you become mine again. I don't know why I'm still here. I don't want to cause you harm. That seems to be all I'm good at." His hand came up to brush gently over the white blouse she wore that hid the scar on her side from his knife, and she felt tingling at the light touch.

"I thought when the Reapers released you, they'd force you to leave the city. Or you'd want to leave, after how they treated you."

"Is that what you want? For me to leave?" Jay asked intently.

"No. I want you stay. With me."

"Even though I'm the enemy?"

Lina stared down at his hands, absently tracing the faded scars and calluses. "You're not my enemy. Even when you betrayed me, I still felt safe with you. Hurt, angry, terrified of the future... But I trusted you to look out for me. You saw the person I was, beneath the insecurities. And I saw you. You're a good man, Jay."

He watched her intently. "Remember that, Lina. Remember that when things here start going to hell and everyone is blaming the outsider. I'm only doing what I have to."

"I already knew it. It was why I could forgive you for stabbing, kidnapping, and dragging me across the continent."

Jay turned his hands over to grip hers. "Well, if we're going to get all sentimental," he began, grinning to cover his uncertainty, "When I was supposed to be undercover, just using you to complete my mission, I liked you. More than just liked. You didn't care about my title. Hell, you thought I was just a gardener and not the son of a national hero and the President; part of the March dynasty. With you, I was just Jay. Probably more myself than I've ever been in my life." His grin faded, his gaze intent. "It made me realize I hated living a lie every day of my life. I wanted to be the man you saw when you looked at me. And when all this is over, I will be."

"You already are."

He pulled her in, kissing her hard on the mouth. "Enough of this sentimental shit. It's giving me a stomach ache. Let's get something to eat."

Lina smiled, rolling her eyes as she let him pull her towards the kitchen.

"Jay?"

"Yeah?" He glanced back at her over his shoulder.

"If you *are* exiled, I'll come with you. I know you gave up a lot to come here."

Jay grinned, a real smile that reflected in his eyes. "I didn't give up anything that mattered."

Chapter 9

"Fear turns everyone to savages, and the warlord sows fear like particles of dust; always, everywhere." - Texican proverb

It was late when Vick pulled in front of Helen's villa. It was dark inside, and he hoped she'd be asleep.

Was he making a mistake, coming here? He'd stayed to care for her when she was ill, but she could easily stay with her family. She didn't need him.

Perhaps you need her, a tiny voice taunted.

Even as he questioned himself, he got out of the truck, heading up the front walk. The door was open, and he entered quietly, standing for a moment in the foyer, a strange feeling of belonging settling over him. Not because of the villa, but because she was here.

"How did it go?"

Helen came from the kitchen dressed in a white robe and neat white pajamas, holding out a mug of something warm. He took it, sipping slowly. His brows raised as he tasted the whiskey-laced tea.

Helen just smiled. "I figured you needed to relax a little."

"It went fine," he answered, raising the mug in thanks before taking a long swallow, scalding his tongue. Damn but the whiskey tasted good. "I'm a little surprised at how many are sick already, but so far the fatalities are low. I'm meeting with the health team tomorrow to find out more details about the virus itself."

Helen nodded, sipping her own tea.

"You should be sleeping. You're not out of the woods yet, yourself."

One elegant brow arched. "While I appreciate your

concern, I'm quite capable of deciding when to rest."

"Fair enough."

"But now that you're home, I'll head to bed. You seem quite familiar with my villa, so please help yourself to whatever you need."

Vick watched her set her mug in the kitchen and turn towards the stairs. He felt like an ass, but he couldn't help the now-familiar desire that unfurled as he watched her walk away, even in the modest robe and cotton slacks and top she wore beneath.

...Now that you're home... The words should have killed his desire, but seemed to be having the opposite effect.

Home, with Helen.

It was just a temporary affliction, he assured himself. Once he was back in Vicksburg and things were back to normal, he'd be able to forget all about this woman.

He hoped.

Helen awoke with a start, hearing noises in the kitchen. It took a moment for memories to return, and realization to settle in.

Vick was staying in her house.

She still wasn't entirely sure how she felt about it, but as much as she hated to admit it, it was oddly comforting.

And it *was* only temporary, after all. Things would soon return to normal, and he would leave.

She tried to ignore the sinking feeling in her stomach at the thought.

She dressed and joined him in the kitchen, getting her own breakfast from the Dispensare. He eyed her white suit with narrowed eyes from where he leaned back against the counter, eating some mixture of egg and potato that looked revolting. She averted her eyes to keep the morning sickness under control.

"Where do you think you're going?"

Helen kept her gaze on her own toast as she answered.

"I told you, I want to help the researchers working on a vaccine. I specialized in medical law, remember. And now that I'm past the illness, the risk to me is low. It would only make sense that I help."

Vick was shaking his head, his normal jovial voice hard. "You're still not well. What if you relapse? You need to rest."

Helen stiffened, her light eyes narrowing. "I'm fully capable of knowing my limits. These are my people falling ill and dying. I'm going to help."

"Even if it endangers your child?"

He knew just the right buttons to push. Her voice grew colder. "I will not put my baby at risk, although I'm touched by your concern."

Vick stood, his height and breadth of frame dwarfing her own petite size. "I could make you rest," he said softly.

"I highly doubt that," she returned, unintimidated. "But you're welcome to try."

His hands clenched, and they faced off for a long moment, the air thick with tension. Then he relaxed, flashing his normal charming smile.

"I'll give you this round. But Helen, I'll be watching. If I think you're overdoing it..."

"Quit worrying."

His eyebrows went up. "I don't *worry*. I express concerns that..." he shook his head, grinning again. "Fine. You win this one."

She smiled slightly back, pleased at his easy acquiescence. He obviously wasn't used to being challenged.

"It's going to be another long day, so don't wait up," he ordered as he grabbed the Virmortus weapon vest he'd taken from the Training Grounds. She shot him a look which told him she was going to do whatever she pleased.

She smiled to herself as he slammed out of the villa. He was becoming easier to manage than she thought. Although she had a feeling that when he really put his foot down, he had pretty big feet. It might be hard to get around them.

She'd worry about that when the time came. Now she needed to get to the lab and see how she could be of help.

*   *   *

"The incubation period is nearly two weeks, and the infected are contagious before the symptoms start to show," the lead researcher explained to Vick later that day. "That is what makes it so difficult to contain."

It was another beautiful sunny day, a salty breeze blowing through the open balcony doors of the Capitol Meeting Room. The same three masked Senators from yesterday's meeting listened intently to the report.

"And a vaccine?" the Health Senator asked.

"We are working on developing one. We have live virus cells from the clinic, and we're studying how they modify. Then we will develop an antigen, isolate the antigen cells, and add the necessary adjuvant, stabilizers, and preservatives. It just takes time."

"How long?" Vick tried to curb his impatience.

"Well," the lead researcher licked his lips nervously, eyes darting to the Senators, "We have a second team using an imitation of the virus, which might allow us to develop the vaccine in a few weeks. It just isn't always as effective…"

"A few weeks? How many?" Vick knew he was growing increasingly harsh, but getting answers from this guy was like interrogating an enemy. He had to pry each bit of information from him.

"Um, probably four, maybe five. And that is assuming it works."

Vick wanted to curse, but knew he needed to maintain his calm. He was supposed to be the damn leader; the one with all the answers here.

The subtle beep of his holoreader interrupted his thoughts, and he answered. It was Chessa, the Virmortus in charge of monitoring the outbreak.

"We've got two more fatalities, sir. And a confirmed case

on the Pleb Terrace."

"Alright, I'll come to the Training Grounds."

"Sir, we've also got a situation on the Pleb Terrace. A small group has attempted to flee the city. The Armati are holding them at the South Gate."

It was beginning. "Alright, send two field assassins – er, agents," he corrected quickly, ignoring the horrified expressions visible above the masks of the Senators.

"Yes, sir, they'll meet you at the Patrician tram."

Vick disconnected, shoving the reader back into his worn jeans. He might be wearing the Virmortus weapon vest, but he was keeping his own clothes.

"Keep me informed of your progress," he ordered the lead researcher, who nodded so fervently the sunglasses perched atop his head fell off. The Senator of Law drew a deep breath as if he were about to launch into a speech, but Vick held up a hand.

"We'll continue this discussion when I return." He left without waiting for a response, his long strides taking him quickly through the understated elegance of the Capitol building into the late morning sun shining brightly outside.

Two more Patricians dead. He had a feeling one of them might be the young man Helen knew in the clinic. The young man, probably not much younger than Vick's own thirty-two years, hadn't looked good when he'd left. He wasn't sure who the other fatality was, and if he didn't know, he wouldn't have to tell Helen.

Coward, an inner voice accused. He wasn't afraid to admit, at least to himself, that he had a healthy respect for a woman with Helen's temperament. She might be tiny, but she had an inner power he'd learned to recognize and respect in others. Tenacity, ambition, fierceness… it was all embodied in that one small package. Tiny yet sexy.

He didn't need to know names of the dead, but what he did need to know was the pattern. Lina had said something about identifying the ill and mapping the pattern of infection.

Maybe they could get some kind of prediction model.

Jay answered Lina's holoreader.

"I need Lina to come to the Training Grounds to set up a system to track the spread of the virus," Vick said without preamble.

"She's resting."

"Listen, shithead, I said I need—"

"Alright, alright, don't get your panties in a bunch. I'll talk to her about it. Maybe tomorrow—"

"Two hours. Tell her to be there in two hours."

"I'll talk to her about it." Jay's voice had gotten cooler, and Vick decided not to push. He might need Jay in his corner, and as crazy as his brother was about Lina...

"Fine, you do that. Tell her two more Patricians have died, and the virus has spread to the Pleb Terrace. Then let me know if you'll be at the Training Grounds in two hours."

Vick disconnected, the small glass tram that was reserved for Patrician use just before him. A paved walk connected the Capitol building to the tram, and a small covered sitting area overlooked the terraces below.

Vick stood at the edge of the cliffside, looking down at the top of the buildings of the Merchant Terrace just below him, and the sprawling Pleb city that stretched another level below the Merchant's small city.

He'd always found the physical segregation of the classes to be a bit of overkill, but he could see an advantage in this situation. It made quarantine much simpler, as long as they could get a good supply delivery system in place. Without the Ferry, which was basically a large two-level tram that could fit e-cars and people passengers, no one would be able to travel between the levels of Alba. The terraces were separated by at least eighty feet in some areas, and closer to 400 feet of sheer rock-face in others.

There was little risk of anyone leaving their Terrace without his knowledge. The biggest concerns were people attempting to flee the city, which was surrounded by walls and had two main gates. However, it would be easy to swim from the beaches, or take a watercraft.

And he had to worry about losing control of the Armati. The Virmortus were so well trained, they'd follow the Alpha to hell itself. But the Armati, the police and standing army of Alba, were a little more uncertain.

A black e-car approached. The Virmortus he'd requested had arrived. Nodding to the two men and one woman, he led the way to the small Patrician tram. Unlike the much larger Ferry, the tram only fit about eight people comfortably.

He scanned the card Marcus had given him, which allowed him to take over control of the tram. It was relatively simple to operate, and soon they were gliding slowly down the mountainside.

"Just follow my signal," he instructed. "I'm hoping to keep this peaceful, but I'll make an example if I need to. Hope to hell we don't need to."

They walked down the center of the main Pleb street leading to South Gate. The large stone wall loomed in the distance, the heavy metal gates sealed shut, containing a small group of Pleb citizens inside. Five Armati guards stood before the crowd at the gate, and the older man in charge looked relieved to see Vick and his small group of Virmortus.

No one else looked very pleased. In fact, the crowd immediately parted, stepping away from them in fear. The weapon vests and black clothing of the Virmortus were quickly recognizable, and struck fear in the hearts of every citizen.

"Sir." The sergeant at the gate hurried over, nodding respectfully.

"Thank you, Sergeant. I'll take over from here," he told the grey-haired man.

He turned to face the crowd of Plebs, many carrying packs of belongings, some with children at their side. They were just people, terrified people, trying to care for their family.

"Citizens, I'm going to make this clear once, and once only, so listen carefully: No one is allowed to leave the city. If one infected person leaves for an outpost town, the infection will spread to the towns in which you're seeking shelter." He scanned the terrified faces of the gathered group, using their fear against them. "How long do you think you'll survive in a town with barely rudimental health care? In a town that probably won't even welcome you in the first place, for fear of infecting their own families? Your best chance at survival is to remain here, and to let the trained health care workers in this city care for you and your family. Follow the instructions to stay healthy, and we will all get through this."

He motioned the sergeant closer, settling his hand on the other man's shoulder in a show of solidarity. "We all want what is best for the people of this city. Go home. Be safe with your families. We will keep you informed of all developments each day at noon, so keep your holoreaders on."

The crowd was beginning to look more confident, more relaxed. Now for the final touch; give them all a task. "I need your help, however. I need each one of you to watch out for your neighbors. Protect one another, and if one of your neighbors should fall ill, call the clinic immediately. Early treatment is the best chance we all have."

The people were nodding, some looking relieved that they could return home. Most Albans had never left the city, and their fear must have been great for them to consider fleeing the only home they'd ever known.

Vick watched in satisfaction as the crowd began to disperse, each heading back towards their home.

"Thank you, sir," the sergeant said in relief. "Our orders were to shoot to kill anyone who flees or revolts, but that sure didn't sit well with me. They're just scared."

"I understand; you did a great job." Vick nodded to him, mentally noting the man's hesitancy to follow the kill order. Might need to replace him.

The other Virmortus followed him silently back through

the city towards the tram.

"I'm going to need a vehicle here on the Pleb Terrace. This won't be the last time we're here," Vick said grimly. Thomas, a short and stocky Virmortus with shockingly red hair, picked up his Com device and began making arrangements.

"I also want that Sergeant moved to one of the clinics, and find someone who isn't going to question orders to guard the gate." Vick looked out over Alba as the tram ascended, a large cloud blowing in from the ocean to cast its shadow over the city.

He hoped Helen's day was going better than his.

"Oh serenity save us," Helen murmured, wishing for once she had Vick's more colorful vocabulary.

"That is what I was afraid of," Terrence, the lab lead, muttered beside her.

The other lab workers, mostly University students and a few Medellas, stood around the counter, all looking at the results projected above the holocomputer.

Helen felt her palms growing damp, and she absently rubbed them on her white lab coat.

"We need to tell Senator Strauss," Terrence said, referring to the Senator of Health.

"And Mr. March," Helen added. She noticed Terrence's face twist slightly at her words. "Is there a problem?"

Terrence coughed, glancing quickly at the others. "Well, I don't know if it's necessary to inform Mr. March. He really is just dealing with security."

Helen looked around. None of the other researchers and students could meet her gaze.

"Mr. March is not only the Alpha Virmortus, but the Interim Consul. He is making all the important decisions for our State, and most certainly needs to be kept informed." Her voice was sharp with suppressed anger.

"I don't know if I would go so far as to call him Interim

Consul. After all, an official vote has never been cast and — "

"Ah, I didn't realize you were suddenly so well-versed in succession law," Helen interrupted. "Please, educate us; who holds the consulship?"

"Well, the Senators are the primary power…" Terrence stuttered nervously. She'd known the overly slender man since she had been a youth taking medical classes under him. The man was brilliant in his research but awkward in most other areas of his life. He'd never taken a partner, married to his work and to Alba.

She tried to keep that in mind, but protectiveness overcame her as she saw the look on the group's faces when they spoke of Vick; the wariness and antipathy.

"We all know Vicktor March has complete control over this city." Helen's voice echoed in the silence that had fallen over the lab.

"That doesn't mean we have to accept him as one of us; as an Alban and certainly not a Patrician," another woman spoke up. Helen recognized her as a medical classmate. "And the winds of power could quickly change, Helen. We might be under martial law now, but the Senators will take back control at any time. Be careful which side you've chosen," her colleague warned.

"I had a feeling this was where the conversation was going. You want to be divisive now? We should be coming together to save our people. Instead, you're worried about petty social issues. Yes," Helen looked right at her colleague, "things are changing. Those who cannot embrace change risk extinction."

"Are you threatening me?" she gasped.

"I don't need to threaten you. That is the reality of this world we are living in."

"She's right." A new voice interrupted the heavy silence that hung over the group, drawing all eyes towards the door.

The Senator of Health entered the room. She was the embodiment of the office she held, perfectly fit, her skin and hair gleaming with health.

"Now is not the time to be divided. Keep your opinions of Mr. March to yourself. He is both Alpha and Consul, and to question him aloud during such a tenuous time could result in harsh punishment. We must work together to fight this new threat, or we will not have a society to protect.

"Without the support of the Virmortus, our leadership is tenuous at best. Do not underestimate their power in this city, regardless of our personal sentiment."

Eyes darted nervously around the room, but no one moved. Disgust, and probably a little morning sickness, made bile rise in Helen's throat. They were all biding their time, using the Virmortus, and Vick, to control the people. Not too long ago, Helen would have thought the same way. Now things didn't seem so straightforward.

Her faith in the Senator's ability to rule was shaken. What Senator Strauss said was correct: without the support of the Virmortus, the Senators wouldn't be able to retain power. Who was really running the city?

Senator Strauss smiled, her eyes lingering on Helen. "Good, now that we've gotten that issue out of the way, why don't you tell me the results of your tests."

Helen watched as the group went through the test results with the Senator. While she didn't think the Senator had ill intentions, Helen planned to share the information with Vick herself.

Surprisingly, in this upside down world of hers, Vick had become one of her most trusted confidants.

*   *   *

Vick drove towards the Training Grounds where he hoped Lina would be waiting. They needed a better system set up to automatically track and report. Too many unknowns were going to make his job nearly impossible.

His holoreader beeped, indicating a call.

"How's the patient?" he asked after accepting the request.

"Terrible." The projected image showing a very ruffled and tired-looking Aerina. "Honestly, can you see Marcus being a good patient?"

Vick laughed briefly. No, his friend would hate being weak and having to rely on others. He could only imagine what he was putting Aerina through.

"I called because I wanted you to know the clinic here at the University needs more doctors."

"Fine, you'll oversee that?"

"Yes. A few Medellas from other Terraces have volunteered to help. We'll need someone to pick them up and bring them up here."

"Send me their ID info and I'll have one of my agents do it."

Aerina looked surprised for a moment. "Agents is an interesting choice of words. But ok, I'll send them over. We'll be at the University clinic if you need anything."

Vick thanked her and disconnected. If it was spreading this quickly and severely here on the less populated Capitol Terrace, it was going to get really bad on the Pleb Terrace.

He needed to make it his priority to keep the virus contained.

"Lina Rhodes?" Vick asked a recruit as soon as he arrived at the Training Grounds.

"She's in the Tech Room," the youth informed him. Relief washed over him as he strode quickly down the stone hall.

Jay lounged in the back of the room, his watchful gaze on Lina as she spoke with some of the other Virmortus. Vick nodded to him as he entered.

"Thanks for coming," he said to Lina.

"We're all in this together," she replied.

"What progress have you made?"

"We're using the Network to build a program that will track the sick. Look here." Lina showed Vick a flat screen with biometrics running across it. "We can identify who is sick by using their biometric readings. We may even be able to determine they are ill before they know it themselves. Our program will automatically send the ID owner's name and location to the nearest Armati post."

Lina waved him over to another station. "Here, we are creating a program that is tracking data. It is recording everything from the biometrics of the ill, the date they fell ill, their location, and when and if they came in contact with other infected. We are hoping to begin predicting where the illness might spread next."

"That's perfect," Vick said, rubbing his hands together in satisfaction. "You read my mind."

Lina smiled, flushing slightly at the praise. Vick squeezed her shoulder. "Keep me informed of its progress. Send the reports to my holoreader."

Lina nodded, still smiling as she turned back to the station. "Sir?"

Vick turned back at the hesitant question. Lina looked nervous but determined. He had a feeling what was coming next.

"Helen can normally take care of herself. But she's fragile right now, being pregnant and after Stephen … well, I just wanted to make sure she's going to be ok." The tall, dark-haired woman's face had turned bright red, but she persisted. "I'm sure you don't mean to cause her harm, but…"

"Yes?" Vick kept his voice relaxed with effort, but every muscle was tensed as if for battle.

"You're not an Alban. And Helen could never survive outside the walls." Lina shuddered as if remembering her own trip outside of Alba. "I just don't want her to get hurt again when you leave."

Vick was silent, noticing the other inhabitants of the room were pretending to be engrossed in their tasks.

"I don't want her hurt, either," he said finally. Lina nodded in relief, turning back to her own task.

Vick turned, eyeing his brother. Jay still leaned against

the wall, large arms crossed over his chest. His younger brother's eyes were alight with mirth. He was enjoying Vick's discomfort.

Jay might be obnoxious, but he was strong, quick, and charismatic. Just what Vick needed.

"I need your help," he stated, standing before Jay. The younger man raised his brows, waiting. "I need someone I can trust to bring supplies from the Aggie Town and distribute them here. We're rationing what we have stockpiled, but most Patricians were accustomed to fresh daily deliveries. We can't last much longer without a delivery system in place."

"You want me to masquerade as an Aggie? Well, that's ironic," Jay drawled.

Vick grinned. "Yeah, hadn't thought about that. You should feel right at home."

"When?"

"Tomorrow morning. I'll have one of my agents go with you."

"Expecting trouble?"

"I always expect trouble."

Chapter 10

"You'll find love again, mi hijo. Embrace it; don't run from it."
-Letters from Matias Emmanuel March

The next few days passed swiftly, filled with tracking the spread of the illness, addressing the people's fears, and seeing to the safe distribution of supplies throughout the State.

The one case on the Pleb Terrace quickly spread to three, then five, and now at least twenty Plebs were in the city clinic. Vick had already ordered an emergency clinic set up in one of the large brothels.

Helen had suggested that when he'd mentioned using a theater or warehouse. There was nothing more disheartening than seeing a large room of sick, and watching neighbors die. It was best to try to keep the ill in separate rooms for morale, she'd explained.

He was constantly surprised by her wealth of knowledge. Not that he should be; he'd already known she was intelligent. But her ability to roll with the punches, and adjust to the swift changes falling upon Alba was a little unexpected. She'd seemed so rigid at first; so uptight. The things that had allowed him to keep his distance were slowly disappearing. It was becoming more and more difficult to keep his own defenses up against her.

His relationship with Helen would have to wait, however, as other concerns were mounting.

Several cases of the sickness had appeared on the Merchant Terrace, but the Agriculture Town remained uninfected. Jay's first trip out to the farm town had been tense, according to his report. A group of farmers blocked the road from him and the accompanying Virmortus. Dressed in the crimson biosuits, the two men stood out like a warning sign to the wary Aggies, Vick guessed. He couldn't blame them for being cautious. The large supply truck they'd driven couldn't get through the roadblock, so Jay had parked and conferred with the farmers from a distance. He'd finally convinced them to leave supplies in the road, and he would load them and drive them into town.

The drop off and pick up had become a daily routine, and Vick was relieved to have someone overseeing the supplies. It was crucial they kept the Aggie Town free from illness. They couldn't survive without food production.

Helen continued to work with the team attempting to develop a vaccine. While he didn't like her risking her precarious health, he had to admit it was beneficial to have her as part of the team. He knew many of the Patricians resented his power and that he was an outsider running their State. Helen made sure he had accurate information regarding their research, which he needed to predict the spread of the illness and make plans accordingly.

The days were busy, but the nights were hell.

Being so close to Helen, so close but so distant, was taking its toll on his temper.

He looked forward to the evenings, when they would eat together, discussing the day's events. She had a sharp wit he found alternately amusing and arousing.

It was in those quiet times together that she let down her guard, and the prickly, independent woman of the day revealed a softer side he'd never seen before.

And every night when she got up to go to her own room, it became harder and harder not to stop her. To beg her to let him in her bed.

But he'd told himself he'd give her space. She was pregnant and her lover had died only a few short months earlier.

He didn't think he could take much more.

Tonight he didn't know if he could keep himself from seeking out the relief only she could offer.

Darkness had just fallen over the city when he'd arrived

home. To her villa, he corrected himself. Thinking of this place as home would be a mistake.

They'd shared dinner and retired to the study to talk, as they did most nights. He couldn't take his eyes from her as she approached, her small feet bare, two mugs of tea in her delicate hands.

She gave him a quizzical look as she handed him one, laced with the whiskey she knew he liked, and he realized he must have been staring.

He thanked her absently, forcing his gaze out the window of the sitting room. The Serenity Garden was beyond, the nearly full moon gleaming off the pool in the center, casting strange shadows from the carefully groomed shrubbery.

He took a swallow of the tea, scalding his tongue, and cursed quietly.

"Is everything alright?" Helen asked, curling her own small form into the chair adjacent his, hands cupping her mug carefully.

"Yes, everything is fucking fantastic," he muttered.

"If you're so over-stressed, perhaps you should go to bed now," Helen retorted sharply.

Vick groaned, the image of his bed, with her in it, popping into his mind. He dropped his head in his hands, rubbing the palms on his eyes, trying to erase the image.

He heard rustling, and felt Helen's slender, cool hand on his brow. He breathed deeply of her scent; sharp and tangy citrus.

"You feel warm, but not feverish."

He laughed softly, mostly at himself.

"Vick, you're worrying me. What...?" Helen gently forced his face up so she could search his eyes, her hands cupping his bearded jaw.

Sparks of heat traveled from where her hands touched his face and her arm brushed his.

He couldn't be the kind, understanding friend she

needed tonight. Standing abruptly, he pulled her up with him. Her mouth parted in surprise, and he gave in to the urge that had been building for weeks. Since the moment he'd first seen her, in fact.

His mouth lowered, not giving her time to protest or pull away, sealing any sounds inside. He didn't waste a moment, his lips claiming hers with force, his tongue sweeping inside. His kiss was fast, almost desperate, for he was afraid she'd push him away at any moment,

She tasted of honey and lemon, her soft mouth taut in surprise for a long moment. Fear mingled with need as he began to think he'd been mistaken; that perhaps she didn't desire him as he did her. He deepened the kiss, feeling as if he were inhaling her essence, breathing the tiny gasps coming from her throat.

Just as he was about to pull away in defeat, she seemed to melt into him, her arms coming up to grip his shirt, her tongue tentatively meeting his.

He pulled her tighter against him, his large frame nearly shaking with need and the effort to go slow; to be gentle.

"Vick," she gasped as his lips left hers for a moment to taste the corner of her mouth, her high cheekbones, and delicate jaw. His hands moved from her shoulders, down her slender sides, and under the satin nightshirt she wore.

She gasped again as his palms grazed her taut nipples, his mouth drinking in the sounds hungrily. He moved lower, and they both froze as he touched the slightly convex shape of her stomach.

He felt her go stiff, her hands lowering from his arms to protectively cover her slight mound. He released her, letting her take a step back, his hands fisting at his sides to keep them from grabbing her again.

Helen swayed slightly, looking bemused, before sinking back into her chair. Her perfectly coiffed hair was mussed, her lips reddened from his kiss, light whisker burns marking her smooth skin.

He knew he should probably apologize; to break the tense silence. But he couldn't. He wasn't sorry for anything. Except that it ended.

"I want you," he finally said. "I want you so damn bad its killing me to hold it in. I'm not going to apologize, and I'm not going to stop wanting to have you, any way I can get you. But I can promise you I won't do anything you don't want. Even if it means keeping my hands to myself." His voice was hoarse as he made the promise that was probably going to be his downfall. He looked out at the damn Serenity Garden, feeling frustrated as hell.

When Helen finally spoke, her words surprised him. "I won't deny I want you, too. But this pregnancy has my emotions so in turmoil, I don't trust myself... I don't know what I really feel."

Vick turned back around, pushing back the strands of hair falling from the leather tie at his neck.

"I'll give you all the time you need to decide what you want," he promised rashly, desperately glad she wasn't demanding he leave her house.

You're a fool, March. There is no way this can end well for you two.

Since when had that ever stopped him? He wasn't looking for any happy endings. His hand went to stroke his beard, feeling the scars running along his jawline. He'd learned to take what joy he could, because life had no guarantees. And he would find a hell of a lot of joy from being with Helen, however she let him.

"You're so generous," Helen said drily.

Vick grinned in response. "A little too arrogant? Running the State must be going to my head. I'm just not used to so much responsibility in my little 'ole town of Vicksburg."

"I can see how it would be a bit of a shock." Her small smile and dry response told him she wasn't offended at his gentle mockery. Damn, another thing he loved about her; her tough skin and quick wit.

Her expression changed, growing serious. She stood, moving close to face him. Her hand lifted hesitantly to trace the same path his often unconsciously took along his jaw.

He almost jerked away as her gentle touch found the same grooves that hid beneath his beard, scars on his skin that ran much deeper. He forced himself to remain still, letting her hand gently trace the damaged skin, following it to the corner of his mouth, moving over his lips. He couldn't stop his jaw from clenching with the effort to remain immobile.

She raised on her toes and pulling his head down, kissed his cheek just above his beard, sending a thrill that wasn't just sexual straight to his chest.

"Sometime, I hope you'll tell me the story of how this happened."

"It's rather dull." He fought to keep his smile in place and his tone light. "Trust me, you wouldn't want to hear it."

"Hmm. I have a feeling I need to hear it," she replied thoughtfully, and he felt uncomfortably exposed under her gaze. "Or perhaps you need to tell it."

Vick opened his mouth with a quick retort, but couldn't force the words out. He turned away with an inarticulate growl. This woman was getting under his skin like no one else had ever been able to.

"Dammit, Helen, just because I want you doesn't mean I'm going to spill my past while you mop my tears." He felt remorse as soon as the words left his lips. But the worst part was that he *wanted* to spill his secrets; to unload on her fragile shoulders. That was ludicrous; he had been self-contained for his entire life. He certainly wasn't going to start needing someone now.

Helen settled back into her chair, not saying anything. Waiting.

The silence stretched and for once Vick couldn't seem to find any blasé comment to fill it. His hand rose to stroke the scar before he stopped himself.

What did it matter? If she really wanted the whole sordid

story, he'd tell her. Maybe then it would help her keep her distance.

To learn how dangerous it was to care about him.

"You want the story of this scar? This is my reminder to never fall in love again," he said finally, wincing at how melodramatic the words sounded.

Helen said nothing, still waiting with a patience that was beginning to annoy him.

Or maybe it was just the anxiety building as he struggled to put his horrific past into words.

"My mother was a monster. A sociopath. But she was also clever and charismatic. A dangerous combination."

"Your mother, President March?"

Vick nodded, beginning to pace in the small study, his thoughts on the day that had altered his life many years earlier. A lifetime, it felt like.

"I loved my mom, regardless of the hell she put me and my sibling through. I don't know why she even had kids; god knows she never loved us. Probably because the mind games were amusing to her. And she was good at the mind games. We were always on our toes, never knowing what side of her we were going to get. Worst of all, we'd come to resent one another, fighting to be the favored one. And she loved it; loved pitting us against one another, and particularly against our father."

Vick swiped his hand over his face as if trying to wipe away the memories. Helen remained silent, her face unreadable in the lamp light. He was relieved she wasn't offering platitudes or sympathy. That always served to make him angry and withdrawn. He didn't want any damn sympathy.

"I had started to figure her out, at least a little. She was pushing me to join politics, like her, once I'd completed my military training. Which had also been her idea. It was a respectable career that would help her campaign. I was popular in school, top of my military academy, and the media loved our family, particularly Jay and I. And she craved the attention, the approval, of the mob. She needed it to win whatever political race she was currently in.

"I'd decided I wanted out; I wanted to travel a little, figure out my own thing. And I'd met a girl. Nina."

Helen shifted slightly, but still remained silent. He almost wished she would interrupt and give him an excuse to stop. To shut up and leave the past where it belonged.

But now that he'd started the story, he couldn't stop it.

"I loved Nina, as much as any nineteen-year-old kid can. I thought we'd get married, travel together, start some kind of life. My mother, however, did not agree. She warned me I was making a mistake. I refused to listen. I wanted out of that toxic family.

"The night before Nina and I were going to elope, we'd gone out to do some last minute shopping. We were jumped. Not by run-of-the-mill street thugs. Trained killers. Military guys."

The night flashed in his mind's eye like a living nightmare he could never wake from. He saw the dark-clothed men walk slowly from the shadows to surround him and Nina on the poorly lit the street. The lights were out, and the block suddenly abandoned. They'd been heavily armed, and the flash of silver in the dim light had been his only warning of the attack from behind. While he'd fought off a few of the older, more experienced attackers, he'd seen two others grab Nina, forcing her against the wall, gloved hands smothering her screams.

He'd been taken down to the pavement and forced to watch as they'd violated the woman he loved with the handle of the knife. Then they'd shoved the knife into her chest. He'd never forget the expression on her face, her dark brown eyes meeting his in a desperate plea to save her; to protect her.

And he hadn't been able to do a damn thing. She'd died before his eyes, the men carelessly dropping her body to the pavement.

They'd turned on him, giving him the mark he carried on his face with parting words he'd known were from the bitch who'd birthed him. *"This is what happens when you cross her."*

"That goddamn bitch killed Nina, and gave me this as a reminder," he choked out the words, filled with the same helpless rage that had overcome him that night.

A sharp pain suddenly penetrated that rage, and he looked down to find he'd shattered the delicate mug in his hand, the ceramic cutting deep into his clenched palm. The whiskey-laced tea mingled with his blood, dripping onto the white floor.

Helen suddenly stood before him, unconcerned about the blood droplet that landed on her pristine white pants. "Let's get this cleaned up."

She led him unprotestingly into the bathroom, running his hand under the water. He watched the blood blend with the stream, disappearing down the drain.

Helen moved efficiently around the small bath, opening a first aid kit, cleaning the cut and applying some skin glue to seal it instantly. He remained impassive even as the antiseptic and glue burned its way through his nerves.

She placed a small bandage over the sealed wound, gently releasing his hand.

"I know you would have died in place of Nina that day. We can't always save the people we love. Sometimes all we can do is love them while they're around. And it sounds like you did that with Nina. I hope someday you can look on that relationship with joy instead of regret." Helen again traced the scar on his jaw before stepping back.

"Goodnight," she murmured.

He watched her leave, knowing she was taking something with her he was never going to get back.

Chapter 11

"We fight for life when we all know death is inevitable. I find it fascinating how we can live so happily every day with death looming over our heads, like the sword of Damocles…"
- Recorded Conversations with Cecilia Delacroix

Morning came quickly after a restless night. Helen groaned at the sound of her holoreader going off. It was a message from Aerina.

Mother collapsed last night. They took her to the emergency clinic. Please come.

Helen got up quickly, her hand going instinctively to the bump that seemed to have popped out overnight.

Good morning, baby. She drew comfort from the bit of light in her darkening world. Emotion ruled her thoughts these days, and an endless tsunami of intense feelings washed over her when she thought of the tiny life inside.

It didn't take her long to dress, as her wardrobe was becoming more limited to the loose clothes in her closet. Her slacks today rode below the small bump, but her normal button blouse fit tightly, making her feel uncomfortable, so she slipped a white sweater on instead.

Vick was already up, normally leaving the villa before her. She hesitated in the doorway, unsure of which side of Vick she would see this morning: dark and brooding or the perpetually jovial.

He grinned as she entered, then glanced down at her midsection. His brows raised as he eyed the bump accentuated by the tight sweater.

"Guess it's really in there," he said. "May I?"

Perpetually jovial Vick it was. Good. She felt more comfortable with this side of him. She wasn't sure yet if she were ready to handle the scarred, broken man she'd confronted last night.

He was waiting, his eyes still fixed on her midsection, and she knew what he wanted. She nodded, and his large hand settled gently on the mound, running over it almost reverently. She fought to choke back the tears that sprang forth unexpectedly. Damn emotions.

"I've never… It's just so… there's really a baby in there," he said in awe, his scarred, work-roughened hand nearly covering her entire midriff.

"She's the size of an orange right now," Helen murmured. He looked up quickly.

"She?"

"Just a guess."

Vick looked back down at his hand, and Helen wondered what he was thinking. He stepped back, and Helen felt a strange sense of loss as his hand dropped away.

"You're up early." His unspoken question reminded her of her friend's message.

"Aerina's mother is at the emergency clinic; she wanted me to come. I'm worried it must be bad."

"If what you said is true, the virus is mutating quickly. Might be becoming more aggressive."

"That is what I'm afraid of."

"I'll give you a ride."

*   *   *

Helen hurried into the emergency clinic as the first forerunners of dawn were casting their light over the city, Vick's truck the only sound in the early morning as it rumbled off towards the Training Grounds.

The University was eerily quiet, although she could see bright lights in the medical wing. Her soft-soled shoes slapped on the tile floor as she walked quickly down the long hallway towards the lights.

An Armati guard stood at the double doors leading into the medical wing.

"ID please."

Helen willingly presented her wrist for a scan, hearing her name and credentials read. He nodded, letting her pass. In one of the labs, she suited up in the red biohazard suit required of all workers and visitors.

Finally she was heading to the desk where one of the volunteer health workers sat in the same suit, entering data into a holocomputer.

"Raina Delacroix?" Helen asked.

The young man looked up, his expression sympathetic. "She just came in last night. They put her in Room 5."

The door was closed to Room 5. Helen knocked softly.

Aerina opened the door, her face pale and blotchy through her face mask, as if she had been crying. Dark circles under her eyes gave evidence to a sleepless night.

They embraced in silence, Helen squeezing her gently before stepping back to study Aerina's mother.

The attractive older woman was sleeping, her breathing slow and ragged through the oxygen mask strapped to her face. A bright red slash across the woman's pale cheekbones indicated a fever that they had been unable to bring down completely.

"I think she's been sick for a few days, but we didn't know; she was busy caring for my father. I just assumed she was tired…" Aerina sank slowly into the single chair in the room, her biosuit crinkling. "She collapsed last night at the other clinic when they were running tests on Father. I think he is going to be cleared today. His sickness seems to be gone."

"How is Marcus?"

Aerina smiled weakly. "He's the same. Still lucid, just very weak. He sent me in here because he doesn't like me fussing. It's so hard to see him frail and helpless…" Tears welled up in Aerina's eyes again, and she pulled open the mask to swipe them away angrily.

Helen didn't say anything about the risk of exposure, checking over Ms. Delacroix's stats, the readouts making her heart sink. Aerina might not be a Medella, but she wasn't an idiot. It didn't look good.

Helen sighed, wishing she could offer her friend some words of encouragement. Unfortunately, the complications from the virus were life-threatening, and resistant to any of the medicine they had. Without a vaccine, there was little anyone could do except avoid those who were sick.

"You might as well head over to the lab. Find us a way out of this hell," Aerina finally said, raising red-rimmed eyes, their blue awash with tears. Helen nodded, knowing she could do nothing here.

"I'm going to do whatever I can. Don't give up hope."

Aerina nodded, rising to give Helen another hug.

"Do what you can and let the rest go," Aerina murmured, almost to herself, as Helen walked to the door. Helen paused for a long moment before heading out and down the long white hallway towards the lab where the team awaited.

Doing what they could to save the State.

*   *   *

"Remind me again how I got coerced into this fucking thankless job," Vick growled into his holoreader.

"Because at heart you're just a hero, like your brother," came Marcus' weak voice in response. Vick let out a bark of laughter.

"You're making a joke; you must be dying."

"Not yet, my friend. I've got too much left I need to do."

"Yeah, like taking back your position. I'm about to appoint one of your scrawny recruits as Alpha and sneak out of the city."

"How are things?" Marcus' voice changed, indicating the moment of levity was over.

"Same as they were yesterday when you asked. Lots of sick, not enough Medellas, and slow progress on the vaccine. But the supplies keep coming in, and no one has revolted yet."

"Good. It will happen. It always happens. Be ready."

"Yes, sir," Vick replied drily. "Just get well and you can

be here, ordering everyone around again."

Vick had just disconnected when his reader started beeping again. He'd been trying to get to the Tech Room for the last hour to check in with Lina. Her program had been surprisingly accurate at predicting how the illness would spread, and tracking the ill.

"Yes?"

"Sir, we've got a situation. Two shops here in the Pleb city have been looted; we've got the looters, but you said you wanted to deal with it personally if it happened."

Goddamn. Not already.

"You're right, Lucien. I'll be there as soon as I can. Hold them and gather a crowd. I need to set an example."

"Yes, sir."

Vick turned, heading back towards the underground garage. His meeting with the tech team would have to wait.

He made it down to the Pleb Terrace in record time, taking the black e-car left at the bottom of the tram towards the city center. He pulled to a halt in the middle of the crowded street, seeing agents Chessa and Lucien standing before the angry gathering.

A man and woman kneeled before Chessa and Lucien, their eyes fearful. The items they had attempted to steal littered the street around them.

Vick took in the situation quickly. The crowd was angry at the looting but uncertain, nervous about the Reapers in their midst. A few had their holoreaders out, broadcasting or writing a holofile to share with others.

Perfect.

"Citizens of Alba," Vick shouted, and the crowd grew silent. "I am your interim Consul and Alpha Virmortus. It is my priority, and my responsibility, to ensure that peace and balance are preserved during this tumultuous time.

"We are all afraid. We are all concerned. But know this: Nothing has changed. I will not tolerate any action that threatens the peace of Alba. Punishment will be swift and severe."

Without hesitation, Vick pulled an EMW from his weapon vest, firing in quick succession. The pop and arc drew shrieks from those gathered. The two would-be thieves jolted and collapsed, their hearts stopped by the powerful currents of electricity.

Shrieks of shock and fear echoed around the packed street as the crowd took a collective step away. Silence descended. The public execution had the desired effect as hundreds of eyes turned to Vick in fear and new respect.

Wailing began, loud in the silence that had fallen over the city square. Two women rushed forward, one falling to her knees beside the dead.

Family of the looters.

He ignored the sick twisting in his gut he'd never been able to shed, no matter how many times he killed in the name of duty. The tone of the crowd changed from respectful fear to angry fear as the wailing women cried over the bodies of the dead looters, their crimes already forgotten.

Lead out the scapegoat. The outsider who would draw their fear and hatred.

He boldly met the eyes of those gathered around, looking for signs of dissension.

A few angry murmurs started to his left.

"…who is he anyway…"

"…just an outsider; he's not our leader…"

"…not one of us…"

"…murdered two Albans…"

Don't do it. Don't fucking do it.

"You can't just shoot a citizen of Alba. They deserved to be heard before a council," shouted one hot-headed citizen from within the crowd. A rippled of assent began.

A young Armati stepped forward, his hand on his weapon. "You're just an outsider. You don't belong here. You can't play executioner!"

Vick turned slowly to face the young man. This moment

could very well decide the future, or downfall, of Alba. If he lost control of the people, anarchy would erupt.

Why did he care? It wasn't his city.

But he did care. He cared about too many people in this city to let it come to ruin. So much for embracing his life as a loner and avoiding these types of entanglements. He was cursed to forever be responsible: For saving people's lives. For taking people's lives.

Que así sea.

So be it.

In one fluid movement, Vick pulled his large hunting knife from his back holster and threw it.

The knife sliced through the air, finding its mark in the young Armati's neck. The man's eyes widened as his hands automatically went to the lodged weapon, clawing at it.

Gurgling and thrashing, he fell to the cobbled street, slowly drowning in his own blood. Vick walked over slowly, bending to pull the knife from the neck of the dying soldier.

"Anyone else have a problem with my leadership?"

The crowd was silent, fear palpable in the bright afternoon air.

Vick turned and headed back towards the black e-car crouched at the curb, leaving Lucien and the other Reapers to deal with the situation.

The bright sun was a mockery; today was a dark day in Alba. And it was only going to grow dimmer.

Chapter 12

"All my fame comes from being a killer. Never forget that even necessary evil is still evil." -Letters from Matias Emmanuel March

Chelsea stepped slowly from the old aircraft. She was still surprised it had managed to get them all the way from the east coast to the wilds of Texico. As relieved as she was to get off that rattling death plane, the scene that awaited them didn't look much more promising.

Heavily armed and unkempt men stood silently before an unusual assortment of vehicles. Each man held a weapon pointed at their small group.

Her mother stepped down, wearing a serene smile, ordering "Do as I say." Jessica, her sister who had joined them on the plane, and a dark-skinned man named Royce flanked her mother as they walked towards the men.

"Hold it right the feck there, lady. You an' yer posse ain't welcome here."

"I have business with your boss, young man," President March responded, her full height making her eye-to-eye with the scruffy mercenary.

"The feck you do. Do you fecking know who our fecking leader is, bitch?"

Chelsea stood as still as possible, hoping to avoid drawing their attention. A near-hysterical smile threatened as she imagined the men gunning them down right here. A fitting end to them all.

"Yes, I know Rey well. He and my deceased husband were close friends."

"Ain't no Rey here."

A second bandit stepped forward, and the two conferred briefly before turning back to face them. "Who was yer fecking husband?"

"Matias Emmanuel March."

A rumble went through the men, and the one who appeared to be their leader squinted, spitting something disgusting onto the dusty ground.

"Alright, you can explain yer business to Jefe. But if he doesn't like ya... all y'all are fecked."

Chelsea found herself being herded along with the others towards the odd-shaped vehicles. Smashed between a hairy, massively built gunner and a wiry man who looked younger than her own twenty-two years, Chelsea tried to breathe through her mouth to avoid the stench.

Mistaking her heavy breathing for fear, the wiry young man patted her shoulder awkwardly. "You'll be alright, missy. Yer pretty. Jefe don't hurt the real pretty ones. Least, not too bad."

"Thanks. That really helps." Her sarcasm was lost on the boy, and he grinned, revealing an unfortunate set of teeth.

The rest of the ride was carried out in silence as they bumped over the desert landscape, occasional springs of water marked by splashes of green vegetation in the endless sea of brown.

Just when Chelsea was seriously considering throwing herself from the vehicle to escape the combined noxious odors of the men and gasoline-powered vehicles around her, rocky walls appeared before them, nearly invisible against the mountain they were built against.

They drove through the open gate slowly. Inside the walls, Chelsea was reminded of an old hacienda, with productive structures, soldier barracks, and a massive manor house all enclosed within the walls.

The walls were manned with more weapon-carrying individuals.

They were unceremoniously pulled from the vehicles and lined up in the courtyard.

A man dressed in a loose white shirt and black slacks

exited the manor. He stood, hands in his pockets, surveying them silently. "Bienvenido. Any friend of Matias is welcome here."

The man looked younger than she expected, around the age of her brothers. His black hair was combed neatly back, his face clean-shaven. Then he turned his head, and Chelsea drew in a sharp breath. The entire left side of his face was badly scarred, the pale lines in his dark skin running from his eye to his chin, marking his ear and crossing to the corner of his mouth. They were deep. When they happened, they must have caused him considerable agony.

As if he heard her gasp, his gaze fell on her, inspecting her. His eyes were a strange amber-gold color, and the way they gleamed in the sunlight made her forget about his scars. Forget about the savages surrounding them. Forget to breath.

"Please, come in," he said more softly, his eyes still on her. "I am eager to discuss business. Or pleasure."

Chelsea sat in the back of the room as her mother and the devil himself discussed plots to destroy Alba. She tried to remain as unobtrusive as possible, but could feel the golden gaze on her again and again.

"And this will be our mole." Her mother's pleased tone grated on her nerves.

"Come, let me look at you." The devil was talking to her. His accented voice was low and smooth, drawing her like a bee to honey.

She rose, walking slowly forward to stand before his seated form.

"You are the mole, hmm? You hardly look old enough to travel the continent and take on trained agents."

"*You* hardly look old enough to lead a bunch of mercenary savages on foolish missions in the desert. Yet here we are."

"Ah, the honeybee can sting." He smiled, the torn side of his face twisting with the expression. "Be careful, abeja. When a honeybee stings, it often dies."

"That is no doubt why most bees save their sting for the perfect time. Or the perfect man."

Jefe leaned back in his seat, folding his arms and smiling even wider. "No woman—or man—here would dare threaten me, abeja. Not just because they fear what I may do to them, but because of what I can take from them." His golden eyes gleamed, a threat and promise.

"I have nothing left for you to take, so I have nothing to fear from you."

At the starkness of her words, the grin on Jefe's face softened, until he was just watching her intently, his golden eyes piercing her armor, *seeing* her. It made her feel naked, standing before him as he read her face, seeming to know her heart.

Instinctively protecting herself, she crossed her arms over her chest.

"You have your father's eyes; his look," he murmured so only she could hear. "We have a deal, Senora Presidenta." His eyes remained on her for a long moment, and then he turned towards her mother, reaching out a lean hand to shake on the deal.

If she had wondered before, now she knew with certainty: Her mother would make a deal with the devil to get her way.

She just did.

*   *   *

After the display in the Pleb city, the day passed swiftly for Vick. He returned to the Training Grounds and finally had the time to meet with Lina and the team in charge of the program tracking the illness.

The images recorded from holoreaders spread quickly. Vick felt the stares of Patricians and Virmortus alike. Fear, respect.

Animosity.

He knew he'd made the correct choice, but it didn't make it any easier to deal with the aftermath.

Lina said nothing about the incident in the Pleb City, for which he was grateful. When Jay returned from his supply deliveries, he'd just nodded to Vick, as if offering his approval.

It was growing dark by the time he headed back to Helen's villa. Exhaustion weighed his steps as he parked his Bronco in the street and loped towards the front door.

The house was silent and dim. If he hadn't already tracked her location before leaving, he'd think she wasn't home.

Helen turned from the lounge when he entered the sitting room, and he saw all he needed in her pale eyes. Sorrow. Pity.

Judgement.

"You saw."

"Yes, I saw it. By now the entire Republic has viewed it."

"I did what was necessary."

Helen looked down at her carefully folded hands. "I knew what you are, but I guess I never really believed it."

"'What I am?'" he repeated incredulously. The anger and self-disgust that had been boiling inside him gladly found another target. "What I am is the man who's attempting to save your goddamn city. A thankless job, since everyone is suddenly an outsider-hating patriot. But not above stealing from each other. Oh no, they'll defend looters—"

"Then just leave. Run back to your safe little town where you have few responsibilities and all the freedoms you want. Where you can hide your scars and keep running from your past," Helen shot back.

"That was a low blow. You'd like that, wouldn't you? Then you could appoint some weak-willed Patrician who's afraid of their own shadow in my place. Then see how they'd protect you and your baby once the uprising begins." His eyes flicked over her slender form derisively. Her eyes were unreadable, meeting his boldly as he leaned close.

"Because that is exactly what is going to happen if

leadership shows a moment of weakness. The "lower classes" or whatever fucking euphemist title you want to put on them, led by a leaderless army, will convince themselves the Patrician lifestyle is much better than their own humble existence. They'll get themselves worked up into a righteous anger until they lose all reason and storm the Capitol. They'll kill anyone who stands in their way, and anyone they might have resented over the years. People like you, Helen, sitting here in your beautiful house with your soft hands and pretty face." He flicked a strand of blonde hair over her shoulder and she shrunk back instinctively.

Good, that was what he wanted. Fear. If she was going to think the worst of him, he might as well give her his worst.

He leaned in closer, until he could clearly see the light blue flecks in her green eyes, trying to intimidate. "Is that what you want? To keep your ideals while your city crumbles around you?

"Because that is how the downfall of this city will begin, and before you know it, Alba will be back in the dark ages; in the war-era like much of the continent still exists." Vick turned away from Helen, unable to meet her eyes. To see the fear and disgust that was bound to be there.

Yeah, he was a killer. He'd always been one. It was frightening how easily it came back to him; the years of training under his father that he'd thought had mellowed. That he'd tried to forget.

"Do you feel any better now?" Helen asked dryly. He turned back in surprise.

She pushed herself off the lounge, letting the light blanket drop to the ground. He instinctively reached out and snagged it, settling it around her shoulders.

Her lips curled up in a half smile and she thanked him, taking another step closer and tilting her head back to look up.

"That came out wrong; I'm sorry. I can imagine this is difficult, and thankless. But you're right: Control is everything at this point. Balance can only be maintained with control."

Vick's own mouth kicked up at the corners. "Don't spout that balance and serenity shit to me. I'll take the sorry and let's leave it at that."

Helen arched delicate brows. "I see you've heard exactly what you want from me. Typical."

Vick's grin spread as elation filled him. She wasn't afraid of the deadly man revealed today. Or disgusted by the broken man exposed last night. "That's the secret to any successful relationship, sweetheart. Selective communication."

"Relationship?"

Vick tried to quickly backpedal. "Figure of speech. Don't read too much into it."

"I won't."

But he could see she did. And she was worried.

Hell, the idea of a relationship scared the shit out of him. He hoped this natural disaster ran its course quickly so he could escape relatively unscathed.

He had a feeling it was already too late.

*   *   *

"Well?" Aerina waited patiently for Marcus to say something. He remained taciturn as always, his dark eyes unreadable.

She was beginning to know how to read his mannerisms. He was relaxed, and his jaw wasn't clenched. He was pleased, she judged.

"You think Vick did the right thing."

Marcus leaned back against the pillow, his large frame rattling the clinic bed softly. "He is the Alpha. It is his decision how to handle these types of situations."

"Mar-cus…" Aerina drawled his name out in frustration.

Marcus finally took pity on her. "Yes, I think he handled the situation well. It was the appropriate action to take. He needs to keep control."

Aerina sat on the edge of Marcus' bed with a sigh, her biosuit crinkling, pulling her head-covering off. "It just seemed so … barbaric."

Marcus raised one brow, his eyes going to her neck. "Public displays of ferocity are necessary at times to retain control." Aerina's hand raised slowly to touch the nearly invisible scar on her neck, both remembering her own near-execution at his hands.

"You still never apologized for that," she said wryly.

"And I won't. You brought that on yourself."

"Yes, well, I'd like to think I've matured since then."

Marcus just raised his brow again in the way that both irritated and sent her heart fluttering at the same time. She wacked his solid arm. "You should be resting; you're not well yet."

His jaw flexed, signaling his own irritation, but he leaned back. He was lucid, but he tired quickly and then the fever would return. She hid her worry behind a small smile. "What do you think about Helen and Vick? Such a strange couple..."

"I try not to think about other people's relationships if they don't directly affect me or my job."

"Well, Helen is my friend. I'm worried your friend is going to break her heart."

"Helen is a big girl. She can take care of herself."

"What about Vick? He seemed awfully attached to her."

"I don't care about the state of Vick's heart, as long as he does the job I assigned him."

"How am I in love with a man who's so heartless?" Aerina groaned. She leaned in to kiss him on the forehead, taking the sting out of her words. He tolerated it as he always did, although she was beginning to suspect he liked her displays of affection more than he let on. "I'm going to check on my mother."

The moment of levity was quickly forgotten as Aerina entered her mother's room, seeing the Medella looking at the computer. The older woman shook her head at Aerina's questioning look, sending a sharp stab of pain to her heart.

She sat beside her mother's bed, carefully peeling the tall red gloves from her hand. Taking her mother's limp, hot hand in her own, she stroked it gently.

"Mama," she murmured, letting the tears fall unchecked.

To her surprise, her mother's eyes fluttered open.

"Lina."

"Mama, I'm so sorry," Aerina's voice was thick with grief.

Raina slowly raised a shaking hand to touch Aerina's covered face. In desperate sorrow, Aerina wrenched the mask from her head, letting her mother touch her cheek. She pressed the trembling hand to her skin, her tears rolling down over their joined fingers.

"You are a strong, brave girl," her mother's voice was weak but determined. "I love you. I'm proud of you; of the life you've chosen even when the odds were against you. It wasn't what I wanted for you, but I can see it made you happy. And that is enough, now." Her mother's eyes went to someone behind her. "Take care of her. Make her happy."

"I will, Ms. Delacroix," Marcus' deep voice promised.

"Mama…!" Aerina cried softly, feeling a large, familiar hand rest on her shoulder.

Marcus gently pulled Aerina up as Anthony was assisted into the room, her father's face pale but without signs of fever.

Anthony settled on the bed beside his wife. He was speaking to her softly as Marcus drew Aerina from the room.

She leaned into him and he stumbled, catching himself against the wall.

"I'm sorry," she said through her sobs. He said nothing, just stroking her back while she cried. She walked back to the doorway of her mother's room, panic filling her as she saw her father leaning over her mother, tears streaming down his face.

"Is she…"

Anthony shook his head. "She's sleeping. But she's so weak. Her blood oxygen keeps dropping … I don't…" he trailed off, gently stroking his wife's damp hair.

Aerina put her hand hesitantly on her father's shoulder,

knowing there were no words that would lessen his sorrow, so they stood in silence. The only sounds were the low beep of the monitor, and her mother's gasping breaths.

Fear held her in its icy grasp. She'd hungered for change and change had come; nothing would ever be the same again.

*   *   *

Helen ran down the long hallway that connected the lab to the classrooms that had been converted to the emergency clinic in the University's medical wing. Her shoes slapped in rhythm on the tile, echoing eerily in the brightly lit passage.

She saw Aerina sitting on the hallway floor, head resting on her upraised knees. She wore the red biosuit, but the head covering and gloves were gone.

"Aerina."

Aerina glanced up, grabbing Helen in a desperate hug, sobs wracking her body.

"I can't believe she's gone. It was just a few days ago we were arguing about my choices; I thought I had years to work things out. I thought..." Aerina couldn't continue, overcome with tears.

"She loved you, Aerina."

"I know. I know."

Helen let Aerina cry herself out. When she subsided to hiccupping breaths, Helen pulled her over to a small lounge, sitting down beside her.

"I don't understand how it happened," Aerina said as much to herself as Helen. "She was strong and healthy; she wasn't a young child or elderly or infirm. Why her?"

Helen answered, even though she wasn't sure if Aerina was really asking or just trying to fill the silence. "The strain has been mutating quickly. Some, mainly those exposed early, were infected with a weaker strain." Helen paused, not wanting to worry Aerina further.

If they didn't complete the vaccine soon, the virus could very well decimate their population. And it would still be weeks, possibly longer, before they would have a viable serum. The team had agreed to only release that information to Vick and the Senators. If the information became public, it would spark a panic that even Vick's harsh tactics might not control.

She had been on her way to speak with Vick in person at the Training Grounds when she'd received Aerina's message.

Studying in the lab had always been soothing; a passion for her aside from her career of medical law. Now it was an obsession. She needed to find a vaccine; to understand this tiny organism that was wreaking havoc on their city.

She put her hand protectively on the tiny mound where her child lay hidden. No matter what it took, she would find the way to beat this.

*   *   *

Helen approached the Training Grounds cautiously. She'd never been so close to the home of the Reapers, much less ventured inside it.

Daring to enter the den of the wolves that prowled the shadows of Alba was another turning point for her. The woman she'd been a few months ago would never have dreamed of risking her reputation in such a way.

She wouldn't lie to herself and deny that she was fearful, but she also would never let fear stop her from doing what needed to be done.

Parking her e-car in the unpaved lot, devoid of other vehicles, she approached the innocuous gate.

I should have just called. But this information was too important to share over a holoreader. She wanted to show him.

And, she admitted, she needed to see him. Raina Delacroix's death had been a shock. The older woman had been a second mother to her, and losing her was another weight on her already heavy heart.

She was buzzed in immediately, and she slowly pushed open the heavy metal door, entering the strange and forbidden world of the Reapers.

If you see a Reaper, death will quickly follow. The old saying was how the Virmortus, which translated as Man of Death, got their nickname. Their presence often meant death.

And here she was, entering their lair.

As she followed a young Virmortus through the second door and into a large stone cavern, she felt little fear. Knowing that Vick was here made her feel safe, and anticipation rose as they passed a vast hole far below into a stone hallway, stopping before an open door.

Helen's heart did a strange flip flop when she saw Vick leaning over a flat screen, talking intently with one of his "agents". He wasn't his normal impeccable self. His hair was disarrayed as if he'd combed his fingers through it, his beard longer than normal. Even his clothes looked wrinkled.

She knew he hid behind the long hair and carefully groomed beard, but he'd never shed the training he must have undergone. His causal clothes were always clean and impeccable, his beard and hair neat. And each movement was careful and precise.

Just like the other assassins he worked with. He might have rebranded the Virmortus from Reapers to "agents", but the wording didn't change what they were: trained killers.

Like most Patricians, she had dismissed the Virmortus as a necessary evil in Alba to maintain balance and peace. But through Vick, she was beginning to see a new side. A more human side.

Vick looked up, his hazel eyes flicking over her. He must have seen something that gave away her distress, for he said something to the Virmortus and paced over to her.

"What's wrong?"

Helen raised a brow, surprised he had seen so quickly beneath her attempt to collect herself after leaving Aerina. Either she was losing her careful control of her emotions, or he was learning her moods. Both possibilities were unsettling.

"I..." her voice broke, shocking her. Taking a deep breath, she started again. "I just came from the emergency clinic. Aerina's mother just died."

Even after viewing the body, and reading the charts, saying those words sounded shocking.

Raina Delacroix was dead.

Vick cursed under his breath, pulling Helen with him from the room. Once in the cool stone hallway outside the busy tech room, he moved to take Helen into his arms.

She resisted, pushing against his hard chest. "I'm fine."

He let his arms fall back, his expression saying he didn't believe her.

"Come with me," he said, turning to head back down the hallway towards Marcus' office.

Vick's office, now.

The office was surprisingly tame in comparison to the eerie hallways, looking like any large office a Patrician might have. Large glass doors opened to a balcony that overlooked the city far below. A table dominated one end of the room, and a large desk on the other side. But what caught her attention was the screen that covered the entire north wall. It looked like a giant topographic map of the city with thousands — no, millions — of moving dots.

"The Network," she murmured, touching the ID chip embedded in her wrist. This was where they tracked the citizens. She'd known about this since Aerina had told her, but seeing it... was unnerving.

"Have a seat," Vick offered, motioning to the chairs placed before the large desk. Helen ignored his offer, feeling restless.

Vick paced to the glass doors, looking out. He was absently rubbing his beard again, touching the scars she'd felt beneath the tawny facial hair.

She walked to stand beside him, so close she could feel the heat radiating from his body; could smell the citrus scent of her own soap on his body.

Her eyes took in his stiff form, the broad shoulders and arms of banded muscle from physical labor. He was so different from Stephen's slender, athletic form. She'd loved Stephen's drive, his intelligence, his dedication to the same ideals she valued.

The feelings swirling in her now were much different from what she'd felt for Stephen. The strange mix of wary respect and earthy lust seemed at odds. She couldn't trust the emotions, but she admitted that she desired him. Even now, with sorrow and fear constant companions, she hungered for this man who was so different from the Patricians she'd always known.

"If you don't stop looking at me like that, I'm going to fuck you on the desk over there."

Helen opened her mouth with a sharp retort, then promptly closed it as nothing came to mind. Instead, all she could picture was Vick's naked body pressed to hers on the huge desk while he —

Shaking her head to clear the image, she took a deep breath to still her racing heart. Turning to face him, she opened her mouth to try again.

Nothing came out. For the first time she could remember, she was at a loss for words.

The emotions sparked guilt, but Helen had always been practical. Desiring Vick didn't mean she'd loved Stephen any less. And the pregnancy hormones were making her feel unbalanced. Perhaps if she had steamy sex with Vick, she could get him out of her head...

Vick growled low in his throat, as if he could read her mind.

"You're not making this any easier on me," he muttered, pulling her up until their faces were mere inches apart.

"If it were easy, you wouldn't find it nearly as exciting."

Vick said nothing, his mouth settling on hers, forcing her lips apart so his tongue could sweep in.

She didn't push him away, welcoming the pure emotion his assault released. The pent up sorrow and fear became an almost desperate passion, driving her on.

"If you don't want this—"

"We're not stopping," she interrupted against his mouth, her hands having found their way behind his neck, now moving beneath his weapon vest and cotton t-shirt.

"Yes, ma'am."

Serenity save her, she was about to have sex with a man who wore jeans and t-shirts. Hysterical laughter bubbled up but she contained it with effort.

Her searching fingers explored the ripples and grooves of his chest that delineated each muscle.

She felt them flex and then he was lifting her, carrying her to the desk, swiping aside whatever was on it. Their mouths remained fused as he lowered her carefully, his hands moving to her knees. He stepped between her legs, the heat of his body pressed to her throbbing core. His mouth moved from hers to trail down her neck, unbuttoning her demure sweater.

The sensation of his beard on her soft skin was startling but only heightened her desire. He'd opened her top, parting it carefully to expose the delicate camisole bra she wore beneath.

Her breath hitched, but she noticed he wasn't any steadier, his large hands shaking slightly as he skimmed her breasts, touching the slight mound of pregnancy.

For a moment, passion morphed into something more, something a little terrifying, as he bent and placed a gentle kiss on the sign of life.

What was she doing?

A quick bout of sex to relieve the tension was one thing. This was more. This was dangerous.

He'll be gone when this is all over. Can I handle another loss?

Fear sparked in her breast as she watched his bent head, a bright contrast to the white of her clothes and skin. His mouth closed over a taut nipple through her lace bra, wringing a gasp from her lips. Her head dropped back of its own accord, and pure sensation took over. His hands touched her sides, her thighs, learning her, worshipping her.

She gasped again as his palm cupped the heat at her center, feeling the warmth through her thin slacks and panties.

Her hands ran through his hair, pulling his head back up to hers, fusing their mouths together again. Using the belt of his jeans, she pulled him against her, reveling in the feel of his hard body against hers, wrapping her legs around his waist.

A knock at the door was like a bucket of cold water.

"Ignore it," Vick ordered.

"No, it might be important," Helen countered, using both hands to push against his chest. For a moment, she didn't think he was going to listen. Then he began cursing softly, adjusting his clothing.

She buttoned her sweater with unsteady hands, hopping off the desk and shaking out her slacks.

Listening to the low voices from the door, she surreptitiously checked to make sure her damp panties weren't going to show.

What was happening to her? This unseemly behavior was completely out of character. Could she keep blaming this on her pregnancy?

At some point, you're going to have to accept that you're not the same girl you were before Stephen died, an inner voice chided. It was true. Not one to duck the truth, Helen admitted to herself that she had been changing; adapting.

"I've got to deal with this." Vick's apologetic voice interrupted her thoughts as he shut the door. "Apparently Aerina's mother wasn't the only death today; a few more of the Patricians who have fallen ill in the last few days are now dead. I need Lina's team to see if they can map a pattern."

His words reminded her of the reason she'd come. "I have some results I need to show you before you go," she said, unsnapping her holoreader from the bracelet on her wrist, and it opened to fill her palm. The holograph popped up at her command, displaying a series of numbers and charts.

Vick came to stand at her side.

Both ignored the electric currents that still seethed between them.

"These are the tests we've run on the virus. See how it has mutated since the first strain sample we collected?" She used her fingers to rearrange the elements in the projection, enlarging a series of slides. Vick gave her a look.

"Alright, let me simplify this. The virus has changed. The early form was not nearly as infectious. It isn't acting like any virus I've seen before. The speed of mutation, which you already knew about, is making it difficult to create a vaccine."

"Are you saying the original estimate of time needed to develop the vaccine is no longer accurate?"

"It is difficult to say, we may have a breakthrough. But likely yes, it will take longer than normal because of the nature of the virus."

Vick ran his hands through his already thoroughly-mussed hair. Grabbing the leather tie, he knotted it at the back of his head in an absent gesture.

"You could cut it, you know. I promise I won't think you're conforming."

Vick looked confused for a moment, then grinned.

"I couldn't compromise my image. How would everyone know I was an outsider if I didn't look like one?"

"You're not an outsider any more than Marcus or any other Virmortus is."

Vick still smiled, but his eyes grew serious. "Unfortunately you're probably right. They're outsiders in their own city. At least I have a real home to return to when this is all over."

"Yes, isn't that fortunate for you." Helen couldn't help the sharpness of her voice. She knew he would return to Vicksburg, but hearing the words still made her stomach drop.

His expression became slightly more guarded, the smile

frozen in place. "Helen—"

"You have things you need to take care of, and I should get back to the lab. I just wanted to show you the results of our recent studies. It should help explain the new trends you're finding today in the spread of the disease. I'll send a full report to Lina, and hopefully she can use it in her projections."

"Thanks."

Helen nodded, heading towards the door, her back stiff and straight as always.

"Helen." She paused at the door at Vick's low voice. "This isn't over."

She knew what he referred to. "That is where you're incorrect. It was over before it even started."

*　　　*　　　*

Vick cursed silently as he strode down the stone hallway towards the tech room. Lina wanted him to see the new projections in person, and he was certain it wasn't good.

He'd fucked things up with Helen. He'd never been good with relationships, which is why he avoided them. But this one, he couldn't avoid. It had dropped in his lap and now he was too enmeshed to shrug it off like he did everything else in his life.

If he was going to pick someone to fall for, why the hell couldn't it have been a simple girl from Vicksburg without all the baggage Helen had? The single women in Vicksburg were always pursuing him, but he kept a careful distance from them all. It had never been difficult before.

Staying away from Helen was damn near impossible.

All eyes turned to him as he entered the tech room. *Shit, this isn't going to be good.*

"Just tell me straight," he ordered.

Lina walked over quickly, a tech Virmortus he didn't know walking beside her.

"We've got some alarming data you should look over."

Vick followed them over to the row of holocomputers

and flat screens. The pile of discarded chocolate wrappers made him furrow his brow. Only one person would dare leave his station in such disarray.

"Where is Simon?"

Lina looked briefly confused. "Simon? He's on the Pleb Terrace, with his girlfriend. He's well, but the quarantine—"

"For god's sake, you're keeping him down there? Send someone to bring him up if he's not sick anymore. We could use the extra help because honestly Lina, you look like shit."

Her face flushed, bringing some color to her pale cheeks. Her eyes were red-rimmed and bloodshot, and her hands shook slightly like she'd been pounding coffee.

"I've been trying to get the system to a place where others can help take over, but right now—"

"I get it. You're working hard. But you need help. And Simon is the best qualified."

"Of course we could use help."

"I can't believe Jay let you leave the house," he muttered, thinking of his own battle with Helen over the same thing. But she wasn't his woman yet.

Yet? He wasn't sure how that word slipped in there.

"Tell me your bad news," he commanded before Lina could take offense at his chauvinistic statement.

"Look at this." Lina pulled up a file, selecting the data to display.

"Are those deaths?"

Lina nodded, making another selection and a second line of data appeared.

"And these are illnesses."

The line increased dramatically in the last day. Just as the death line had.

"How many?"

"Nearly one hundred."

"One hundred people died from influenza?" Vick couldn't keep the disbelief from his tone. He could see this happening in a place like Vicksburg, which only had rudimentary health care. Or in any other outpost or town across the old North American continent.

But in Alba? How could their advanced medicine not be able to stop such a simple virus?

The virus is not acting like any virus I've ever seen. Helen's words ran through his mind. This wasn't a simple flu virus.

This was something far more sinister.

Chapter 13

"We will breed strength and intelligence into our citizens. Each match will be monitored; each new immigrant tested and scored. The end of the world is Darwinism at its finest."
- Recorded Conversations with Cecilia Delacroix

The sun was barely peaking over the hills when Helen walked into the lab the next morning, looking around the room for one of the trained Medellas helping with the vaccine. The team had all been working long hours, some staying the night, to make progress on the vaccine. So far, they'd had nothing but roadblocks. And while they struggled in here, Albans were dying all over the city.

A lone inhabitant worked at this hour. Helen recognized one of her medical professors in back, running some slides. She groaned inwardly. Agatha was straight-laced and power-hungry. But at this point, Helen was desperate for some answers.

"Agatha, I need a favor," she asked in an undertone.

The silver-haired woman looked up. "Yes, of course, Helen. What can I do?"

"I need some tests run. On me."

Agatha looked surprised. "I thought you already had the illness? Are you thinking—"

"No, it's the baby. I've been having cramping and light spotting." Helen contained the fear that ran unchecked through her body, trying to appear calm.

"Oh." She glanced down at Helen's slightly rounded belly.

"I hate to ask, but I don't want to bother anyone at the clinics right now, and I thought..."

"Yes, of course. I can run a few quick tests. But my dear, you were very ill. That can have some severe consequences to a fetus," Agatha warned.

"I know." *That is what I'm afraid of*, she added silently.

Agatha led her to an empty lab room, helping her get settled on one of the tables. Helen lay down, her heart pounding heavily in her chest.

Please let my baby be alright.

Agatha gently probed, feeling around her belly, checking the baby's heartbeat. Thankfully, the heartrate was strong and normal. Helen felt the huge weight of fear lift slightly from her chest as she heard the quick staccato that indicated her baby still lived.

But that didn't explain the spotting, and it didn't mean her baby was unaffected.

Agatha brought out the sonogram, taking careful measurements. All the while, Helen felt the fear coursing through her veins, thick and dark, threatening to rise up in her throat and choke her.

Please, please, please...

"I'm going to take some fluid," Agatha murmured, drawing out the long needle used for amniocentesis. She was quick yet careful.

Helen gritted her teeth against the discomfort, even after the Num ointment was applied topically.

Agatha sat down beside Helen, pushing away the sonogram machine. The look in the older woman's eyes was one Helen knew well; the look of pity.

"Helen, I know—"

"Please, just tell me." Helen's voice cracked slightly.

Agatha sighed. "I can't say for certain at this stage; it is so early. But I am afraid your baby might not be ... normal."

"Normal? What do you mean?"

"Well, your sickness affected the blood flow to the baby, and your low oxygen levels, and high fever, may have caused some damage in your child's neural development."

"No," Helen whispered in denial. "How abnormal were the measurements? Will she survive?"

"The measurements were only slightly outside the normal range, so it is possible there is a margin of error. Again, it is difficult to say at this stage. But Helen," Agatha took Helen's hand in hers, "Perhaps you need to view this in a different light. I know you wanted to keep this child, because of Stephen. But to raise a child alone, as an unwed mother ... perhaps this is for the best. You can move on and live your life free from the difficulties your situation will bring—"

"Are you suggesting I abort the child because it might be handicap?" Helen's voice cut through the woman's gentle words.

Agatha continued cautiously as she noticed Helen's rising agitation. "There is nothing wrong with choosing to humanely remove a fetus that has little likelihood of surviving and living a normal life—"

"I will not kill my baby. I don't care what is wrong with her, or what I have to do to save her. She will live, and I will give her the best life I am able." Helen felt anger burning in her chest. To suggest it would be easier to end the tiny life growing inside her, and move on as if it had never been created made rage burn in her chest, replacing the fear.

Never. She would sacrifice whatever necessary to bring her baby into the world.

"Thank you for your help, Agatha. I trust you will keep this confidential. Please let me know the results of the amniocentesis labs."

Helen didn't wait for a response, slipping off the table and exiting the room with her head high. They could all think what they wanted of her. Keeping her baby was right and no one could convince her otherwise.

*   *   *

Vick watched Helen cut and eat her food mechanically, her eyes staring at the plate but not really seeing it.

"I know this is a stupid question, considering the situation, but is everything alright?" he asked finally after her knife scraped the plate with unnecessary force for the third time.

Helen set her utensils down, wiping her mouth with a napkin and tucking it beside the plate. Vick watched in fascination at the ritual, knowing it was one of many she used to hide her emotions.

"Everything is fine. Except the obvious, of course."

Vick wasn't buying that answer for a second. "Right. You look like you're wound tighter than a tick on a Texican."

Helen looked up, taken aback for a moment. "That is a disgusting phrase."

Vick grinned "My dad used to say it. At least it got you to stop glaring at your plate."

"My, aren't you the clever one." Helen rose, carrying her dishes to the cleaner, sliding them in before turning to leave the kitchen.

"What the hell. Is this about what happened in the office?" Vick's voice started to rise slightly. Maybe it had been stupid for him to try something, especially with her being pregnant and all, but damn, it hadn't been just his hands and mouth active in that office.

"Oh for serenity's sake, of course it isn't about that."

He felt relieved, but pressed on, needing to know what was bothering her. *Why should I care? It's her own damn business, and she doesn't want me part of her life, anyhow.* Yet he still found himself following her out of the kitchen and into the study.

"Then what?"

Helen turned to face him in frustration. "I told you I was fine. Absolutely fine."

"I heard what you said," Vick's voice was soft, "But your actions are telling me otherwise."

"Now you're an expert on women's emotions and body language? Please." Helen's laugh sounded forced, and Vick said nothing, just folding thick arms over his chest, waiting.

Helen's expression was mutinous as the seconds ticked by, but then he saw something crack, her shoulders slumping slightly. "I might be a little agitated because I found out the baby might be ... might have something wrong with it."

The words hit Vick like a blow, and he sank into the overstuffed chair behind him. The baby wasn't his; should mean nothing to him.

But it did. He'd come to think of the life as a little person, a miniature Helen with silky blonde hair and pale green eyes, adorable little stubborn features... Thinking of that child — Helen's child — at risk twisted his insides.

"Are you sure?"

"No, but it wouldn't be unexpected after my illness."

Vick stood, taking a step toward her, wanting to offer comfort but not knowing how. "Helen, I'm sorry. What are you going to do?"

"Nothing. People get sick, war happens, and some babies don't make it. That's life."

"Don't give me that shit. You care. You're torn up." Frustration warred with sorrow in Vick. Why wouldn't she just cry it out like a normal woman, dammit. Then he could offer comfort, and maybe this wrenching in his gut would subside.

"This might be for the best," Helen was saying distantly. "Without a father, this baby would just complicate my life; make me an outcast. I'll be better off without her." Helen's voice wavered slightly on the last words, but she kept staring out at the Serenity Garden, barely lit by a fountain light in the growing darkness.

Frustration became anger, and Vick ran his hands through his hair. He needed her to admit she cared; *she* needed it. "So you're just going to toss Stephen's child into the trash, and move on with your life? Sounds like a great idea, actually. You can start fresh with a new Patrician; have the life of respectability and power you've always dreamed of. Who needs some baby clinging to your tit, ruining your chances to be Senator, dragging your good name into — "

A loud crack interrupted his derisive words as Helen's

hand connected with his face.

"Get out of my house." She stood before him, her chest heaving.

Damn.

"I'm not leaving."

"I said get out!" her voice became a hoarse cry as a few tears escaped to find paths down her hollow cheeks, dripping from her delicate jaw. This was what he wanted, some honest emotion. But he had to be careful, if he pushed too hard, he'd destroy the fragile bond they'd formed.

He stepped forward, carefully pulling her in. She fought back, her small fists beating his chest as tears became full blown sobs.

"I really hate you," she cried against his chest.

"I know, sweetheart, I know."

He continued to hold her, rubbing her back gently as her tears subsided. Once she'd gained a little control over her emotions, she pushed back and tried to repair herself.

"Better?" he dared to ask.

Helen looked up quickly, her mouth opening with a scathing retort. Then he saw the fight leave her. "Yes, I suppose I needed that. Thank you." The words came out so grudgingly, Vick couldn't help but laugh. He hugged her again, ignoring her small struggles to escape the embrace.

"We're going to get through this. You, me, and little Helen. Got it?" He tilted her chin up, meeting her light green gaze, still awash with tears.

Helen said nothing, searching his face. Then she nodded, straightening her already taut shoulders with determination. "Yes, we will."

"That's my girl." He squeezed her once more, kissing her forehead before releasing her.

"I've been so wrapped up in my own issue, I never asked about your day. Any new developments on the battle front?" Helen asked as she sat, still trying to scrub away the remaining evidence of tears.

Vick walked over to the desk, pulling the decanter of whiskey from the bottom drawer and pouring a healthy splash into the glass tumbler. Stephen's tradition, she'd told him, keeping whiskey in his desk drawer.

He would have gotten along well with the man, Vick thought. He had great taste in whiskey. And in women. He almost felt guilty for his growing relationship with Helen, but brushed the feelings aside.

No time for guilt or regrets. Stephen was dead, and if he was as great a guy as everyone said, he wouldn't want Helen alone in this slowly crumbling world.

He took a sip of the whiskey before answering Helen's question, debating about how much to tell her. She obviously had a lot to deal with right now, but she'd want to know. An indomitable will was contained in that tiny package.

"Unfortunately, I don't have any good news. You were right about the virus. It's much more potent on the newest patients. We've had a large number of deaths in the last twenty-four hours."

Helen tucked her feet under, drawing a white blanket around her shoulders. "That is what we feared would happen. Prevention is the best cure right now."

Vick nodded. "We've instigated a curfew on all terraces except the Agriculture Town. As far as we know, they're still virus-free."

"That is amazing. I suppose our segregation has helped to contain the spread."

"Guess the founders weren't just classist assholes after all," Vick added, earning a reproachful smile from Helen. He turned the subject. "How is Aerina doing?"

Helen frowned. "I haven't spoken with her today. I was so concerned about the baby ... Is her father doing better?"

"Senator Delacroix appears almost fully recovered. That leaves us with four Senators. Unfortunately, the new Senators appointed by Marcus haven't been able to travel here from their respective terraces."

"You won't make an exception for them?"

Vick shook his head, draining the rest of the whiskey in a single swallow. "If I start making exceptions, everyone will expect it. The few people I'm allowing to travel are essential to our survival. More Senators will just cause dissension at this point."

"It is still so hard to believe we are in this position. What are the chances that Jay would become the carrier of an illness right before traveling here, and pass it along to infect our entire nation?"

"Good question," Vick said softly. "I'm curious about that myself."

Chapter 14

"Don't be afraid to die. There are worse fates, believe me. Be afraid not to fight." – Letters from Matias Emmanuel March

The morning of Raina Delacroix's memorial was cloaked in a cool haze. *Even nature mourns her,* Helen thought as she followed the few Patricians allowed to leave their homes for the brief wake.

Raina's ashes were spread into the wind from the Memorial Garden tower. A single individual could fit up the tower, and Aerina's father ascended slowly with the small glass box containing the earthly remains of his wife.

Lina, Helen, and Aerina stood at the base of the tower, a Virmortus standing respectfully at a distance to ensure the strict quarantine was adhered to. After the short ceremony, the attendees were required to return immediately to their homes.

Each memorial was treated this way, and a Senator's wife was no exception.

A slight breeze stirred the heavy air, helping to spread the ashes towards the large Serenity Pool in the center of the garden.

Lina hugged Aerina close as she broke into sobs. Helen watched impassively, keeping the swirling maelstrom of emotions locked tight. Stepping forward, she helped still-weak Senator Delacroix from the lift that had taken him back down from the tower. Linking her arm with him, she walked him to the e-car waiting to return him to the clinic. Aerina and Lina followed, both sliding in the vehicle.

"Are you coming?" Lina asked as she got into the driver's seat.

Helen glanced at the Virmortus that had followed them.

"I'll walk back to the lab after this. I need to make a stop first."

She watched the e-car disappear out the gates of the gardens, turning back to the tiled path.

"I'll just be a moment," she told the Virmortus. The black-clothed man nodded, following as she walked the tiled path, past the tower, towards the back of the elaborate gardens where a large statue stood amidst flowers and shrubs.

Stephen's memorial. A statue for a hero of Alba, the white stag in a defensive stance, massive horns lowered to battle an unseen enemy. Stephen's name and the date of his death were engraved on a golden plaque.

Helen sank slowly to her knees before the towering statue, her fingers brushing the flowers planted along its base.

"I'm sorry I haven't visited before," she murmured. "I didn't know what to say until now.

"I'm sorry I couldn't open up to you; that I didn't trust you completely. I was afraid; afraid I would be forced to give up my dream of being a Senator, like my mother did when she had me." Helen's laugh had a bitter tinge. "How silly I was; how naïve.

"I told a friend to forgive himself so he can think of his loved one without regret. I realized I needed to do the same. I loved you as best I could, and I'll love our baby. I don't want to have regrets, Stephen. I'll remember you with joy, and tell our daughter of the great man who fathered her, and who saved us all."

A drop darkened the marble beneath her, and Helen realized it was a tear, her tear. More joined the first, and she let them fall unchecked, finally grieving for the man she'd loved. The tears served their age-old purpose, to wash away the pent-up sorrow, lightening her soul of its weight.

Helen felt certain that their love could have grown, and trust would have come with time. Time they'd never have, but she could now look on their brief relationship with happiness, without the guilt casting a pall.

Helen rose, absently brushing her white slacks clean. The

Virmortus still stood behind her on the path, his back to her, giving her privacy.

She nodded her thanks as she walked past him, planning to walk the half mile to the University grounds.

"Ms. Vanderbuilt, can I offer you a lift?" The young man's voice was surprisingly deep. Helen turned, really seeing him for the first time. His eyes were dark with an emotion she felt certain was sympathy. She was again reminded that these killers were first people, even if Patricians were raised to view the Virmortus as tools of the Republic, their only purpose to maintain peace and order; a necessary evil.

This young man was more than just a killer.

"Yes, I would appreciate a ride," she responded, falling in step beside the black-clothed Reaper.

*　　　*　　　*

Vick arrived at the Training Grounds to find Jay already there. He'd asked his brother to meet him first thing in the morning in his office.

Marcus' office, he corrected himself. He didn't want to get too comfortable here. Marcus was improving, and hopefully it would be only a matter of time until he could turn this job back over to the rightful leader. Then he could disappear back to Vicksburg.

He was becoming awfully good at disappearing when things got tricky.

Jay glided from the shadows of the dimly lit hallway to join Vick in the office, looking every inch the agent today in his dark clothes, complete with combat boots and EMW at the small of his back.

Vick settled in the chair across from Jay, eyeing his brother, his mind on the new issue that had arisen. How should he approach it without offending him?

"Jay, I need a little more understanding of how this virus came to Alba."

Jay said nothing, waiting for Vick to ask a question. Vick

grinned. He had to remember Jay went through the same training he did. *When interrogated, answer direct questions but do not offer additional information. You can learn much about your adversary by the kinds of questions they ask.*

"Before traveling here, when was your last contact with the former President?"

"You mean our mother?" Jay asked sardonically. It was Vick's turn to wait in silence. "I already went over this with Trent. Trust me, he was quite thorough."

"I know. I watched. But he was focused on your involvement; your movements. Something here just isn't adding up. I want to walk through it again."

"You really think she has something to do with this, even from prison?"

"Do *you* think this is really just bad luck?"

Jay shrugged, obviously not wanting to commit. "It was the day before I left. I visited her in the mental facility where she was being detained. She never came outside of the holding cell, and I kept my distance. There was no way she could have infected me or planted anything on me."

"And then?"

"I went to her home, stole her private jet, and flew to the outskirts of Alba's radar. My pilot, Stix, dropped me and headed back. He's got family he moved into my estate, and was going to keep an eye on things. I hiked to the front gate, where I was met by Trent's friendly welcoming committee."

Vick leaned forward, resting his forearms on his knees, rubbing his hands together slowly as he contemplated Jay's response.

"Do you trust the pilot?"

"Yes," Jay answered before Vick had even finished.

"Who else did you see the day before you left?"

"Just people I trust; people who hate her as much as I do. They knew about my plans to take her out."

"Give me names."

Jay leaned back in the chair, his hands going to the sides

of his head. "James was still recovering from his injuries. Just Thomas, Stix, and ... Shit. Holy shit. She did it. You'd think I'd have learned to not underestimate her... Shit," Jay said again, rising in his chair and stalking to the window. Vick waited patiently.

"I met with my team before I left, sort of a last goodbye. They were my family. But one man, Royce, was also there. He came late, right before Stix and I flew out. I was a little surprised, since he'd only been with us on the last mission. In fact, he'd only been added at the last minute, and while he seemed smart, he hadn't added anything to our team. And he'd insisted on sharing a parting drink, when he'd told me once he didn't drink alcohol. Shit."

"Who added him?"

"The President's lackey, the General."

Vick looked down at his hands, clenching them together to stop the movement. The bitch was still fucking with his life, even after all these years. That narcissistic sociopath who masqueraded as his mother would do anything to get back at people she thought had wronged her.

Like her son. He would know; he'd been the victim of her ruthlessness on more than one occasion. His hand went to the scar on his chin, remembering again the reason he'd vowed never to be close to anyone.

As long as she was alive, no one would be safe around him. And now it appeared Jay had fallen under the same family curse.

He needed to kill his mother. It was the only way he'd ever be free.

"Let's run the scenario. She is involved. It is a test tube virus. This could have a silver lining: There must be a vaccine in the Southern Empire. And you have her jet?"

"If I could get a satellite signal, I could reach Stix, and he could be here in a day. That's approximately three days to get a vaccine, assuming we could find it."

"Much quicker than the weeks or even months the lab is

telling us," Vick finished.

Both men stared at each other in silence for a long moment.

"It's worth the risk. We can head outside and get a signal; direct Stix to meet us south of the city to avoid detection."

"You going to come?"

Vick hesitated. He hated to leave the city. But they might need someone to identify the vaccine, to make sure they took the correct one. That meant they'd need a Medella.

"Let's just see if we can contact Stix and go from there."

"There is one thing you might need to deal with before we go."

"What now?"

"I've been making the run to the Aggie Terrace, picking up the food at the drop point. Yesterday, they left fewer rations. I thought maybe it was a mistake, but today was the same. If I had to guess, I'd think they're testing your control."

Angry frustration made Vick's hands clench. The last thing he needed was their food source being compromised. He'd have to address this before he did anything else.

"Alright, let's go."

He met Nemo in the hallway, Helen not far behind. Panic and another emotion he hated to admit rose. Fear.

This is why you swore never to care about anyone. Because everyone you've ever loved, that bitch has taken from you. Don't you have enough ghosts to answer to?

"What is it?" He didn't bother to hide the impatience in his tone.

"Sir, Ms. Vanderbuilt wanted to speak with you."

"I'm sorry to interrupt, but I have some new information about the vaccine I thought you'd—"

"I don't have time for this," Vick interrupted Helen's explanation.

Her already cool voice became frosty. "Again, I'm very sorry to interrupt you. You asked to be kept informed—"

"Send any future data directly to Lina. She's in charge of the Virus Program until Simon returns." Vick walked past her without a second glance, ignoring her confused and offended expression.

Jay followed, offering an apologetic shrug to Helen.

Regret twisted in Vick's gut as they slid into his Bronco in the garage below.

If his mother was coming … she'd use any leverage she could against him. Helen was his weakness, and he was determined to protect her.

It was best for them to cool things now, anyway. Before she got hurt.

Too bad it's already too late for you, his inner voice taunted.

Yeah, too damn bad.

At least Helen was still alive. That was enough for him.

*   *   *

They took the service road that was an unkempt two-track leading out past the Training Grounds. The Virmortus were the only ones that used the concealed trail. To the south, the road went to the Crow's Nest, a lookout and security station. To the north, the road went down the mountain towards the Agriculture Town.

The Armati patrolled the Aggie's town, but security was much less apparent there than in the city. Stone walls surrounded the sea-level Pleb City, and the other terraces were cut into the stoneface of the mountainside, creating a natural barrier of rock wall around each level of terrace.

"This city really isn't very secure," Jay commented. "My men used these access roads all the time to meet with me. The Aggie town was more challenging, because the farmers and hunters knew everyone's comings and goings there."

"The walls are meant to give people a sense of security. The real security is the Virmortus, who keep an eye on the city and its surroundings constantly. Obviously their system wasn't failsafe, however, since you got in."

"Just goes to show how truly amazing your little brother

is at being a Top Agent." Jay grinned as Vick rolled his eyes.

"Yeah, you're a real winner; homeless, living off your girlfriend."

Jay still grinned, unfazed.

"We're gonna have to ditch the vehicle soon and hike in. I want to do a little reconnaissance first. See what we can learn."

Jay nodded, all joking forgotten. Both men were calm, controlled; predators ready for the hunt.

The day was still dark when they reached the outskirts of the town. In honor of their mission, Vick had donned dark pants and shirt with his weapon vest in lieu of his normal t-shirt and jeans. Jay was dressed similarly.

The men blended well with the shadows, avoiding the farmers still working in their fields, or the people milling around the town's shops. They were headed towards the warehouse that stored the food to be sent on the truck into the Pleb city.

They neared the warehouse, seeing the truck already outside, waiting to be loaded. They slipped unseen into the warehouse. It appeared full, no obvious shortage that might explain why the drop point had been missing the normal amount of rations.

A man and young woman were talking near the large loading doors.

"Devin is speaking at the Meeting Hall in a few minutes. Let's head over there before we pack up the truck."

"Yeah, it's not like they can do anything if we're late," the girl laughed, following the older man out.

Vick waited a few moments before motioning Jay to follow him out the same doors the Aggies had taken.

The Meeting Hall was in the middle of town, and it was a test of their skills to remain unseen as they approached, entering through the back.

"I've heard stories from friends in the city." A large man was speaking, a brawny, tanned Aggie not too much older than Vick. "They're dying. Some illness has been spreading, and it isn't safe for us to venture near. What might be a sad time for many is an opportunity for us." A murmur spread through the crowd, some faces looking uncertain, others excited.

The man continued, "Since the city began, we've been the menial caste. We've worked long, hard days to feed the people of the city. We give the Patricians their fresh food and raw materials with very little thanks or payment. We don't have the luxuries of the Capitol Terrace, and I can promise you the Senators think of us last when casting their votes."

Muttering and angry agreement began to spread, discontent growing from the man's seeds of discord.

"I say we demand change. Quit giving them the results of our labors. We can rule ourselves; become independent from Alba. What do we need them for? All they do is take from us!"

A roar of approval sounded from the small crowd packed into the meeting hall. From the corner of his gaze, Vick saw Jay rolling his eyes at the group's ignorance.

"We'll keep the food we've grown for ourselves, and force them to trade with us! We'll become wealthy and self-governed!" The man was shouting now to be heard over the loud approval of the gathering.

Time to snuff this flame before it went anywhere.

Vick kept clapping, slow and loud, after the other cheers died down. All eyes turned towards him, and the sight of him in his black clothes and weapon vest elicited a few gasps of fear.

A Reaper in their midst.

"Great speech, Devin. You know how to get a crowd riled up. Too bad it's all bullshit."

Murmurs of both antagonism and panic swept through the group, and Devin's face grew red. Vick guessed it was both anger and a healthy dose of fear.

"You all want to secede from Alba and become your own

state? Let's talk about that for a moment. What Devin here has failed to tell you is how long your state will last."

Vick swept the room with his gaze, making sure he had everyone's attention. His voice dropped a little lower, making the room strain to hear him.

"What do you think will happen once the world outside learns of your wealth of food? Without our protection, how long do you think you'd last? Do you know what bandits do to towns like yours? To the women? To the children." He made sure to smile at a young woman holding a small child on her hip.

"You're just an outsider; what do you know of our people? Of our politics?" Devin wasn't ready to give up this bit of power he'd snatched from the tragedy occurring in Alba.

Vick took a few slow steps forward, and the other man, who matched his size, took an instinctive step back. The people in the room could clearly see who held power here. "I *am* an outsider. That is why I know how the world works, in your state and outside the walls. Do you know why you've been able to thrive here, sheltered from the brutal realities of the modern world? Because you sit in Alba's shadow, with their impressive might and technology protecting you.

"Without Alba's help and technology, my own outpost would have been eviscerated long ago; the men killed, the women raped and stolen, and the children... well, there are some groups that enjoy coming up with new and creative ways to gut the children."

Gasps of horror went through the crowd.

"I've buried the dead myself; felt their blood on my hands, picked up the pieces of children before the scavengers could finish devouring them." Vick held up his hands as if the blood of the dead still stained them.

"So by all means," he raised his voice a little louder, "please vote. Try your hand at democracy. Do you want to learn the price of independence, or do you want to remain fat and happy under the watchful eye of Alba?" His gaze landed on a heavy woman holding the hand of a chubby little boy. "Cast your vote. You'll get no repercussion from me."

"We'll need to set up a program on our holoreaders, and cast our votes in private."

Damn Devin, are you really that fucking stupid?

Vick's smile changed to a regretful grimace. "Oh, I'm sorry, I forgot to mention that you'll need to return every piece of Alban technology, including your holoreaders, textiles created in the city's factory, the paper your inspiring speech is scribbled on … and anything else Alba has shipped here to your charming little town."

"I vote we remain part of Alba," the overweight woman shouted out with a fearful look at Vick, clutching the confused-looking boy's hand.

"I second that," the mother with the baby on her hip added in a wavering voice.

"Enough of this foolishness. The fear and uncertainty has gone to our heads. We are Albans. We must stick together during this trying time." The old man from the warehouse spoke up this time, his eyes also darting to Vick as if gauging his response.

A round of "ayes" sounded from the group. Devin's blustering had dissolved into alarm and he edged towards the back of the crowd.

Vick's hand caressed the knife in his belt as he considered his next move. Could he afford to let this man live? Or should he make an example here as he did in the Pleb city?

Jay's hand settled on his arm, and his brother spoke up finally. "Remember that Devin nearly led you down the road to ruin. The acting Alpha has granted you all your lives, when Devin would have cost you them, as well as the lives of your children and neighbors. Do not stand by idly while rash men incite foolishness. Protect your town, and your State, by standing strong. Stand against traitors who would undermine your great nation. If you are to remain great, you must return to your roots: Respect your leaders, and uphold peace."

The fear in the room faded to indignation and pride. And anger, now all directed at Devin. Vick cast a wry look at Jay. His little brother always did have a way with people. But it was also strange that the younger man was pushing old Alban ideals, when change had been swiftly spreading through the city under Marcus' rule.

He'd worry about Jay's political motivations later.

He was just thankful he hadn't been forced to kill anyone today. At least not yet. It was still early, after all.

The trip back to the Bronco was much quicker, and soon they were heading along the rocky trail towards the Training Grounds.

"We should be able to access the signal from the trail east of the city. It was where I could sometimes get a signal, and Alban radars couldn't intercept."

Vick nodded, taking the eastbound trail once they were partially up the mountain. The fewer people knowing of this mission, the better. He didn't want to give false hope of a vaccine that might not even exist. Or incite fear of the Southern Empire when the people were still recovering from the last battle.

Jay pulled out a large, square device from the pack he'd brought.

"You're using a prewar ham radio to communicate? No wonder no one could intercept." Vick couldn't keep the awe from his voice. He'd been looking for one for years.

"Yeah, we've been working with these for awhile. You'd be surprised how many small-time outposts have these things. Only way to communicate after the first blasts, I guess. This one is authentic pre-war. Stix has one that was made more recently."

Vick touched it reverently, impressed at the great condition it was in. "Let's just hope your friend has his on, and is monitoring it."

"He will be," Jay said confidently.

Sure enough, they heard back immediately from what sounded like a young girl, promising to locate Stix.

"Probably one of his daughters," Jay said as they waited. A few minutes later, the broken, raspy voice of Stix came across. He agreed to meet them at coordinates near Vicksburg late that evening.

He sounded like he was trying to say more, but the signal began breaking up, and Jay gave up, tucking away the device. "We'd better head out if we're going to make it."

"We'll need to bring a Medella with, to identify the correct vaccine."

Jay looked at his brother. "Why not bring Helen? She's the most trustworthy—"

"No, she's not going." Vick's tone allowed no argument.

"I get it. I wouldn't want my woman on this mission, either. But she's our best bet."

Vick felt the familiar panic rising at the thought of bringing Helen any closer to his mother.

He couldn't risk the life of another woman he loved.

He'd admitted it. He loved her. God*damn*, he was a fool. He was going to protect her from himself, whatever the cost.

"Who do you suggest we take? Perhaps we could just kidnap another Patrician. That worked out well for me last time," Jay said sardonically.

"No. We'll take the head of the lab, Terrence."

"That weasely little shit? He's afraid of his own shadow. He won't agree to come."

"I can be persuasive."

                    *   *   *

The days spent in the hidden hacienda passed slowly for Chelsea. She avoided contact with anyone, which proved easy to do when it came to her mother and sister, who couldn't care less about how she spent her days.

But the man, the disturbing, fascinating man who went merely by Jefe, or Boss, was not so easily dissuaded.

It was afternoon, and she had been wandering through

the immaculate gardens along the cliff-side. A dark shadow fell over her, making her gasp and turn, terrified of being caught off-guard.

It was him, watching her as she brushed the leaves of a climbing bean plant.

"Do you enjoy gardening, abeja?" he asked, referring to her with that mocking name he'd given her the first night. Honeybee. Only from his lips, it sounded more like an endearment than mockery.

"Don't all bees like gardens?" Sarcasm helped her keep her distance; it made her feel safer.

"When we came upon this abandoned estate, we meant to only spend the night. But it was your father who explored the grounds and discovered the hidden spring within the mountain. It is why we have chosen this place, and why our little garden is able to flourish in the middle of the desert."

Chelsea's heart panged at the mention of her father. She'd barely known him. The larger-than-life figure that had dominated her early years was absent most of her childhood, and dead throughout her adolescence.

"You knew my father well?"

Jefe nodded, coming up behind her and snapping a bean from the plant, offering it to her. She shook her head, and he took a bite, his even white teeth contrasting with his deeply tanned skin.

Chelsea instinctively took a step back, not liking having anyone too close. To hide the action, she turned down another row and pretended to inspect the cherry tomatoes hanging from a chest-height plant.

"He was a frequent visitor to our region of Texico," Jefe said, his golden gaze missing nothing. "He was a good man, your father."

The sorrow in Chelsea's heart twisted to bitterness. "I didn't know him well."

Jefe prowled among the greens, inspecting and touching the growth. She kept her gaze on the tomatoes, but felt his presence as he approached, his shadow falling over her.

He reached his hand out to touch her cheek, and she forced herself to remain still, feeling the callused palm brush a loose strand of tawny hair behind her ear so he could clearly see her face.

"I am sorry. It is a shame his death came too soon."

Chelsea nodded jerkily, refusing to give in to the self-pity that was attempting to blossom.

Jefe's hands went to her shoulders, and afterwards Chelsea didn't know if he were attempting to offer comfort, or trying to make a move, but survival instinct kicked in as a man, a powerful man, seemed to surround and engulf her. Lashing out blindly, her fist connected with a hard cheek, and she ducked away so quickly she stumbled.

Her chest heaving, Chelsea stared at Jefe. She'd offended him. He stood stiffly, his hands fisted at his side, his scars white as his clenched jaw.

She wanted to apologize; to tell him it wasn't him. But the words remained locked in her throat, terror still controlling her.

"What's the matter, abeja? Is a warlord not good enough to touch your pretty white skin? You can tolerate my help, but not my touch?"

He paced closer, and Chelsea's eyes widened further, terror completely taking over as memories blended with reality.

Large, clammy hands on her arms, holding her, placing restraints on her. Touching her, making her skin crawl... "What's the matter, you little cunt; do you think a March is too good for a man like me? Well your own mother told me to do whatever necessary to convince you to behave. Anything, Chelsea. Do you know what that means?"

Before he could touch her, a distant voice interrupted, speaking rapidly in Spanish. Jefe's expression became controlled again, the liquid gold of his eyes cooling to burnished amber. "It looks like you are needed, abeja. Come, we will prepare you for your mission."

*   *   *

"Everything is progressing as we planned. Fear is driving the citizens to search for change; to thirst for the peace and safety of our roots as a nation. The unpopularity of Vicktor March as Alpha will only help our cause when the time comes."

"The Council will be pleased," the messenger murmured, starting slightly at a distant slam of a door that echoed eerily through the stone tunnel.

The man in shadow also turned. "I cannot be seen here; I have things to accomplish and will be out of touch briefly. Soon, I will be able to report to the Council directly, and these clandestine meetings underground will no longer be necessary."

The messenger nodded. "The Council is just as eager for that day as you are."

"Will they take care of the current Alpha, as I requested?"

"Yes, they plan on using the former President of the Empire. It was a simple matter to allow her to escape. She's a bit of a loose cannon, as you know, but we are confident we can deal with her once she's completed the actions we need, and further weakened Alba's current leadership. With her and her barbaric army at the gates, you will easily gain the support of the Alban people. Then you can deliver the promised goods."

The man in shadow nodded. "Yes. Alba's great secret will be yours. And a very profitable relationship will be rebuilt after all these years."

Chapter 15

Each citizen will perform the duties assigned to them within the caste of their birth. Citizens may petition Population for assignments outside of their caste. Any attempt to change castes without consent, or to masquerade as another caste, is punishable under the Law of Death. – Law of Segregation, Alban Charter of Government

"Is there a reason you're leaving?" Helen watched as Vick threw clothes into a bag. "Is this something we can discuss?"

"I told you, sweetheart, I just felt bad abandoning you when you were sick. You seem to be doing fine now, and its best if I stay elsewhere. I'm sorry your feelings are injured—"

"My feelings are hardly injured just because you're leaving," Helen interrupted coldly, her heart feeling like it was being squeezed by an iron fist.

"That's right, you don't need anyone, do you Helen? I thought maybe we could have something hot in the sack, but probably best if we forget about that, too. This situation is complicated enough. It's best just to cut each other loose."

Helen said nothing, the pain caught in her throat, trapping the chilling retort that would normally pass her lips. She fought back the tears with effort, not willing to show him a bit of weakness.

I thought this was going somewhere. That he felt something for me. How could I have been so wrong about him?

The pain was crushing. When she'd lost Stephen, it had been devastating. But she'd accepted it. He'd died doing what he wanted, as a hero for their state. He was gone, and she could do nothing about it.

But this. This was different. It was devastating but also … ruining. She could feel her soul shriveling with each efficient movement as he packed his bag, not even caring to glance at her.

He'd forced her to feel, to face her emotions. He'd teased, comforted, actually *seen* her, not just the façade she wore for everyone else. Even Stephen hadn't delved below the prickly exterior she'd worn.

But Vick had. He hadn't just dug beneath, he'd blasted the façade to smithereens, laughing while doing it.

Perhaps it *had* been just a game to him; a challenge.

It hadn't felt like a game, though. It had felt real.

He looked so arrogant and unconcerned, checking his weapons and tucking them in the belt at his lean waist. His movements were quick and efficient, emphasizing the careful control he maintained over his honed body. Light from the window gleamed on the gold streaks in his tawny hair, catching the golden flecks in his hazel eyes. She'd dismissed him at first, thinking him too rough and unkempt for her. But the last few weeks, she'd seen the intelligence and humor behind the rough exterior; the gentleness he tried to disguise.

Had she seen what she wanted? Did the man she'd come to know over the past few weeks even exist?

Clenching her small hands into fists, Helen forced herself to turn away. Leaving the room with her head held high, she went into the kitchen to fix dinner. Only she had no appetite.

A short while later, she heard his footsteps on the stairs as he descended. She sensed his presence behind her as he paused in the doorway, and she held her breath, waiting for him to say something. Anything that would help her understand.

But he said nothing, and soon she heard his nearly silent retreat, then the quiet closing of the door.

Putting one hand on her stomach, she laid her head on the table and wept.

*   *   *

Vick looked at Helen's back, the slender lines of her body stiff with anger. He felt a wrenching in his chest as he saw her small hands shaking slightly as she stirred a mug of tea. She made tea to comfort herself, he knew. One of the many little things he'd learned over the past weeks with her.

His hands clenched into fists at his side as he fought back the words of apology; the words begging her to forgive him and forget everything he'd just said. Words begging her to come with him and never leave his side.

Forcing himself to turn away, he stepped through the front door, closing it quietly behind himself. He gripped the handle, knuckles white. He couldn't make himself let go. Leaning back against the door, he laid his head on the cold wood. The muffled sounds of sobbing filtered through, making the pain in his chest intensify with each breath.

This is why you're leaving. To protect her. To keep her and the baby safe from you. You're no good at relationships. You're better off alone.

He pushed off from the door and loped down the steps to the Bronco. Turning the key, he watched the front door of Helen's villa, almost wishing she would appear.

But she didn't.

He drove away, ignoring his brother's obnoxious, knowing grin and the muffled sounds of struggle from the back seat.

This was best, he told himself. He just hoped he could believe it.

Turning his mind with effort to other matters, he focused on the man in the backseat.

Jay had been right. The head of research at the University had flatly refused to come. Nothing they said changed his mind. So Vick had followed Jay's plan B: Kidnapping.

The plan was simple. Drive Jay to the drop point, spend the night in Vicksburg and return the following morning. Jay and their hostage were going to continue on to the Southern Empire, head to the Center for Disease Control, which Jay told him ironically was located in the same building in Atlanta from the prewar era. Most of the same diseases were even there, still alive, because the Center had some truly impressive generators, hardened against the EMP blasts.

"Lina is going to kill me when she finds out I went back to the Empire," Jay said absently, watching the rocky terrain pass quickly.

"What did you tell her?"

"I tried to keep the details to a minimum. I love the girl, but she can't keep a secret to save her life. And I mean that literally. I just told her we had to meet with Stix about something going on in the Empire, and we'll be back in a few days."

Vick nodded, silently hoping the trip really would be as innocuous as he'd made it sound.

*   *   *

Helen sat in the Serenity Garden, oblivious to the warm sunshine and merrily chirping birds flying amongst the flowers and low trees.

Her eyes felt dry and scratchy from crying, exhaustion weighing on her limbs.

This was ridiculous. How could a person allow themselves to be brought so low because of foolish emotions? She hardly knew Vick. He should be nothing to her.

Her hand subconsciously went to her stomach where her baby rested. Determination fluttered to life, overcoming the sorrow that had settled in her heart.

She owed this baby more than this. Enough self-pity.

Getting up, she left the room to take a shower and head into the lab.

Helen was just grabbing her things when the door announced a visitor.

Lina Rhodes.

Helen frowned. Something must be important for Lina to break curfew to come here. She hoped this wasn't more bad news. She had talked to Aerina that morning and her friend had seemed to be holding it together.

Opening the door with some trepidation, she motioned

Lina inside.

"Please tell me what Jay and Vick are up to," Lina said without preamble.

"What do you mean?"

Lina narrowed her eyes, her hands clenched. "I know no one trusts me to keep quiet. But I can't stand not knowing. And I might be naïve at times, but I didn't buy a word of Jay's story about meeting with someone from the Southern Empire."

"They're meeting with someone from the Southern Empire?"

Lina's guileless brown eyes narrowed in confusion. "Vick didn't tell you anything? He and Jay are leaving the city. According to Jay, they're just meeting Stix about some issue in the Empire. Jay thinks I'm still the naïve girl he could lead around, but I know him well enough now to see when he's not telling me the whole truth."

"They both left this morning?" Helen asked, her mind working quickly.

Were Jay and Vick working with the Empire? Was this whole thing a set up to steal the Technology and destroy Alba?

"No," she breathed.

"What?" Lina demanded.

Helen shook her head, not wanting to even say the words aloud.

"Helen… for peace's sake, tell me. I have to know or I'm going to lose it," her voice hitched.

"Calm down," Helen snapped. She needed to think. If Jay came here to plant the virus and weaken Alba, it would be simple to take a vial of Technology and hand it off to the Empire. And Vick was in the perfect position to facilitate, as the interim Consul and Alpha. No one would—or could—question anything he did.

"Lina, are you certain Jay is coming back?"

"Of course," Lina responded defensively. "Why

wouldn't he?"

"Did you see what he took with him? Did you see him leave?"

"He left from the Training Grounds with Vick. I know he's hiding something, I just don't know what... Why, what do you know?"

"It might be possible that Vick and Jay are working together to steal the Technology, and deliver it to the Southern Empire."

Lina looked at her, aghast. Then she began shaking her head. "No. Jay is done with the Empire. He would never do it."

Helen bit her tongue to keep from yelling at her friend to stop being so naive.

"Let's think about this. Both men left together to meet an agent of the Empire. They are both citizens of the Empire; sons of the deposed President. And they were secretive about their mission. What else could they be doing?"

Lina just shook her head again, her long dark curls swinging around her head. Her rejection of the Patrician style of short, neat hair was only one of the many changes Helen had noticed in her friend since returning from captivity in the Empire.

She might be different, more confident and courageous, but she was still loyal and would never betray her people. But that didn't mean her boyfriend wouldn't. Jay had used Lina before to get to the Technology. What was going to stop him from doing it again?

"We'll go ask Marcus. If they are on a mission for the State, he'll know." Lina turned, not waiting to see if Helen followed.

Helen followed her, getting into the passenger side of Lina's e-car.

They drove to the University in silence, suiting up and heading straight to Marcus' room. The large man was alone, sitting up in the bed, typing furiously on a virtual keyboard, a holoscreen projected before him. His appearance shocked Helen for a moment. His face had thinned, and sported a dark shadow. His eyes were red-rimmed.

Helen only glimpsed an image of reports and projections before Marcus minimized the screen, raising one dark brow in question.

"Marcus, we were hoping you could clear up a misunderstanding. Vick and Jay are meeting with an agent of the Empire, and we want to know why. Or at least know that it is Alban business. Helen here," Lina cast an evil look at her friend, "is convinced the men are working with the Empire to steal the Technology."

Marcus' dark eyes settled on her, and Helen barely contained a shiver. She understood why people were terrified of this man. Just that gaze alone was enough to freeze her blood.

"How did you come to this conclusion?" Marcus coughed, the entire bed shaking with the dry sound.

Helen cleared her throat. "It isn't a conclusion, merely a supposition. I just don't know why else they would disappear in the middle of this crisis to meet with an agent of the Empire."

"Well Miss Vanderbuilt, I suggest you keep your *suppositions* to yourself." Marcus' low voice had turned dangerous, a side she rarely saw of the man. She swallowed quickly, telling herself she wasn't afraid of him.

"Very well," she said stiffly, turning to go.

"Marcus, please, can you tell me that they are ok?" Lina pleaded. Helen didn't wait to hear his response, walking down the long hall towards the lab.

She wasn't sure what she believed. Marcus hadn't seemed concerned, but he was hardly going to give anything away. And how cognizant was he of what was going on in Alba?

Could Vick be capable of something like that? Betraying an entire nation of people? What would he gain from it?

President March was his mother. He'd claimed to hate her; to fear her, even. Had that all been a lie?

She had believed he cared about her, and then he had walked out without an explanation, catching her unaware. If she misread him that completely about their relationship, she might have seen what she wanted to in other areas, too.

But could he really be working for the Southern Empire?

The uproar in the lab interrupted her worried thoughts.

"Terrence is missing!" one of the students helping them exclaimed. "He never came in this morning."

"Has someone gone to check on him, to see if he's ill?"

"Yes, and he's not in his villa. No one can reach him."

"And the virus test tubes are gone!" another researcher called.

What in the name of peace was going on?

"Has anyone been running tests outside of this lab?" Helen asked, scanning the faces of everyone in the room. They all shook their heads.

"Terrence told us not to remove the vials. We needed to contain everything here."

If Vick was involved, why would they take the virus? Why get rid of Terrence? To keep them from finding a vaccine? Stealing the vials wouldn't stop them completely, but it would certainly set them back a few weeks; they would need to start over.

"Are there security recordings here?"

"You think someone took them?" a tech asked fearfully.

"Someone did." Helen's tone was grim.

"I believe the recordings are sent directly to the Virmortus," the same tech said.

That meant Lina would be able to access them.

Heading back down the long hall, she found Lina talking to a Medella.

"Lina, I need your help."

"I'm not going to investigate Vick and Jay. Marcus told me to trust them, and I do. I know Jay is doing what he thinks is best, even if it does drive me crazy that he can't tell me the whole truth."

Helen nodded. "I understand. If you're right, then you can ease my mind, too. Please?"

Lina looked at Helen, her eyes softening. Helen imagined what she saw; her own gaunt, pale face, eyes red from her earlier tears and lack of sleep. Lina might be a little savvier and confident now, but she still had a soft heart.

"Of course."

An hour later in the Training Grounds, Lina played the recording of the past twenty-four hours from the lab. Helen's heart sank at what she saw. Jay and Vick entered the lab, where only Terrence worked during lunch. Vick talked briefly with the slender man, and it appeared that they were arguing. Terrence turned away, dismissing the men.

Vick looked to Jay and then moved quickly, grabbing the Patrician and pulling the man towards him in a violent embrace. Terrence collapsed, appearing unconscious, and Vick tossed him over his shoulders. Jay went through the carefully labeled vials, grabbing the ones she'd seen missing and storing them carefully in a refrigerated case. They disappeared out the back.

"What are they doing?" Lina asked in shock.

Helen said nothing, crushed beneath the weight of her own shock and despair. How could she have so completely misread him? She had cared about him, and believed that he cared about her and the baby.

She had been so wrong; so foolish.

"There must be some reasonable explanation."

"Wake up, Lina." Helen couldn't keep the anger inside from spilling forth. "Didn't Jay already betray you once? They obviously planned something. Who knows how long they've had this prearranged. Possibly since before Jay left the Southern Empire. Maybe even longer."

"I can't believe it." Lina's voice had grown soft. "Until

Jay tells me himself, I won't believe it. They must have had some logical reason for taking Terrence and the vials."

"Fine. Believe what you wish. But I'm going to do something about this. We can't afford the time this is going to cost; the lives that will be lost."

"What are you going to do, follow them to the Empire?"

"If necessary," was Helen's grim response.

*   *   *

"Your reports look great, sir. You could probably go home tomorrow, granted you take it easy for a little while," the Medella told Marcus, clicking out of the holoscreen displaying his vitals.

Marcus grunted in response, irritated he had to wait another long day in this tiny room.

"That's wonderful!" Aerina exclaimed. Marcus looked over at her, noting the dark shadows beneath her eyes. She'd taken her mother's death particularly hard.

Lina and Helen had been surprisingly absent, although with their responsibilities, he understood that they were busy elsewhere.

He just felt so damn helpless when it came to comforting Aerina. Dealing with emotions had never been something he'd concerned himself with until recently. He mostly avoided it, letting Aerina talk when she needed, or evading the situation entirely where her friends were involved.

But this … he certainly couldn't avoid this issue.

Surprisingly, Aerina hadn't said much, but he could tell she was suffering. He hadn't been able to attend the memorial with her, and the resulting feelings of helplessness morphed into anger. Anger, he found, was a much more palatable emotion than helplessness.

At least he could get out of this damn prison and start taking over responsibilities again. He'd have to confer with Vick about whether or not it would be worth another transfer of power, but his friend seemed to be doing a sufficient job keeping everything under control.

"Sir." One of his young recruits stood in the doorway.

"Yes?"

"There is a bit of a situation, and Mr. March is unavailable. I wanted your guidance."

Marcus raised a brow, waiting impatiently for the man to tell him what was going on.

The young man's gaze skipped to Aerina for a moment before fixing on Marcus' chin. "Ms. Vanderbuilt has been causing a problem. She's trying to get the jet ready for a flight to the Southern Empire."

"Explain." Marcus' voice had dropped dangerously low, the even tone hiding his rising fury. That meddling bitch was always causing problems. If she wasn't Aerina's friend…

"She won't go into detail, but she's been ordering the men to prepare the jet. She says it is under Mr. March's orders, but I don't think that is the truth. I can't reach him to confirm."

"Tell her I want to see her at once," Marcus ordered. The young Virmortus nodded, leaving the room quickly.

"What do you think she is doing?" Aerina settled back into the chair beside the bed.

"She was in here earlier ranting about Vick and Jay working for the Empire. Perhaps she's trying to go after them." The woman had guts, he'd give her that much. He felt a grudging respect for her tenacity. Marcus threw his legs over the side of the bed, hating that he was still so weak.

"I can't believe he didn't tell her his plans. I thought they were … together."

"Relationships are always a problem," Marcus said darkly, rising. He wore grey drawstring pants and a black t-shirt, but he still felt naked. He needed his uniform and weapon vest.

Pacing the tiny room slowly, he looked out the small window that faced the circular drive. Aerina's concern was written clearly on her face as she watched him.

He didn't have to wait too long. Helen's small white e-car pulled into the turn-around, and the petite blonde woman exited, determination visible in the taut lines of her body.

A minute later she appeared in the open doorway.

"You summoned?"

Marcus leaned against the wall, folding his arms over his chest. A tense moment passed. Then another. She waited him out, her pale green eyes meeting his unflinchingly. Marcus had to admit he was duly impressed. Most opponents would be talking, trying to fill the uncomfortable silence.

"What are you trying to accomplish?" He kept his voice low and even.

Helen glanced at Aerina before looking back at Marcus. "I'm going after Terrence and the test vials. We need both to successfully create a vaccine."

"And what do you think happened to them?"

Helen opened the holoreader snapped on her bracelet, selecting a file, opening a recording. Marcus recognized it from the security tapes. Vick and Jay were in the lab, talking to Terrence before taking him, unconscious, and the test tubes they were using to develop the vaccine.

Marcus had to admit it looked damning. He felt another grudging bit of admiration.

Helen closed the reader, reattaching it to her bracelet.

"They did kidnap Terrence." Aerina sounded shocked. "Why would they do it?"

Marcus felt his frustration rising, but he kept it tamped down. "He probably wouldn't come willingly." He turned to Helen. "Go home, Helen. Do the job you're assigned."

"I can't. Not without those vials."

"Why don't you try trusting your lover." Marcus put a note of reprimand in the statement.

Helen stiffened, her hand resting protectively on the growing bump that was her child. "Vick is not my lover. We are … were … merely friends. Apparently not even that, if he's been plotting against Alba this entire time."

"Do you really believe that?" Aerina asked gently.

Helen looked at her, strain becoming evident on her features.

"I don't know what to believe anymore." She was struggling to control the emotions Marcus saw clearly rampaging beneath the surface. He felt a tiny spark of sympathy, banishing it quickly before it could spread.

"Helen, Vick isn't in league with the Empire. He's—"

Marcus interrupted Aerina before she could explain the details to Helen. "His plans are none of your concern. Go home. Rest. Tomorrow, return here and we'll discuss your use of the jet."

"But each moment matters! People are dying." Helen's gaze again flicked to Aerina, and Marcus saw the sorrow etched on his lover's face at the reminder. Goddamn Vick, why couldn't he leave his personal shit out of this situation? The last thing Marcus wanted to deal with now was complications from Vick's emotional impotence. Helen clenched her fists, her voice growing quiet. "I can't just go home and—"

"You can and you will." Marcus could see she wanted to argue, but she didn't, nodding. Aerina hugged her quickly, and Helen forced a smile.

"Why didn't you tell her Vick's plan?" Aerina asked him after Helen had left, exasperation clear on her face.

"Because Vick had his reasons for keeping it from her."

"I don't care what Vick's reasons are!" Aerina angrily ripped the biosuit head-covering off. "You saw her, Marcus. Helen is fragile right now. She should be home, resting, eating right, not running around trying to save our city when it doesn't need to be saved! And why in the name of peace did Vick kidnap Terrence?"

Marcus shrugged. "Probably because he wouldn't go willingly. He needs a Medella along."

Aerina sighed. "I suppose it doesn't matter. *I* know Vick isn't in league with the Empire, but I don't think Helen is thinking clearly right now. Why did you stop me from telling her anything?"

"Vick deserves someone who is going to put her trust in him, not turn on him the moment things get shaky."

Aerina looked over in surprise. "That is amazingly insightful, for someone who hates 'emotional entanglements'. And it's very sweet of you to look out for your friend." Marcus scowled, prompting a small smile from her. "That's why I love you. Beneath that gruff exterior beats a good heart."

Marcus said nothing as she embraced him, pulling her in close. It never failed to surprise him how much those simple words — *I love you* — warmed him. He found they still stuck in his throat when he considered uttering them back, but he figured Aerina knew. She'd never pushed him, at least not yet, to return the sentiment.

They're just words, he tried to tell himself.

But they weren't. They were a sign of vulnerability that he wasn't sure if he was ready to embrace. Not yet. Not now.

He'd told her what mattered: that he was never going to let her go again; that he would die for her.

He hoped that was going to be enough.

"This looks cozy. No wonder you're healing so fast, with this kind of nurturing," came a deep voice from the doorway.

Marcus released Aerina and stepped forward to clasp hands with Ramus.

"It's good to see you back."

"Ramus! I'm so glad you're well," Aerina echoed, moving in to give the large man a hug. He stood awkwardly in her grip for a long moment, patting her gently on the shoulder until she stepped back.

"When the fever finally broke, I opened my holoreader and thought I was still hallucinating when I saw you'd turned over control of this great State to someone else. To an outsider," Ramus said, his tone questioning.

"Vick has been a valuable asset to Alba for years. You know as well as I do that he is trustworthy, and as much as I hate to say it, most fit to lead after you and I were out of commission."

"Yes, of course, I didn't mean to question your decision. It just drove home the extreme situation we're facing."

Marcus nodded. "But you make an important point. We need a better succession plan in place. This damn illness could have killed us both, and who would take over as Alpha then? Not to mention appointing a Consul. I've been dragging my feet about it, and I need to make a decision. I sure as hell don't want the job any longer."

"How about Vick?" Ramus began, pausing for a moment to cough. "He sure seems to be doing a bang up job."

"He's itching to get back to his own little town. Even if the Senators would be on board, which wouldn't happen, Vick would never take the job."

"What about you, Ramus?" Aerina asked, handing him a glass of water. "You're a smooth talker, and the people would love that handsome smile."

"You think all I am is a pretty face?" Ramus feigned injury.

Marcus, as usual, ignored the banter. "That is an interesting suggestion."

"Hey, I've got my eye on your job."

"Since I plan on living a long time, you might have a long wait."

"I'd drink to that," Ramus murmured, downing the water in his hand. "But let's get this situation straightened out, and then we can talk about succession and consulships.

Chapter 16

For a man to know peace, he must fight. Peace is the result of battle, either in secret or on a large scale, and only the conquerors will find it. -Virmortus Training Manual

Vick and Jay rode most of the distance towards the meeting location in silence. The Head Lab Technician, whose name was as unmemorable to Vick as the man himself, had been given a sedative and slept in the back during the bumpy ride.

They arrived ahead of the Southern Empire jet, waiting at the coordinates just outside of Vicksburg, each lost in their own thoughts.

Vick thought of Helen. Had it been a mistake to crush her so completely? He was leaving at the end of all this, anyway. But why couldn't he have left her with a few good memories and ridden off into the sunset, like a cowboy from the pre-war western movies he'd watched as a child.

The truth was, he'd panicked. It hadn't been for Helen's sake he'd cut ties. It was for him.

You fucking coward.

The sound of the jet approaching interrupted his morose thoughts. The gentle hum grew to a roar as the aircraft hovered before slowly descending, dust blowing in a small maelstrom that temporarily blinded him.

Once the dust had settled, the door opened. Vick and Jay glanced at each other as two figures exited the cockpit, both short, but one definitely feminine.

"Chelsea. What are you doing here?" Jay asked as they drew closer. He shot Stix a dark glare.

"She begged me to come. I've never been able to say no to a pretty girl," Stix rasped, apology evident in his broken voice.

"We'll deal with her later." Vick's eyes remained stuck on his little sister. He hadn't seen her in nearly a decade. She'd been a child then, full of curiosity and hero worship for her father and older siblings. She had blossomed into an attractive woman, with the same golden brown hair he and his brother sported. She hadn't inherited the family height, her petite stature reminding him of Helen's delicate build. But her green-gold eyes, a lighter shade than his, had the same bitter gleam. She'd seen the evil in the world.

He wondered what horror his mother had inflicted upon her in the intervening years.

And how she fit into the scheme their progenitor had devised now.

Dragging his gaze away, he turned back to Stix.

"Well? What news do you have that you couldn't discuss over the radio?"

"She's gone," Chelsea answered for the wiry little man, her arms crossed defensively over her chest.

"Who?" Even as he asked, Vick knew.

The devil had escaped.

"Your mother." Stix affirmed his fears.

"You should have killed her," Vick growled, glaring at Jay. "How?"

"Two of the guards let her out. You know how persuasive she can be. Probably thought they were doing their patriotic duty, poor fucks. She killed them. Found their bodies myself just a few days ago," Stix said.

"Why didn't you tell me sooner?" Jay asked.

"I've been trying to keep it quiet, and you know how many outposts are scanning the radio channels, picking up whatever news they can. Royce was traveling to Texico and offered to contact you by Com device when he was in range."

"Royce." Jay said the name like an expletive.

"Told you he seemed too smooth," Chelsea said.

The men ignored her. "Let's assume Royce is involved. And they are heading to Texico. What's her goal?" Vick crossed his arms over his chest, hiding his clenched fists. He knew they'd never be free of that bitch. Not as long as she lived.

"She's got contacts in Texico; our father's family," Jay offered.

"Mercenaries; raiders and men who'll do anything for the right price." Stix's gravelly voice grew even harsher.

They all knew what this could mean for Alba in its weakened state.

Vick's mind worked quickly, running through scenarios. "Here's the plan. Stix, you take Jay back to grab the vaccine with our reticent friend there to identify it." He motioned to the unconscious man still in the back of the Bronco. "I'll head back to Alba and begin working on the State's defenses and trying to locate former President March. And this time I'll kill her myself," he added grimly.

"What about me?" Chelsea asked.

Vick's gaze flicked to his little sister. He was about to tell her to return with them, but something stopped him. "I'll bring you back to Vicksburg. You can wait this out there."

"Can't I remain with you?"

"No."

Chelsea opened her mouth, obviously wanting to protest, but the look on Vick's face warned her to remain silent.

Jay hauled the heavily sedated Patrician out of the Bronco, tossing him over his shoulders and carrying him to the jet, Stix following.

Vick and Chelsea waited in the Bronco for the jet to lift into the air, shading their eyes from the swirling dust stirred up by the forced air engines. As it disappeared into the western horizon, Vick started up the engine. The shadows were growing long. It would be dark soon.

"Welcome to Vicksburg," he said a short time later as they entered the wooden gates of the small town. He felt the same surge of pride he always did upon viewing the ramshackle town. It wasn't much to look at, but the people were well-fed and safe. Which was more than many outposts could claim.

Children ran excitedly to greet them, while adults paused in their chores to wave.

"Vicksburg? Did you name it yourself?" Chelsea asked dryly.

"As a matter of fact, the people named it. It started out just me in the old winery main house, and I started letting people stay in the outbuildings from time-to-time. Some of them started lingering, and I quit kicking them out. Vicksburg was born."

"My, aren't you the philanthropist."

"When did you get to be so cynical?" Vick glanced at his sister in bemusement. She wasn't the inquisitive little thing he remembered. She'd grown some teeth.

"When everyone abandoned me to the care of the monster."

Vick winced. She had a point. He'd been wrapped up in his own issues, and his father might have tried to shield his older children from her, but the older man had already given up by the time Chelsea was growing up. Had been spending considerable time in Texico with his "other" family. As had Vick.

And then their esteemed mother had had their father murdered, Vick had gone into hiding, and who the hell knew what went on in the March estate after that.

"Chels, I'm sorry I wasn't—"

"Please. Enough with the post mortems. It's done. You're probably incapable of ever having a normal relationship with a woman after what happened to Nina, and I'm depending on pharmaceuticals just to get through the day. We're both fucked. Why dwell on it?"

Vick's mouth snapped closed on his apology. Damn. A sad but true assessment of the legacy their mother left them.

He pulled up in front of the old winery main house, the stone building as beautiful today as it must have been a century before. It had long ago been stripped of anything of value to survivalists, but the eclectic art and daily items had been left behind, much to his antiquing delight.

He imagined Helen's voice chastising a frivolous activity like collecting old junk. A guy had to have a hobby. He couldn't focus on murder and mayhem all the time. Then he'd turn out like Marcus.

Was he never going to be free from Helen? This house had been his sanctuary from the ghosts following him; now it seemed it would be haunted by Helen's memory.

"Come inside and make yourself at home. We've got an energy box that gives us running water and electricity. Should be some food in the Dispensare—"

"The what?"

"Dispensare, food dispenser. Damn Albans and their Latin words. As if that makes everything better. If you need anything, you can trade with the townspeople."

"What do you trade?" Chelsea reverently touched an old Route 69 sign welded with other metals and glass to form a wall-hanging.

Vick dumped his bag near the main floor bedroom, shrugging. "Services, I suppose. I fix things, run security, act as judge when necessary..." He cast a considering eye in Chelsea's direction as he flipped on an old wall sconce. "You can probably run off my credit for now, but you'll need to find something to trade."

"I'm not sure if my hunter-gatherer skills are up to par," she said wryly.

"You'll figure something out. As long as it isn't selling your person," he added darkly. Chelsea just rolled her eyes, moving on to inspect the next antique.

"I need to check on a few things, then I'm going to bed; I'm leaving early in the morning to get back. You'll be better off here than in Alba. We'll talk about long term when I get back."

Vick headed out to meet with his "assistant mayor", an

older woman who managed things when he was gone. He felt a tinge of relief to be out of the house; seeing his younger sister brought back unwelcome memories of his youth. Painful memories he preferred to forget.

Memories that had become his personal nightmare.

*   *   *

It was dark when he returned to the old estate house. Chelsea had already retired for the night. He poured himself a tumbler of the Alban whiskey he'd swiped. It was good stuff. The Aggies might still be on his shit list after trying to secede from Alba under his watch, but they sure distilled excellent hooch.

He settled into the chair before the massive stone fireplace in the main room, watching the flames flicker. It was warm enough to go without a fire, but he needed to relax. His eyes swept over the room filled with antiques collected over the years from his own travels and visitors who'd passed through his town. He often accepted unique artifacts in exchange for food and shelter, much to the amused disgust of his citizens.

As long as they could keep growing enough food to sustain them, and had shelter over their heads, Vick was content to live simply. He never wanted to live in a place that glorified wealth like his old home.

Even Alba was too civilized — too modern — for him.

Just another reason why he couldn't have Helen. She'd never want to leave the prestige and culture of her home. Certainly not to live in this ramshackle town.

Alba wouldn't be so bad. Not if he were with Helen. Emptying the tumbler in an effort to banish thoughts he had no right contemplating, Vick's eyes fell on the old Route 69 sign Chelsea had been studying earlier. Rising, he walked over to straighten it.

He noticed the dust, which accumulated quickly in his absence, had been disturbed. Running his hand along the back of the sign, he pulled out a small cord. Carefully removing the sign, he turned it over.

Wrapped around the hook on the back was a device he recognized well from his agent days.

Damn. He hadn't seen that one coming.

Sighing, he put the cord back and re-hung the sign. Sitting in the darkness for a long time, he considered his next move.

He needed to lure the monster out into the open and attack where she was most vulnerable.

Her pride.

The rolling darkness within him was surging towards the surface, threatening to burst forth. The poison of anger, hate, and fear—yes, fear—that he'd kept carefully bottled over the past decade needed to be drained if he was to live any kind of normal life.

And have any kind of normal relationship. For years, he'd been content to be alone, to play the role of benevolent leader, keeping his distance from everyone.

But not anymore. After playing house with Helen, imagining what it would be like to have a life with her, he would never be content to sit in this big empty house night after night, alone. Not as long as the monster was out there, threatening the only things he cared about.

The wind picked up outside, whistling through the old grape vines that grew untended in the valley behind the house, bringing the aroma of the backyard honeysuckle into the manor through open windows.

He breathed deep of the familiar scent, but peace remained elusive.

A plan formulated as he sat in the dark, drinking another tumbler of whiskey, inhaling the scent of honeysuckle.

He was going to find peace, through the monster's death or his own.

Chapter 17

"Fear is the worst epidemic we could face." -Recorded
Conversations with Cecilia Delacroix

The smoke from the crematorium was a dark shadow
against the clear spring sky. A rare lack of breeze had the
ominous cloud hanging low over the city, symbolic of the
pestilence that was wreaking havoc on the inhabitants.

Vick re-entered the gate he'd exited less than twenty-four
hours earlier, wishing he could have remained longer in
Vicksburg.

Alba's atmosphere tasted of despair. The acrid scent of
smoke seemed to linger, even though it was hovering far to
the north of the city. The normally busy streets were empty
but for patrolling Armati enforcing his edict for all residents to
remain in their homes. Only workers essential to the running
of the city were allowed out, and they had all been issued
biohazard suits. The crimson stain of the suits against the
backdrop of the city was another reminder of the death
creeping nearer.

As Vick cruised slowly towards the Ferry to take his
vehicle back to the Capitol Terrace, he passed a sobbing man
and woman, handing a tiny wrapped bundle to a red-suited
Armati.

A baby. His gut twisted, and the image of Helen's
rounded stomach flashed in his mind. His callused hands
gripped the steering wheel, turning white from the force.

His mother was doing this, all this, to gain back power.
To satisfy some psychotic idea of revenge. She'd see the dead
baby and shrug, considering it a worthy sacrifice for her sick
ambitions.

The anger he felt was like a sickness; a fever that burned

so hot he thought it would consume him. She'd taken everything from him, and now she was doing the same to these innocent people.

He was going to stop her. Because Chelsea was right; he was never going to have a normal life while his mother still lived.

Ten years was a long time to run. He was done running. He'd already put his plan in motion that morning, telling Chelsea what he wanted the monster to know. His mother was a vulture, circling, waiting for her weakened prey to fall so she could swoop in and reap the harvest.

And when she swooped, that was when he planned to strike.

High on his hopes and full of determination, Vick scanned his card on the Ferry, overriding the hold placed on the large tram that ferried people and cars between the terrace levels.

He felt like he was going home. Because Helen was beginning to feel like home to him. And maybe it was time to stop running from it and embrace it.

*   *   *

Helen drove towards the University medical wing, exhaustion and frustration combining to make every nerve feel on edge.

She'd hardly slept the night before, thoughts of Vick and why he would betray her and the city running endlessly through her mind.

It isn't like he really betrayed you. He never made any promises, the same inner voice that had haunted her throughout the night continued to taunt.

Trying to put the distracting thoughts from her mind, Helen exited the car, straightening her white suit top and smoothing the skirt as she entered the guarded door to the emergency clinic.

"Could I have a biohazard suit? I'm here to see Mr. Trent," she informed the receptionist.

The young man looked up in surprise. "Mr. Trent was released and has already gone home. He did leave a message for you to join him at once, Ms. Vanderbuilt."

"Thank you," Helen murmured, biting her lip to keep from muttering her real thoughts. He could have sent her a message so she didn't drive here first.

She drove the distance to Marcus' villa quickly, paying little attention to her surroundings, still wrapped up in the turmoil of thoughts still plaguing her.

Aerina opened the door, ushering her inside. Helen absently answered her greeting, her eyes widening in shock as she noted the extra inhabitant in the room.

Vick.

"What are you doing here?" Her voice was sharper than she intended, anger hiding the shock.

Vick's eyes narrowed. "Just going over some things with Marcus. I could ask the same of you."

"Marcus asked me to come." Helen glanced at Aerina, who was trying to appear busy with the breakfast dishes.

Vick leaned back in the kitchen chair, thick arms crossing over his chest. Helen knew his façade of relaxation was just that, a cover for his real emotions. What was happening? Did he dare return to Alba because he was assured that no one believed he was guilty?

A niggling feeling of doubt began to rise, mingling with unexpected hope. Perhaps she had been wrong. Perhaps there was another explanation behind the overwhelming evidence against him.

Marcus finally broke the taut silence in his normal blunt manner. "Helen here thinks you and your brother have been in league with the Southern Empire and your recent trip just reaffirmed her suspicions. That and the recordings of your activities in the lab before you left."

Vick's face darkened, and Helen could have sworn she saw pain flash in his hazel eyes for a moment before he smiled. But that was impossible, she reminded herself. He didn't really care for her. Not like she'd thought…

"Ahhh. Clever girl," Vick murmured, rising. Helen stiffened as he approached, his size less intimidating than the gleam in his eyes.

She met that intense gaze with effort, standing her ground. The other two people in the room were temporarily forgotten.

"You figured it all out, hmm? Did it feel good to be right all along about me? I'm just a devious drifter; a selfish piece of shit. Did it make you feel *safer*, Helen, to be able to hate me?"

The gently mocking words had the desired effect, filling her heart with guilt. Because he was right. It had allowed her to turn her confusion and hurt into righteous anger. To change the feelings of rejection to ones of recrimination.

The urge to lash out at him was nearly unbearable, shocking her with the intensity. She'd never had the desire to physically hurt anyone. Not until Vick entered her life. Her small hands clenched into fists at her sides. She wanted to wipe that derisive grin off his handsome face.

He was angry too, but he was hiding behind his own false amusement, the hypocrite.

"Go ahead," he urged, reading the look in her eyes. "It'll make you feel better."

Helen spun away, taking in Aerina's sympathetic look and Marcus' unreadable one. The only thing worse than this horrendous scene was that it was being carried out before an audience.

Aerina seemed to take pity on her. "Marcus, didn't you say you wanted to get to the Training Grounds early?"

Marcus nodded, saying nothing as he grabbed his weapon vest and followed Aerina towards the door. Aerina cast one more sympathetic look towards Helen, and a glare at Vick, before they exited.

Helen heard the door close behind them. Silence hung over the room, heavy and charged.

"Why?" she managed to ask.

"Why did I kidnap Terrence? I needed—"

"No," Helen made a swiping motion with her hand, "why didn't you tell me? I'm not the only one who's been lying to themselves to feel safe. Why did you suddenly shut me out of everything?"

"Why were you so quick to believe the worst of me?"

Helen turned back to face Vick. "Don't put this on me. I wouldn't have thought it had you told me the truth in the first place!"

Vick swiped his hands through his tawny hair in frustration, the false smile disappearing. The mask was gone and the real Vick stood before her, all six feet of infuriated man staring her down. "You thought the worst of me. You thought I was a fucking traitor; the enemy." His hazel eyes had darkened in anger, his hard jaw clenched.

But Helen was angry too. She stepped forward again, tilting her head back to meet his angry gaze. Her voice was clinical as she explained. "I observed. I made a supposition based on your actions. What did you expect, Vick? I've only known you a few months. I liked you. I thought you were interesting. Sexy. And then you just walked out and told me it was fun, but not fun enough. What did you expect?" she asked again in a louder voice. Her hands came up to push against the hard chest before her, the need to let out her frustration, hurt, and anger too great to control.

Her shove barely moved his muscled frame, and he grabbed her shoulders.

"This is the real Helen, isn't it? You want to be cold, but you burn hot beneath that chilly exterior."

"It doesn't matter. You're not interested, remember?"

"I didn't say I wasn't interested. I just said it was never going to work and I didn't want to waste our time."

"Then what are we still doing here?"

"Hell if I know," he muttered, slowly backing her into the wall. He planted a hand on either side of her head, caging her there. She couldn't help but notice that even in his rage, he was being incredibly gentle with her.

How could she have doubted him? The man before her now would never betray people he cared about. And he did care, more than he wanted to admit. About Alba, about Marcus, Aerina … perhaps even about her.

The thoughts fled and Helen's breath hitched in her throat as he leaned in close. "I guess we'll just have to fucking hate each other," he said. "Or love fucking each other."

She wanted to push him away. To tell him to he was the last man she wanted in her life, or in her bed.

But she couldn't. Because it was a lie. Even now, her body was throbbing for his touch. Her fast breaths and pounding heart stemmed from desire rather than anger.

It was irrational. Unhealthy. And completely idiotic.

She didn't care.

He was still there, waiting. "What are you waiting for, permission?"

She saw his grin, and then she tasted it as his mouth crushed hers.

It was heaven. She couldn't stop the small moans that escaped, and he drank them in like a drowning man.

The heat of anger had turned to a new kind of passion, and it raged between them unchecked. Helen gripped the strong forearms still caging her to the wall, wanting them on her body.

As if he read her mind, his arms suddenly pulled her forward and up. Instinctively, she wrapped her legs around his lean waist and he gripped her bottom, still pressing her to the wall. She ground her hips against him, desperately needing to be closer.

He pulled his mouth away, both panting for breath. He stood, frozen in place.

Helen tried to pull his head back down. He resisted.

"What?" she gasped the question.

"I don't… I…" One hand lightly touched her rounded stomach. "I don't want to hurt—"

"Shut up and keep going," she interrupted. "I'll be fine."

"Yes, ma'am." His hand moved up, deftly unbuttoning her blouse one-handed and reaching inside to cup her enlarged breasts.

He dropped to his knee, supporting her on his other thigh. He gripped both breasts as his mouth kissed the exposed skin of her stomach, her skirt riding up to her waist.

She gasped at the combination of sensations. His hard thigh between her legs, his hand tugging her nipples, his hot breath on her skin as he kissed lower...

"Vick please," she begged, mindless with the need to feel him against the painful throbbing of her center. Her hands fumbled with his t-shirt, pushing it up and running her hands over the warm ridges of muscle beneath.

He pulled off his shirt while her hands moved lower to undo his belt and the buckle of his jeans. The evidence of his desire strained against the material, and he groaned as she reached inside to touch his hard length.

She glanced at his face, tight with the strain of holding onto his control.

She wanted him to lose control.

Pushing him back onto the floor, she kissed his flat stomach, feeling the muscles clench as he groaned again. She kissed lower, breathing heat onto the bulge still covered by his jeans.

He cursed, a jumble of words that made no sense, as he stood, pulling her up with him. In a moment, he was naked. Ripping off her panties, he pressed her against the wall again. She gasped as she felt the head of his shaft pressed against her throbbing core. She was so swollen and ready, she *ached*.

He seemed to be hesitating again. Using her legs that were again locked around his waist, she squeezed, forcing him inside. Pleasure surged through her, and her head dropped back against the wall.

"Don't stop. Don't you dare stop," she murmured. And he didn't. His control gone, he thrust madly, his hands gripping her hips with bruising force.

She didn't care, her own nails digging into his bulging biceps that flexed with each lift of her body against his.

His thrusts became almost frenzied, and she matched each one, the pleasure building, building...

The climax burst forth, drawing a shrill gasp that didn't sound like hers. Distantly, she heard his own deep groans echoing her cries of release.

Both gasped for air in the aftermath, and he lowered his head to rest against the wall beside hers.

Her legs were shaky as he gently lowered her so they could reach the floor. She fumbled with her clothes, lowering her slim skirt that was still twisted around her waist, and searching the ground for her panties.

The white lace underclothes appeared before her face. She snatched them, pulling them up and buttoning her blouse with shaky hands.

Vick picked up his own clothes, and she couldn't help but steal a few glances at his unclothed body. He was strong and bronzed, his body moving with an innate fluidity. The short ponytail at the nape of his neck and close-cropped beard made him look rugged, and her eyes were drawn to the lighter patches where his strong body was scarred from his past. When he turned away to grab his shirt, she noticed the star of the Empire tattooed on his right shoulder.

Vick shot her a knowing look before pulling the shirt over his head. The air was still charged with the currents that continually flowed between them. Their lovemaking had done little to alleviate the tension.

"I suppose we just needed to get that out of our system," Helen said, needing to break the electric silence. "Now we can be a little more dispassionate about the situation."

Vick lowered his shirt with unnecessary force, his head still averted. He nodded brusquely. "Whatever you say, Helen."

Her heart sank at his words, but she ignored it. She

hadn't really expected him to argue; to claim their encounter had been more than just passion sparked from anger.

"So assuming you're not working for the Empire—"

"Yes, let's assume that."

"—Where did you go then, Vick? And why kidnap Terrence?"

Vick was silent for a long moment, pressing a few buttons on the Dispensare and digging around in the cupboards. He approached, holding out a mug.

Tea. With just the right amount of honey and lemon.

He sipped his own coffee before speaking. "We needed a doctor who could help us identify a possible vaccine. When Terrence proved ... reticent ... about our invitation to travel, we were forced to take him against his will. But don't worry," Vick added wryly, "Jay can be very persuasive. I'm sure he and Terrence will come back good friends."

"You've found a vaccine?" Hope burgeoned from the tangle of emotions swirling insider her.

"We don't know yet. But we will in a few days. Don't hang up your biosuit yet."

Helen was silent, warming her hands on the mug, considering the possibilities if a vaccine existed in the Southern Empire. Jay was returning to his old home in an effort to locate the vaccine for a city that had imprisoned and rejected him. Both men were risking their freedom and their lives to save Alba.

Did she believe him?

Yes.

Helen finally admitted the truth to herself. She'd wanted him to be guilty so she would have a place to direct her hurt, anger, and sense of betrayal. And a reason for his rejection.

But she'd never really been convinced he was the enemy.

Words of apology hovered on her tongue, but he spoke before she could utter them.

"If your concerns have been addressed, you may as well return to your duties at the lab." The dismissal in Vick's voice was obvious. Helen stiffened, unconsciously smoothing the suit over her bump. Her hand lingered, drawing some comfort and control from the tiny life.

Nodding, she walked swiftly towards the door, wanting to escape the uncomfortable scene. She felt Vick's eyes on her back as she yanked at the handle, almost desperate to get out so she could think.

Yes, she'd misread Vick. Perhaps she should have trusted him even in the face of overwhelming evidence.

Did it make you feel safer?

Vick's question echoed in her mind as she strode down the walk towards her e-car. She stopped beside the door, her hand on the handle, her eyes staring blindly ahead.

It had made everything easier to tell herself she'd been betrayed. To see things in black and white again. To feel justified in hating him.

She honestly didn't know what to think anymore. She felt controlled by her emotions, swept along like a surfer caught in a riptide. The more she struggled against the onslaught, the more ensnared she became.

A heavy hand on her shoulder wrung a gasp from her lips as she spun around.

Vick stood in the street behind her, his normal mask gone. He looked exhausted, angry, and ... sad.

His muscular frame dwarfed her own petite size, but she'd never felt fearful of his size, or worried for a moment that he would harm her. Even knowing of his dangerous past, she trusted him to always be gentle with her.

She trusted him.

"I know things between us are uncertain, but I never expected you to think the worst of me," he said.

"It was a natural assumption, based on the evidence I—"

"Just stop. Everyone else who saw the same evidence gave me the chance to explain myself before assuming the worst. But not you, Helen." His eyes were dark with an emotion she could have sworn was pain.

Did he care more than he let on? Was he just putting up a shield to protect himself, like her?

"I thought that… hell, forget it. I just wanted to know if you're ok. I was rough—"

"It's fine. I'm fine."

"And the baby?"

Words swirled around in Helen's mind, things she wanted to say to Vick, emotions she couldn't express. They all stayed locked behind the wall she'd built over the years. Helen didn't know how to let down her guard, let go of her pride, and tell him the truth.

She cared about him. She was sorry.

Instead, her eyes fixed on the beard he hadn't trimmed in days, unable to look at the unguarded emotion in his eyes. "There is still a chance of some lasting effects, but the tests so far have been encouraging. Now I just have to wait until she's born to know."

"If she's even half as resilient as her mother, she'll be fine." His tawny head lowered, his lips moving slowly over hers as if memorizing their shape; their taste. She stood immobile beneath the gentle assault until he pulled back, his hands cupping her cheeks for a moment, and then he was gone.

She was unable to formulate a response as he sprinted to the Bronco she now saw parked at the end of the street. In a few moments, he was gone, heading north. No doubt back to the Training Grounds. To his job.

I should have apologized for thinking he was a traitor, she thought remorsefully. *I shouldn't have let pride and insecurity get the better of me. I should have trusted him.*

Sliding into the driver's seat, she held the frustrated tears at bay, driving aimlessly. It wasn't until she'd pulled in front of a familiar house that she realized she'd had a destination in mind the entire time.

Heading up the walk with slow steps, she didn't knock, opening the door and entering her childhood home.

"Helen!" her mother exclaimed, coming from her office. Without pause, she walked forward, taking her daughter's hands in both of hers.

Helen looked at their joined hands, so alike but for the extra wrinkles lining the backs of her mother's. Suddenly their hands blurred, and tears streamed unchecked down her cheeks.

"Come, darling, I'll make you some tea," her mother offered, gently ushering Helen into the kitchen.

Helen got herself back under control as her mother efficiently brewed tea for both of them before joining her at the table. They sat in companionable silence for a few minutes while Helen worked out what she wanted to say.

"I thought I had everything planned perfectly. I worked so hard for so long to be selected as the Medella of Law. I was the first to be recruited directly from University for that position." Helen recited the accomplishment emotionlessly. Her mother nodded. Everyone had been proud of Helen's success.

"I chose Stephen, another successful Patrician as my mate. We would both have become Senators, I have no doubt. I always said the right things, followed the laws, exceeded everyone's expectations..." Tears continued to fall as Helen put her head into her hands.

"Where did I go wrong, Mama? I thought if I was responsible, smart, and worked hard, I'd be happy. But I'm not. I'm alone. I'm pregnant. The laws are worthless in the face of this disaster, and our entire State is falling apart. I don't know what to think anymore. What to believe."

Her mother gently touched her bowed head. "Darling, you did nothing wrong. We all change as we grow. The person you would have been with Stephen is not the same woman you are now that he's gone. The world around you has changed, and you have adapted." She used one hand to raise Helen's face so their eyes met. "Embrace the person you are becoming. Someone who can see the gray areas of life. A woman that can bend a little, and appreciate that we all make mistakes. Let yourself make mistakes, my love. Sometimes mistakes lead to the best parts of our life."

Helen smiled through her tears, knowing her mother spoke of the baby growing inside her. She rested her hand on the bump that seemed to give her strength even while it wreaked havoc on her body.

"Stephen would have wanted you to be happy, no matter where you chose to find happiness," her mother added, taking a careful sip of hot tea. Helen nodded, keeping her eyes on her own mug. Her chances of happiness with Vick had been over before they'd really even begun.

"I was so afraid of giving up my dreams for a man; for a child. I thought being in love meant I'd have to give up everything, like you did." Helen met her mother's eyes, seeing the love shining there. Love for her. "Now I understand why you did it. I finally know what my dreams really are. Being a Senator wouldn't bring me the joy you and Daddy have. I'm just so afraid I realized it too late. I didn't trust enough, and now…"

Helen couldn't continue, putting her face in her hands, breathing shakily.

"It is never too late, darling. Dreams can change, but you have not. Fight for what you want, just as you always have."

Chapter 18

"A wise man once said 'fuck this shit' and lived happily ever after." – Texican Saying

Vick cursed again as the Ferry slid slowly down to the bottom terrace, slamming his fist on the thick-paned glass.

He'd hoped the bout of fast, steamy sex with Helen would have gotten her out of his system.

The opposite was true. The last barriers he'd had against her had been broken down by her uninhibited response. He was doomed. Regardless of how he felt, she still saw him as an outsider, like everyone else in this damn city.

The hope for a future with her was crushed before it had even taken root. He felt like a fool.

He felt like shit.

The twisting in his stomach wasn't from too much coffee without breakfast. It was regret. Regret he hadn't tried harder with Helen; that he had killed the one chance at love he might have had. The weight in his gut was nothing compared to the painful ache in his chest. After being so careful to protect himself for years, she managed to bring him low with little effort.

He watched the Pleb city grow with the slow, steady descent of the large tram.

What was he doing, trying to save these people's ungrateful hides? He had more than repaid any favor owed to Marcus. What he wouldn't give to return to the comfort of Vicksburg and forget all about Alba.

All about Helen.

But it was too late for that. Helen had stolen a piece of his soul. If for no other reason, he needed to finish this for her. And for the child he stupidly fell in love with before it was even born.

He might be an idiot when it came to love, but he was still a warrior. The dark side he'd thought was permanently laid to rest had awakened during his short reign as Consul.

He was going to end his mother's reign of terror once and for all. He'd laid the snare in Vicksburg, now he just needed to wait for the jackal to sniff her way there.

In the meantime, he was going to try and stop an uprising. *If this damn Ferry could move any faster, that is.*

Taking Marcus' black e-car swiftly down the eerily empty streets, Vick made it quickly to the north gate. He saw the crowd from a distance. The remaining loyal soldiers had managed to hold off the mob with their weapons, but the unruly crowd hadn't been deterred by the few unconscious bodies of their fellow protestors strewn in the street.

"No more curfew!"

"We need a real leader!"

"Justice for Alba!"

There was nothing more unpredictable than a mob. Driven by fear and adrenaline, they would be unorganized and rash. Any bold idiot or closet sociopath could become a leader just by being the most aggressive. He'd rather face an army any day instead of a fired-up mob.

Vick stepped slowly from the low, black vehicle that was Marcus' trademark. The crowd grew quiet, although he could hear the few rumbles of discontent when those nearest realized it was him, and not Marcus.

He shouldn't have told Marcus he would handle this. But After Helen had left, he'd needed something to vent his rage. He'd thought knocking a few Pleb heads together would be the answer. Now, however, he was worried he might take his anger too far. Apparently he was already quite unpopular with the citizens of this fair city.

Guess he had nothing to lose. Not anymore.

"This is your only warning," he raised his voice to be heard. "Disperse immediately. You are in violation of curfew."

One bold young man stepped forward, although Vick noticed his hands were shaking.

Dammit, kid, I don't want to kill you.

"Who are you to instill martial law here? We're citizens of Alba, and you're just an outsider."

Vick strode forward until he was in the kid's face. The younger man was trembling, taking a few steps back before gaining enough courage to stand his ground.

From his left peripheral, Vick saw a small grouping of young men dressed in long slickers. Dockworkers. To the right, another group with cropped hair of Armati in plain clothes inched closer.

This wasn't going to end peacefully. His hand slid down to rest on the hand-held EMW tucked in the front of his vest. The kid before him saw the movement and took another step back.

Sorry kid, your boldness is going to cost you.

The dockworkers moved first, one coming up with illegal contraband no doubt found on a fishing voyage down the coast; a ballistic weapon.

Fuck. I should have put on the bullet-proof black suit Marcus told me to wear.

That was his last thought as instinct took over. Lunging forward, Vick dove into the crowd rather than stepping back. The idiot with the antique Glock fired into the mass after him.

The weapon misfired, and the man holding it struggled to discharge the magazine to check it. In the few seconds he fiddled with his faulty weapon, Vick was on him. He didn't mess with the EMW at such close range, just grabbing the man's head and making a quick twist right and then harder left until he felt the bones give.

Before the body hit the cobbled street, Vick had his EMW pressed to another's forehead.

"Think long and hard about your next move," Vick warned.

The man stood frozen, eyes wide. Vick could hear the

muttering of the crowd growing to a roar. A show of aggression wasn't enough to make them back down today. Fear of the disease killing their family and neighbors was greater than their fear of Vick.

He sensed the shift, fear becoming anger. And they were directing it all at him.

Time to retreat.

Using his free hand to grab the long-barreled EMW from his back, he fired at the building directly ahead. The blast made windows explode in the stone structure, reigning glass down upon the crowd.

Amid the screams and confusion, Vick headed towards the alley beside the building he'd damaged. The screams turned to shouts, and the group of off-duty Armati in the crowd charged after him. The rest of the crowd followed.

Bursting through the first door, he entered what looked to be a theatre. It was empty, like most buildings were now. The side door took him past eerily silent practice rooms and to double doors leading to a large stage. He eyed a small room atop the balcony where sound and lights were controlled. He could hunker down and repel the enemy from there until reinforcements came, or they retreated in fear.

These people aren't your enemy, he reminded himself. Running his hand over his face, he forced the old instincts back into the compartment of his mind where they belonged; his past.

He was responsible for the safety of those people. Even if the ignorant bastards *were* trying to kill him.

Heading through the theatre, he exited another door on the other side. This alley was nearly empty, and by the time the few stragglers of the crowd realized it was him, he was already headed down another street.

The only sounds were distant shouts of the mob, and his own boots pounding on the cobblestone street. The midday sun was concealed by slight haze, making the whole city seem to waver around him.

Bursting free of another alley, he was suddenly in the city center. The twisted and blackened debris from the battle with the Southern Empire months before had been mostly cleared away, but the remaining rubble and empty space was a stark reminder of the short but deadly battle that had cost many Albans their lives.

And the Empire still isn't done yet wreaking havoc here. No wonder they hated outsiders. If they knew he was the son of the woman responsible...

Pausing for a moment, he pulled out his holoreader, ordering it to call Marcus.

"Bit of a problem, my friend. They're out for blood, and some of them are armed. I'm afraid I had to tuck my tail and run."

Marcus' projection remained impassive but for the tick in his jaw. "The Alpha should never show weakness."

"Well, I could go back and start killing them all, but I hardly think that would help at this point. They're scared, and they need someone to blame."

"Alright, I think I have a solution. Sit tight there for a half hour and I'll send reinforcements." The image winked out as Marcus disconnected.

"Sure, no problem," Vick said wryly, clipping the reader back to his belt. Resting the heavy long-barrel on his shoulder, the hand-held in his other hand, he scanned the open space for a good place to hold the mob at bay.

A large pile of building materials offered a possible bunker. Vaulting over lumber, he settled in amongst bundled boards and bags of mortar. Removing his weapons, he set them out carefully, charged and ready.

He could have easily disappeared into the city. But that would have solved nothing. The crowd would still be rampaging, looking for someone to blame. Looking for something to fight.

War gave people an enemy. But the devastation of disease offered no one to fight; no adversary to demonize.

Fear and helplessness could be debilitating, so people often would seek out an enemy.

Like him. The outsider.

He understood. He didn't even blame them. But he sure as hell wasn't going to die here today.

He still had to kill his mother.

Leaning back, he propped his feet up on a stack of mortar mix bags. A hero from one of the pre-war films he collected would be smoking something with tobacco right now, waiting for the adversary to find him.

All he had were his weapons and holoreader. And so he waited, sunglasses protecting his eyes from the glare of the hazy sun as he studied the west part of the city, waiting for the crowd to emerge.

It didn't take long. The young soldiers in the group appeared from the alley first, scanning the city center for him.

They couldn't find him. Vick rolled his eyes. He needed them to stay here until back up arrived. This showdown would end today, hopefully not with their deaths.

He knew Marcus wouldn't hesitate to decimate the crowd if they wouldn't back down. If they lost control of Alba, it would be catastrophic for the citizens. Order would break down, the flow of supplies would be interrupted, and the sick would go untreated. People often longed for freedom, but true freedom was a fantasy. All anyone ever finds is a different kind of oppression.

The growing crowd drew his attention again. Aiming, he fired the long-barrel EMW, the high voltage current striking the building across the open space. The pop and arc was followed by the crack of artificial thunder. The bolt struck the building, lighting it up as it traveled through various pathways to the ground.

Confusion ensued, the people scattering to escape the currents running through the building into the ground, and the debris from exploding windows and over-heated brick.

Vick set down the hand cannon, as it was commonly

called, and picked up his hand-held EMW. This smaller version of the weapon was meant for individuals. Dialing down the voltage, he set it on stun. He didn't want to kill anyone. Just slow them down a little.

The crack and pop of the gun was less impressive than his hand cannon, but it still had the desired results. Bodies dropped to the newly-laid cobblestones, unconscious.

The minutes ticked by, and the bodies on the ground continued to multiply.

Where the hell was Marcus?

He knew a few of the military-trained in the group were making their way around to try and flank him. If they made it here before reinforcements did, he'd probably have to kill the damn kids.

Fuck playing a hero. If they wanted a bad guy, they'd get one.

Chapter 19

"Presence is just as important as action. Psychological warfare is the first step in overpowering the enemy and controlling the masses." -Virmortus Training Manual

A low rumble began in the distance, and everyone looked to the sky. A jet approached them, hovering overhead for a moment then lowering to land right in the middle of the open city center.

Vick hoped the people didn't realize it was the jet that had belonged to former President March.

The crowd backed away to give the jet plenty of room, looking uncertain.

Wind from the forced air engines blew bits of debris everywhere, and those closest shielded their eyes.

Then the engines went silent, and the hatch opened. After several long moments, a familiar figure strode out, wearing a black Virmortus suit and weapon vest.

Jay held a refrigerated case in his hand, and behind him came Terrence, the Head Lab Technician.

Before the mob could decide how they felt about it, two squat black vehicles pulled into the square.

The first door opened, and out stepped Ramus. His height and bulging arms were intimidating enough without the black suit and weapon vest he wore.

The large, ebony-skinned man took in the scene swiftly before stepping back to open the rear door.

Even Vick was surprised to see the Senator of Health emerge, her white suit perfectly crisp, skin glowing with vigor.

Murmurs began spreading through the mob. From the second car, another Virmortus emerged, along with the Senators of Law and Population.

Jay spoke into a voice-amplifier, and those in the crowd began recording his speech on their devices. The tone shifted dramatically; fear and hate turning to hope.

"Citizens of Alba. I am Jayden March, an Alban agent that has been under cover in the Southern Empire. I'm also the brother of Vicktor March, the interim leader of your State. While you have been plotting treasonous acts against your leader, he sent me on a mission to the Empire, the land of our enemy, to find the vaccine for the illness laying our people low."

Holding the case high, he motioned Terrence close, saying something to the smaller man. Terrence nodded, taking the amplifier.

"We believe we have succeeded in finding a vaccine," Terrence claimed, clearing his throat nervously as he scanned the audience. The Senators, flanked by Ramus and his Virmortus, walked up behind them to show support. The Senator of Health took the megaphone from an overwhelmed Terrence.

Cheers spread through the crowd at the news, everyone pressing forward eagerly in an attempt to see the cure.

She raised her hand to greet the crowd, nodding her head and smiling.

"Dear people of Alba. I hear your cries for help. You want answers. You *deserve* answers. Extraordinary measures have been taken to survive these trying times. But now that we have uncovered a cure, our great nation will once again return to the days of peace. The rightful leaders of Alba will again be protecting our people, and the ideals we've always upheld, to keep peace and serenity for all."

Renewed cheers spread at the words of the Senator. Her healthy face glowed with assurance, and a few rays of sun slipped through the clouds, making her white suit appear luminescent.

Damn, she was good.

This was his cue in the performance. Putting his weapons

back in his vest, Vick stood, walking towards Jay.

His little brother was a born leader, right down to his perfect white teeth.

Jay extended his hand to Vick, pulling his brother to his side. Vick took the offered case, holding it high. He then accepted the voice amplifier from the Senator.

"Citizens, difficult times can bring out the best in us, and fear can bring out the worst. My last act as temporary Alpha and Interim Consul will be to pardon you all for your treasonous acts today. If we are going to survive this, we must stand together, against our common enemy.

"Don't let fear get the best of you. Then the enemy wins without even firing a shot."

Silence filled the damaged city center, the stark reminder of the enemy all around them in the un-cleared rubble and half-repaired buildings.

As if they had pre-planned it, a third military vehicle arrived, and Marcus stepped out. Amid cheers of the crowd, which Vick was certain was a new experience for the Reaper, Marcus strode up the open hatch.

Vick felt the weight of responsibility lift from his shoulders as leadership was transferred back to Marcus before the gathered crowd and remaining Senators, who looked on with grudging approval. Only Anthony Delacroix was absent, as he was still mourning the death of his wife.

"Only you could make *me* the good guy," Marcus murmured as the two men shook hands to solidify the amicable power change. Vick grinned at the rare attempt at humor from his friend.

"All part of the outsider leadership service. Don't think I won't be sending you the bill for this. You *owe* me."

The Senators stepped forward, each addressing the people in turn. They seemed to be looking to the Senator of Health as the spokesperson, and she definitely had what it took to a leader. Poise, control, and the obvious respect of the people.

His attention turned as Ramus motioned Vick to follow him.

"Glad to see you're feeling better," Vick said as they walked to the first vehicle.

"Couldn't leave Marcus to clean your mess up by himself."

Vick grinned. "What mess? I planned this little scene perfectly."

"Is that so? And here I thought we came to save you from an angry mob."

"Had it all under control. But I sure am relieved to let Marcus take his city back."

Both men slid into the military vehicle, heading back towards the Ferry.

"What's left of the city," Ramus muttered, cruising the empty streets.

"I hope to hell Jay really did find a vaccine."

"We'll know soon enough."

*   *   *

Jay disembarked his mother's former jet for the second time that day. This time, he was on the roof of the Training Grounds, rather than in the middle of an angry mob.

He'd rather face the angry mob again. He rolled his shoulders to relieve the tension building as he anticipated facing Lina and explaining where he'd been.

He was the son of a powerful and dangerous leader, an agent who'd killed and face many dangerous foes. But the strange vulnerability he felt with Lina was terrifying.

It amazed him how easily she had forgiven him everything. After all the horror he'd put her through, she still looked at him with the same sweet trust she'd had at the beginning, before he'd betrayed her and her nation.

He was terrified of losing that faith. Of seeing her expression change to hatred or mistrust. Part of him felt it was inevitable. Someone as smart as Lina—and as principled—would eventually figure out he wasn't good enough for her.

Lina felt the pull of the systems around her, working carefully to filter only the networks she wanted to access from the hundreds of others at the periphery of her consciousness.

It was sort of like focusing on a conversation in a loud room. Her mind could automatically filter the unwanted information out, allowing her to concentrate. Although she had to admit, sometimes the other conversations grew increasingly loud, and it was difficult to focus. She could only imagine if more people had the same ability; it would become a cacophony of noise. No wonder the world had been in shambles because of the Technology.

Right now, she was focused on using the data they'd gathered from the network to map out the spread of infection. The virus was contained to a few specific neighborhoods in the Pleb City and Merchant Terrace, but on the Capitol Terrace it rampaged throughout the villas unchecked.

Lina frowned, wishing Helen were here to bounce ideas off of. She hated the riff that had formed between them, but she couldn't understand how her friend had been so quick to assume the worst of Jay and his brother.

Their actions did look bad, but Lina knew Jay. She knew he would do what he believed was right and necessary to complete the mission he set himself on.

That didn't mean she wasn't furious at him for going without telling her the truth. He could have saved her a lot of needless worry, not to mention poor Helen. The petite woman had looked awful, so tired and thin. Lina made a mental note to stop by and see her after she was done here, to make sure Helen rested and avoided a relapse.

Leaving the computer busy processing the most recent vital data from citizens, Lina went back to the grid that showed the movements of each citizen. Zooming in on the Pleb city center, she watched the crowd slowly dispersing with relief. Ramus, recently back from his own battle with the illness, had left to pick up Marcus from the Capitol and help

Vick with the quickly escalating situation.

She heard the door to the Tech Room open behind her, not looking up from her work. She assumed it was Simon, who'd left a few minutes ago to find "a snack." In the two days she'd worked with him, she was amazed at the amount of calories the tall, lanky man consumed. And it wasn't the healthy foods Patrician preferred, but candy, potato sticks, and other disgusting snacks she knew were popular among Plebs.

"Did you bring me anything?" she asked, her stomach rumbling softly at the thought of food.

"As a matter of fact, I did." The familiar voice made her head whip around, and she turned so quickly she stumbled. Strong hands steadied her before dropping away.

Intense relief brought tears to her eyes as she looked over Jay, from his tawny head down his muscular body clothed in Reaper's black, to the combat boots he'd kept from his days as the Empire's agent.

"You lied to me!" she burst out, anger warring with affection. The latter won out, and she threw herself into his arms, ignoring the weapon vest that pressed uncomfortably against her.

His arms closed around her. "I didn't lie, exactly. I just didn't tell you the whole truth."

She glared up at him. "A lie of omission is still a lie."

"I'm sorry. I had hoped I'd be there and back before... well, without out setbacks."

"Setbacks like Helen?" Lina asked, her voice muffled against his chest.

"Yeah, like Helen."

"Aerina told me how upset Vick was when he found out. He must care about her, to be so hurt that she didn't trust him. I don't know why he just wasn't honest with her in the first place."

Jay winced. "Point taken. But my brother's issues are his own. I'm just damn glad you didn't think the worst." He leaned back so he could see her face. "Do you trust me, Lina? Even after ... everything?"

"I must, or I would have been as angry as Helen when I saw that footage of you two stealing the test tubes and abducting poor Terrence."

"What did you think?"

Lina stepped back, sensing that the holocomputer had finished acquiring the vital stats and commanded it to process the information to determine who was most susceptible to the illness, and begin mapping the spread of infection. "I was hurt that you hadn't told me what was going on. But I knew you were doing something to help, in your own way. I told you, I trust you, Jay."

Jay studied her, his face impassive. Then a wide grin spread, and he hugged her close again, kissing her hard on the mouth.

"Thank glory, I thought you were going to toss me on my as-er, ear after pulling that stunt. That's why I love you, *bella diosa*, you'd forgive the devil if he came with a sincere apology."

"Let's not get carried away," Lina said. "Just because I trust you doesn't mean you're completely forgiven for not telling me."

"I'll make it up to you, I promise." His voice lowered, and he pulled her in, his mouth moving over hers more gently. She let him weave his spell over her, helpless under the onslaught of emotion.

"Of that, I have no doubt."

He pulled back. "But first, now that we've put that little issue behind us, I have something else to talk to you about."

Lina stiffened at his somber tone, stepping back to see his face. "What now?"

"You're not going to be happy. But I am trying to be more honest. Just hear me out."

"Jay, you're scaring me. Just say it." Lina felt prickles of ice traveling her spine as she waited for Jay to explain his ominous words.

"I might need to leave the city for awhile. I know you've got an important role here, and I don't expect you to leave if you don't want to." Jay plunked a heavy object wrapped in a blanket on the desk beside her. "This here is a little incendiary device; a bomb meant to start a large fire very quickly."

Chapter 20

"Control is an illusion. You're never in control of your environment. Just yourself and your own reactions." - Letters from Matias Emmanuel March

Helen ignored the first message from Aerina to come to the Training Grounds. Immersed in the molecular structure of the cells under her microscope, she was trying to forget she had a life outside of this lab.

A life that felt as if it were quickly falling to ruins.

Fight for what you want, just as you always have. Her mother's words echoed again, and she raised her head for a moment, her eyes staring unseeingly at the bustle of the lab.

What did she want? Her baby, certainly. The respect of her peers. The Senator role she was slated for.

But did she really want that? As an unwed mother, she'd already fallen from grace in the eyes of many Patricians. Surprisingly, she didn't care as much as she'd expected to. She felt mostly disgust towards the small-minded individuals who looked down on her decision to keep her child.

She wasn't even sure if becoming a Senator mattered as much anymore. The thrill of prestige, the challenge of such responsibility, no longer filled her with excitement.

"Helen, are you alright?" Helen started slightly at the question from one of the lab workers. She had been staring into space, her hand on her rounded stomach, for several minutes now.

She smiled slightly at the young man, nodding. "Yes, thank you." The athletic University student nodded, hesitating for a moment before going back to filling vials with more test samples taken from recent victims.

Helen's gaze was snagged by Agatha, the older woman who had run the tests on her. Terrence's absence had created a vacuum of authority, and no one had stepped in yet to claim it.

Helen knew she had the natural leadership qualities, but Agatha had more medical experience. *What a stupid power struggle to have at this point.* She decided to avoid the issue altogether by naming Agatha as Head of Lab until Terrence returned.

If he returned from whatever forced mission Vick and Jay had sent him on.

Another summons beeped on her holoreader, and she glanced down as she made her way towards Agatha.

I need your professional opinion. Please come to the Training Grounds.

This was the third message from Aerina. The last place Helen wanted to be was at the Training Grounds where she might run into Vick.

I'll be there soon, she responded finally.

"Agatha, I wanted to talk with you for a moment, if you have time?" Helen forced her voice to be as cordial as possible.

Agatha looked at her with suspicion, but nodded, leading Helen to the refrigeration room where hundreds of vaccines and diseases were kept.

Helen shivered, her thin biosuit doing little to keep out the cold. Her breath fogged out as she spoke.

"Our team needs a leader until Terrence returns. I was hoping you would be willing to take on that role; you have the most experience, and the others look up to you."

Agatha's expression was startled, but pleasure was quick to follow. "Yes, of course, I will be happy to take on the role of Head of Lab until Terrence returns. I hope they can discover what happened to him, poor man."

I'm sure you're waiting with baited breath for his return, Helen thought sardonically. Aloud, she said, "Thank you, this will be such a big help." The walls of the frigid, tiny room began closing in on her, and Helen turned quickly to exit.

"Helen," Agatha's voice made her pause. "Your test results suggest your progesterone levels are low, which might account for the spotting. You can get the supplement from the pharmaceuticals storage room. I hope your child is healthy. I truly do."

"Thank you," Helen murmured. Would the woman have told her about the test results had Helen not approached her?

It doesn't matter. Your baby still has a chance. That is what is important.

Her heart feeling much lighter, Helen headed towards the pharmaceuticals storage room.

* * *

"Helen! You're here." Aerina jumped up from the chair in Marcus' office. Marcus sat at the desk, reading through something on the holocomputer. A short, unkempt man sat at the meeting table, eating a plate of pasta. Terrence sat with them, looking disgruntled.

The travelers had returned. Did they find what they were looking for?

"What is going on?" Helen asked.

"This is Jay's pilot, Stix." Aerina introduced the unkempt man, who barely looked up to nod before returning to his food. "They just returned from the Southern Empire. They brought a vaccine with them. And Terrence here, of course." Aerina was watching her carefully for a reaction.

"Let me see it."

Aerina smiled in satisfaction, going to the Dispensare in the corner, typing in a few codes and producing a bottle.

Helen took the bottle. "I'll need to return to the lab and run some tests. Are you sure...?"

Terrence finally spoke up. "Yes, we are quite certain. With the help of these...barbarians—"

Stix just grunted at the insult, continuing to eat.

Terrence pressed on, "...we were able to locate their center for disease control, which was shockingly well organized. It made the act of acquiring the vaccine for our illness quite simple. Were you aware it was a bioweapon, engineered for quick dispersal amongst a population and difficulty in developing a vaccine?" He seemed both horrified and fascinated with the finding.

"I can't say I'm surprised. As soon as we run the proper tests in the lab, we can begin the mass development of the vaccine at once," Helen responded. Hope burgeoned in her chest. This nightmare was finally going to come to an end.

"Enough chatting. Take the vaccine and run your tests," Marcus ordered.

"Of course," Helen said coolly. She knew Marcus wasn't her biggest fan, although beyond her mistrust of Vick, she couldn't imagine what problem he had with her.

"I'm coming with you," Terrence said.

"You've been working hard; you should rest," Aerina said.

"I'll rest when my people are safe," Terrence said piously.

Aerina nodded, and Stix muttered something under his breath before stuffing his face with more noodles.

Helen just motioned for Terrence to follow her out.

"Keep me posted on the results," Marcus ordered. Helen nodded, not looking back. She couldn't help but wonder where Vick was. Had Marcus taken back control? Wouldn't they need to make an official announcement?

Sighing, she waited for Terrence to settle into her e-car before starting it up with a quick swipe of her wrist. When all this was over, she and Vick could talk it out like adults. Now she would focus on getting the vaccine tested, and creating enough for the citizens of Alba as quickly as possible.

Agatha would be disappointed that her control of the lab was short-lived.

*   *   *

Vick drove the large Bronco across the rocky terrain, the warm wind from the ocean grabbing hold of his hair and whipping it around his head. Normally he lived for these moments of solitude. Not today. He was focused on his mission.

He was going to destroy the monster.

The only emotion he felt was cold determination. Nothing was going to stop him. Only after she was dead would the people he loved be safe.

How had this happened? How had he come to care so much for the small group of Albans when he'd been so cautious all these years about forming connections?

His feelings for Helen were the biggest mystery. He hadn't known her long, only several months, but already he knew she was his weakness. Leaving her behind, and the baby growing inside her, was one of the hardest parts of his decision.

But this was right. He couldn't risk anyone else's life. The monster needed to die, and he would be there to watch her burn.

Even if he had to burn with her.

It was just a few more hours now and he'd intercept the former President's small army of mercenaries several miles outside of Vicksburg.

It was a beautiful day to die.

*   *   *

Leaving the vaccine development in the competent hands of the lab staff, Helen headed home for some much-needed rest. They'd celebrated the successful injection of the first patient from the initial batch taken from the Empire. It wouldn't take them long to create enough for the entire city.

Now that she'd left the bustle of the lab, her thoughts inevitably turned to Vick. Where was he? She'd finally watched the broadcast of him officially stepping down, and Marcus taking over control of the State again.

Had he returned to his personal escape, the small outpost he ran? She knew he missed his home, and had been counting the days until he could return.

Where did that leave her?

Alone.

Taking a deep breath to combat the lump in her throat, she pulled in front of her villa. It looked dark and lonely, knowing Vick wasn't going to be waiting inside or coming home.

Except this wasn't his home. His home was hundreds of miles south in Vicksburg.

Pulling her exhausted body from the car, she lifted her chin and headed toward the door.

Fight for what you want.

Was this what she wanted? An orderly, predictable life as a Patrician?

No, something inside her responded. *I want the passion I glimpsed with Vick.*

Would it be too late?

*   *   *

The delicate chimes of her holoreader woke Helen from a deep sleep. She sat up, disoriented, fumbling around on the table beside her bed for the source of the sound.

Accepting the call, Helen squinted at the projection of her father's smiling face.

"Your mother and I just got our vaccines. We wanted to call and tell you how proud we are of your hard work."

"Thanks," Helen said, clearing the sleep from her voice. "But I can't really take the credit. Vick and his brother are the real heroes."

"Where is your young man?" her father asked, looking as if he expected to see Vick hovering behind her.

She wished.

"He's not mine, Father. And I'm not sure where he is now."

"Oh, I see." He looked disappointed. "Well, we were just checking in." He appeared to be studying her projected image. "Are you alright?"

Helen forced a smile. "Yes, just over-tired."

"If you need anything—"

"I know, I'll ask. Thanks, Father."

Dressing, Helen left the depressingly silent house, heading once again to the Training Grounds. She was going to talk to Vick; to find out if they had any chance of a future once this was all over.

*   *   *

"What do you mean, he's gone?" Helen felt her stomach drop at Aerina's words. She didn't know where Vick had been staying since he left her villa, but she had felt some comfort thinking he was in Alba; that she could see him if she needed to.

"He's gone to meet the army that President March is bringing from Texico. He wanted to try and face them alone." Marcus didn't look up from his holocomputer as he answered her.

Helen had found Aerina working with Lina in the Tech Room, and had convinced her to bring her to Marcus so she could find out Vick's location.

"You let him go alone to face an army?"

"Vick is a trained professional; he does what he wants," Marcus answered. Helen shot him an angry look, fear and frustration churning within. Vick was going to face his mother; the object of his nightmares. She couldn't let him do it alone.

"We need to help him. *I* am going to help him," Helen said with finality.

"This is his show right now," Marcus countered in a low voice. "He's doing what he has to."

"He doesn't plan on coming back, does he." Helen reeled away, her hands going to clasp her stomach, unconsciously trying to draw strength from the tiny life inside her. Pressure on her chest made her breaths come fast and shallow.

Aerina came up behind her, laying a hand on her shoulder. "Helen, I'm sure he has a plan—"

Helen threw her hand off. "Don't humor me. He's been running from that sociopath for over a decade, and now he's gone alone to face her. He is going to kill her, and we all know the odds of him getting out alive are slim. Not against her army, and not without our help."

Aerina turned to face Marcus, her eyes narrowing. "Is that true, Marcus? Is Vick going to martyr himself?"

Marcus' jaw flexed as he regarded the women before him.

"His plan was to lure her in and kill her. If he can't take her out, he has a backup. With so many variables, I can't predict his odds of survival."

"And you let him go?" Aerina asked incredulously.

"It isn't my call."

"I am not about to let another man that I- I … care about martyr himself for this State. I'm going after him. And I have a better plan. That ignorant hillbilly and his dreams of a shoot-out are going to have to wait. I'm not letting him die."

Aerina's eyebrows shot up, and Marcus' jaw stopped flexing, his mouth curving into his version of a smile.

"I am beginning to see what Vick likes about you," he said.

Helen ignored that, turning to leave. "Well? Are you coming?" she demanded.

Aerina's mouth snapped closed, and Marcus' smile tightened.

"I'm giving him the chance to do this on his own, as he requested. Any interference now could be disastrous for him."

"I'm not going to leave him out there to die," Helen hissed.

Marcus stood, his full height towering over the diminutive woman. "You don't have a choice."

Aerina interceded before the argument escalated further. "Helen, Marcus is right. We can't risk Vick's life by interfering. Trust him to know what he's doing." Taking Helen's arm, Aerina led her towards the door. "I'll ride home with you. Marcus plans on staying late."

Helen allowed herself to be escorted to the lower garage,

panic pinching her chest tight, making it difficult to breathe. What if something happened to Vick while she sat here idly, unable to tell him her true thoughts?

She couldn't stay here. She couldn't let him face his mother alone. She'd go alone —

"Alright, we aren't going to have much time," Aerina muttered, interrupting Helen's anxious thoughts.

"What do you mean?" Helen watched dumbly as Aerina slid into a black e-car. Marcus' vehicle.

Aerina shot her an exasperated look. "We're going to help Vick. But you'd better have a plan, or we're not going to make it out of this alive. Mainly because Marcus is going to kill us, but also because we're going to face an entire army of hillbillies, armed with nothing but our good looks and brilliant minds."

"The easiest thing will be to just give her what she wants."

"The Technology?" Aerina navigated the e-car out of the garage with ease.

"Precisely."

*   *   *

Vick saw dust rising from the distant army. He sat, parked, his arm resting on the Bronco's steering wheel. Summer had come early to the coast, the Santa Ana winds blowing warm air across the valley.

He'd chosen this spot to face the army, a dip nestled between towering rockface on either side. This had once been a road, cut through the hillside, although the asphalt surface had long ago been covered by blowing dust and overtaken by craggy vegetation.

Pulling out the bottle of whiskey he'd swiped from Helen's villa, he took a long swallow. The liquor felt good running down his throat, taking the edge from his anticipation.

He didn't want to die; martyrdom had never been his thing. But if his plan failed … he wasn't leaving this valley unless the monster was dead, even if it meant his own life.

Que asi sea.

She'd terrorized the continent long enough. Had terrorized *him* long enough. His only regret was that he hadn't done this years ago, after she'd killed Nina.

Better late than never.

He no longer needed the zoom feature on his Alba-crafted sunglasses to see the vehicles approaching. His mouth quirked up in a grin as he watched. Texico's vehicles never failed to amuse him. They were so like the vehicles depicted in the Mad Max pre-war films he enjoyed, it was almost as if they had watched it and used them as a blueprint.

The strange mix of trucks and cars from the pre-war era had been welded together, and an assortment of weaponry and armor were also soldered on in as many places as possible.

Hillbilly tanks, the Albans called them. It was a perfect description.

Setting the whiskey bottle between his legs, Vick pulled a cigar from the console. One of his farmers in Vicksburg had started growing a little tobacco and rolling his own cigars. Vick had avoided the nicotine sticks popular in the Southern Empire, but found he enjoyed the cigars.

Lighting the end with the Bronco's cigarette lighter, he took a long puff. It was almost show time.

*   *   *

"Are we close?" Helen couldn't stop the question as she sat anxiously beside Aerina in the oversized off-road vehicle. She didn't understand Aerina's obvious enjoyment as she controlled the strange hybrid vehicle that bumped easily over the rocky terrain.

Anxiety warred with fear. Helen kept her eyes locked on the refrigeration case held in her lap, too terrified to glance out the windows and see the landscape bounce past.

"About forty minutes more," Aerina answered. Helen nodded jerkily, her knuckles white on the case. She was terrified of crashing, but even more terrified of not making it in time.

Are we too late already? Vick didn't have an ID chip, so they had no way of tracking him or knowing if he was still alive.

They did have a lock on the army approaching, and it was still moving northward. That gave Helen hope that they hadn't encountered Vick yet.

Or they've already killed him, the voice of fear whispered.

Helen ignored it, staring blindly at the case in her lap. This had to work.

*   *   *

The convoy of vehicles stopped a short distance in front of Vick's Bronco. Slowly, he lowered his legs from the dash, keeping the cigar clenched between his teeth as he stuck the whiskey on the floor.

The door opened from the first vehicle, and the woman of his nightmares regally descended.

Vick's fingers itched to grab his EMW and fire repeatedly, to watch her statuesque body perform the macabre dance of death from the high-powered voltage.

But he knew the moment his hand even twitched towards the weapon, the army surrounding him would fire, and this whole endeavor would be wasted.

Patience.

Moving slowly, he exited the vehicle, keeping his hands in sight. He wore his usual jeans and white t-shirt, tight enough to reveal the lack of weapon strapped to his side or chest.

"Well, if it isn't my first born son, as brashly stupid as always," she said as they drew closer, the well-modulated tones grating on his nerves.

"And Mother, you're looking old," he replied, and was rewarded by the cracking of her cool façade. Anger tinged her cheeks red, and she brought herself back under control with effort.

"Something you'll never live to be, my son. It is a shame that all of my children turned out to be such disappointments. But I suppose I shouldn't have expected more, considering how disappointing your father was. I keep hoping I can bring Chelsea up to snuff. She did a fine job pinpointing your little outpost hideout and sharing your whereabouts with my army." She shook her head with false regret. "At least I've finally found some benefit from your father's connections." She indicated the army behind her.

A man approached, about Vick's age, with long scars covering the left of his face. His black hair, gleaming amber eyes, and disfigured face made him look like the devil himself.

"You must be the paid help."

The man just smiled, revealing surprisingly white, even teeth. The expression only served to make him more foreboding.

Vick knew everything he needed to about this man. He was a mercenary, first and foremost. He offered his services to the highest bidder, and had no allegiance to state or person.

That was what Vick had counted on. She couldn't have chosen a better man to fit his own plans. He just needed to cut off the head of the snake, and the body would die. The drums in the back of his Bronco containing a lethal mixture of chemicals were plan B.

"You should have had the intelligence to remain dead, Vicktor. I have no business with you, so unfortunately I'll have to do myself what the Albans failed to do years before."

"We do have business. As the leader of Alba, I've come to ask you to surrender yourself immediately."

She laughed, holding up a hand to stop the man at her side from firing his weapon. "You? How did you mange that? I'll admit, I'm impressed. This does change things. You know why I'm here. Hand over the Technology and I'll consider letting your Albans live."

Vick noted that she didn't promise to let him live. They would both know that to be a lie.

"Give me the vaccine, and I'll consider making a trade."

She laughed again. "I've heard of your epidemic. Not so mighty now, are those Albans? As much as I'd love to claim the credit, the virus wasn't mine. But I'll certainly take full advantage of your misfortune and take that worthless city and everything of value in it."

She was so full of hubris, Vick thought. So smug in her perceived victory. Why wouldn't she take credit for virus obviously planted in the city?

"Unfortunately for you, I don't think I'll need to bargain for the Technology. I'm going to enjoy destroying that ridiculous city. By the time I'm done, I'll be able to walk in and take what I want. I'm sorry, son, but I just don't see a need for you. Say hello to your father for me."

As her companion raised his weapon again, a loud crack resounded in the man-made canyon. The warlord stumbled before catching himself as a bullet traveled through his leg, and his weapon moved from Vick to the fallen boulders lining the old road.

"The next shot will be the center of your forehead, you old bitch." The feminine shout came from not far behind Vick.

Goddammit.

"Chelsea, I wondered where you'd hidden yourself," their mother said. Vick clenched his jaw. This was a complication he didn't need. "You've done a great job convincing your brother to take you in and reveal his location. I'm proud of you. Come on out, darling, and you can work by my side from now on. You have more pluck than all your siblings combined."

Vick wondered how Jessica felt about that. His other sister, whom he could see sitting in one of the other vehicles, had stood with their mother since the beginning. The monster had twisted his sister's mind; he knew Jessica would never be free from her grasp.

The mercenary still stood, blood slowly dripping down his pant leg. "That is quite a sting, abeja. Come out," he finally spoke, his voice smooth and accented. "I want to see your face, or I will have to have my men blow you and your delightful brother to bits."

"Do as he says, Chelsea!" Vick ordered, gritting his teeth. If they fired anywhere near the Bronco...

After a long moment, his sister's tawny head appeared from behind the boulders. She looked nervous but determined as she walked forward slowly, the antique gun he'd kept on his mantle held at her side.

"Come here, abeja," the man coaxed. "Put your toy down and come to me if you want to live."

Chelsea's hands were shaking and she dropped the gun beside the Bronco's front tire, walking forward until she stood beside Vick.

"No, no, abeja, I want you here," the man ordered.

"Forget it. You'll have to shoot me," Chelsea said, crossing her arms over her chest.

The man made a tsking sound. "What a waste that would be of such spirit and belleza."

"Listen to him, Chels. You've already fucked this up enough," Vick ordered under his breath. Chelsea cast him an injured look.

"I'm sorry I lied to you. But I just saved your life, you ungrateful bastard." With that, she stomped over to the mercenary, stopping a few feet short and turning her back to him. He gripped her arm, pulling her close.

"Much better," he murmured. Chelsea said nothing, her eyes meeting Vick's.

"If you're done molesting my daughter, perhaps you can take care of her so she doesn't become a problem." March looked offended at all the attention Chelsea was getting.

The mercenary smiled, his face twisting. "She's a useful hostage. I think I'll hold onto her for now."

Silence lengthened, the idling motors of the motorcade stretching behind his mother the only sound in the early afternoon. Vick waited for ballistic fire from one of the heavy guns on the trucks to level him and his little sister.

Any fire would trigger the firebomb in the Bronco. At least if he died, he'd go knowing he took her, and some of her makeshift army, with him. Alba would be safe.

Helen would be safe.

Into the charged near-silence came the hum of another approaching vehicle, this from behind him.

What the hell?

He glanced back to see an Alban off-road vehicle roll into the canyon. It pulled to a stop several hundred feet behind them, sitting for a long moment while the dust settled.

"Is this the cavalry?" his mother mocked. Vick said nothing, waiting to see who exited.

Aerina stepped slowly from the vehicle, her reddish-blonde hair gleaming like fire, looking regal in her Emissary garb. She held a weapon in each hand pointing towards the ground. She was ready, but telling the nervous gunners on the hillbilly tanks she wasn't going to fire.

The passenger door opened, and his heart froze when he saw the familiar blonde head appear.

Helen.

He had difficulty believing what his eyes told him were truth. Why the hell would Marcus allow the women to come? He'd known Vick's plan. Known it was deadly.

Goddamn, couldn't a man execute a plan without a whole crowd of unwelcome guests fucking it up?

What were they thinking?

Helen approached confidently with Aerina, a large case carried by her side. With her light hair, pale skin, and white pantsuit, she looked like an angel in the bright rays of sunlight streaming down into the canyon.

"President March," she said in her clipped voice, "I have something here you want. I'm prepared to make a bargain."

The older woman raised one brow, her eyes on the refrigerated case. "And who are you to bargain with me?"

"I've been appointed temporarily as Consul, and I have

here samples of our MTI, Alba's exclusive Mind Technology Interface. I'd like to talk licensing of our proprietary technology in a way that is beneficial for both parties. You will have access to our support team, and we will provide you with the Technology."

"And what do you get, *Consul*?" March cast a mocking glance at Vick.

"The Senators of Alba are tired of war. We have decided it is in our best interests to release our Technology and form valuable alliances."

"What is to stop me from killing you and your little group here and just taking the Technology?"

Helen smiled slightly. "How confident do you feel in your understanding of this Technology? We have perfected it in our undisclosed lab. You risk losing years of information and put the Technology itself at risk." Helen stepped forward, her expression all business. "I know you're a woman of business first, and you understand the value of time. I feel confident that with our support, you will achieve the level of success you desire with our Technology in a very short time. We obviously would not have approached you were we not confident in our ability to deliver."

Vick could see his mother wavering; Helen was quite persuasive. Vick himself was beginning to wonder if it was all bullshit, or if Alba really did have a lab developing the Technology over the years.

He was watching his mother's face closely, and a look he recognized all too well came over her attractive features.

Fuck.

"If what you say is true, we have no need for this worthless vagrant." March nodded again to the devil at her side holding Chelsea, and a shot rang out from the man's old-fashioned hand gun.

The bullet struck Vick with shocking force, sending him backwards into the Bronco. His last thought before blackness overcame him was that he hoped to hell Helen was as smart as he thought. Or they were all doomed.

*   *   *

"Sir, you need to see this."

Marcus looked up from the topographic map he and a few other Virmortus were reviewing, planning their attack on the small army approaching from the south.

Turning impatiently, he took the holoreader from the young recruit, seeing Chessa's face in the projection.

"What is it?"

Chessa turned the camera towards the supply truck behind her at the Ferry. It had been part of her job to oversee inspections of everything traveling between the Terraces until the disease was contained.

"Sir, we found this amongst the supplies."

Marcus studied the miniature projection, finally recognizing the small, oval-shaped object lying amongst the piles of produce and frozen meats.

An incendiary device. Compact. Lethal.

"It was from the Aggie Terrace, sir," Chessa told him in a low voice.

"Who is picking up the supplies from the Aggies?" Marcus asked, although he already knew the answer.

"Jayden March, sir. The Confederate."

Goddamn traitor. He should never have allowed that bastard in Alba.

"Where is he?"

"We believe he is at the Training Grounds with Ms. Rhodes."

Marcus turned, leaving his office and striding down the cold stone hall towards the Tech Room where Lina had been practically living lately.

Jay came around the corner, Lina at his side. Without hesitating, Marcus' EMW was in his hand, and he fired off a shot.

Jay's reflexes saved him as he dove behind the stone wall and back into the Tech Room he'd just exited. Lina's scream echoed off the bare stone as chunks of rock flew from the EMW blast.

"What are you doing?" Lina gasped as Marcus continued pacing forward, the EMW in one hand, his sica blade in the other. "If this is about the bombs in the produce shipment—"

"You know about that?" Marcus paused, his dark gaze narrowed dangerously.

"Jay was coming to tell you!" Lina drew up to her full height, but was unable to stop the trembling of her hands as she tried to block Marcus' path. "He didn't plant it. He just uncovered it, and was coming to tell you!"

"I told you this was a bad idea," Jay's voice called from within the Tech Room. "That bastard is going to kill me and ask questions after."

Marcus said nothing, his weapons gripped tightly, ready. But his gaze fell on the rounded object wrapped in a blanket that Jay had dropped on the floor. It looked just like the device his Reapers had found.

He heard a movement in the Tech Room and pressed his back to the stone wall, considering his next move.

"Lina, get the hell out of here," Jay called again. "I don't want you hurt."

Instead of backing away, Lina took a step forward, planting herself in the center of the doorway. Her face was pale, and her dark eyes wide with fear, but she stood her ground.

"Marcus, just listen for a moment. Jay came across that in a shipment, and was waiting to see who had planted it. He knew it would make him look guilty, and so was trying to determine their origins on his own before he was sent by Vick to the Empire to find the vaccine."

The story rang true. Why would someone bent on destroying Alba bring back a working vaccine? And Jay had been smart enough to avoid capture for months the first time in Alba; why would he be so foolish as to stash the devices where they would immediately implicate him?

Unless someone else was hoping to make the Confederate take the fall if the devices were uncovered. Someone else who was plotting against Alba.

Damn. It would have been so much easier if it had just been Jay. Now he would have to launch a new investigation to uncover the traitors in the city. And that also meant someone else was trying to destroy them.

He lowered his weapons slightly, and saw Lina release a pent up breath.

"Sir!" Nemo came with another of his men from the direction of his office. "Your car has been stolen, and a guard just called in his report that he allowed it to leave the city!"

God*damn*, now what? "Who?"

But he already knew the answer.

"Ms. Delacroix and Ms. Vanderbuilt, sir."

He was going to kill her. At the very least, he was going to chain her in one of the interrogation rooms for a month. The fury that swept through him wasn't what made his hands begin to shake.

It was fear.

"Have this destroyed immediately," Marcus ordered, scooping up the fire bomb and handing it carefully to Nemo. "Get a team together to start searching out any more that might be planted around the city. Tell Ramus he's in charge of the city's defenses until I return." He shoved his weapons back in his vest, turning to head back towards the garage.

"Need backup?" Jay exited the Tech Room cautiously, his hands held slightly to the side to show he was unarmed.

Marcus deliberated for a moment. "Probably. Come on."

"I'm coming, too," Lina said.

Jay shook his head. "Stay here. You're more valuable working behind the scenes than in battle. Believe me."

Lina frowned, but nodded. She looked almost relieved. "Bring them back safe."

Jay kissed her and headed after Marcus, who was already in the stairwell.

Marcus considered the remaining e-cars. Not fast enough. He needed to be there *now*. The maelstrom of fear and rage threatened to overwhelm him as he imagined Aerina driving rashly into danger with only fragile, stubborn Helen at her side. And his only back up was an outsider of Alba, something a year ago he would have found unimaginable.

He headed up to towards the roof where the jet waited, taking two steps with each stride, Jay close behind. Regardless of how the epidemic and impending attack turned out, Alba was going to be forced to undergo significant changes to survive in the new world emerging from its post-apocalyptic shell. Isolationism wasn't going to be an option any longer.

Unless the world was once again plunged into war on a massive scale. Then they'd all be set back a century.

Who would build Alba this time? Because it sure as hell wouldn't be him.

Chapter 21

"Pride goeth before destruction; a haughty spirit before a fall."
- Proverbs 16:19, The Bible, Old World Religious Text

No!

Helen contained the cry of anguish with effort as she watched Vick's body slump lifelessly from the grill of the Blazer to the rocky ground.

She was too late.

Chelsea screamed as her oldest brother lay still in the dirt, running forward. The scarred man stopped her, grabbing her arm and hauling her back to his side with a quick jerk. She turned on him, but he subdued her struggles easily, his weapon remaining steady at his side.

She had heard Aerina's choked cry beside her and refused to look at her friend, knowing if she saw Aerina's sorrow she'd lose her own battle with control.

You need to live, to save Alba. To save your baby. Thoughts of her unborn child gave her the boost of strength she needed to look dispassionately on the scene.

"That was messy. Hopefully we can deal a little more civilized from this point on. I would feel better if your ... companion ... waited in the vehicle," Helen said coolly, meeting President March's icy gaze. What kind of monster was she facing, that she'd commanded her own son's death without batting an eye?

The President smiled, appearing satisfied at Helen's response. "Yes, I'm very sorry about that unfortunate display," she said dismissively, her gaze going to the case at Helen's side. "I'd like to see the Technology."

Helen said nothing, opening the case and pulling out a holder containing six small vials.

"I can inject you immediately, if you wish," Helen

offered, pulling out a syringe and loading a vial containing the swirling amber liquid.

March's eyes gleamed with avarice as she watched, walking forward slowly.

She stood before Helen, her height even more impressive up close. "It doesn't look like I had anticipated," she murmured as if to herself. Without warning, President March grabbed the syringe, shoving it into Helen's neck. Burning pain spread from the injection site as the vial's contents entered her bloodstream.

"I'm sure you understand, I had to be sure it wasn't a trick," March said gently as she removed the needle.

Helen nodded, gritting her teeth against the momentary discomfort, her hand gripping her neck. They had planned for this, but uncertainty made her heart quicken with fear. There was no way to be absolutely certain she was safe from what was contained in the vials, and that it wouldn't harm her child.

It was too late to worry about that now. She could still save Alba from this army of mercenaries.

Even if she was too late to save Vick.

Anguish twisted in her, and she was careful to keep her gaze downcast, fearing her adversary would sense her hatred; would smell her fear like the jackal she was.

March waited, watching her carefully for signs of any adverse effects. Helen remained standing, getting her emotions under control and calmly returning the older woman's gaze. March slowly reached for a second vile, loading it into the syringe.

"Finally," she breathed, closing her eyes in anticipation, then injected the fluid carefully into her own arm.

Helen's eyes flicked to the scarred man who had shot Vick, hatred swirling just beneath her calm exterior. "Does anyone else want a sample?"

The dark man with the gleaming eyes just smiled, a terrifying expression on his broken face. He knows, Helen thought. Knows of my hatred. She carefully averted her gaze to include others.

"I'll take the remaining vials, and expect you to produce several hundred more in the next week," March instructed brusquely, taking the case from her hand.

"We have a few dozen vials on hand we can deliver immediately, but the production process is rather complex and it may be several months before we are ready to deliver that large of a shipment," Helen told her.

The President's eyes narrowed, but she nodded. "Fine. We'll take up residence in his quaint little town." March indicated Vick's prone body with a casual flick of her lean fingers.

Helen's stomach twisted as she imagined the woman who had destroyed Vick's life taking over the town he'd loved so much.

"Send the vials you have. Once you've delivered the first set, I'll see about getting your people the vaccine to that nasty little virus I hear is decimating your state."

"Ms. March—"

"President March. I'll soon have a new nation to run," the conceited woman interrupted. Helen nodded.

"President March, if you could humor me, I find myself fascinated by this illness you've planted in our city. How did you manage to engineer a sickness that mutates so quickly?"

March smiled, obviously amused by the question. "Well, my dear, I've already told you I was not responsible. Perhaps you should look a little more closely at the new members of your little nation. Confederates are big on loyalty, you know. Even if it isn't loyalty to their own mothers."

"What do you mean?" Helen asked, watching March closely. She had begun licking her lips repeatedly, and was now flexing her fingers. Mentally she checked her own vitals. Everything seemed stable. The antidote was working. And apparently so was the poison. "Do you have information about a traitor in Alba?"

"We'll discuss that once the Technology vials have been delivered," March snapped, appearing more agitated. "What the hell is wrong with me?"

"The Technology does have some mild side effects as it binds with your synapses. You may experience discomfort and tingling." Helen watched as March swallowed repeatedly, touching her face with a shaking hand.

"How long does it last?" she asked.

Helen looked at the man standing behind March, seeing the smirk on his disfigured features. How much did he know? He made no move to signal his men, and Helen released her breath slowly.

Soon. Just keep it together for a little longer.

She couldn't look at Vick's body or she'd break down right now. She could grieve after her baby was safe.

"Something is wrong," March gasped, her hands on her throat. "You little bitch. What have you done to me?"

"I don't know what you mean," Helen answered softly. "You injected me with the same substance. I feel fine."

"Jefe, if I die, kill them all. Starting with that pale whore." March raised a shaking hand, backing away. She grabbed for the scarred man, and he shrugged off her grasping hand. She gaped at him as she collapsed to her knees, no longer looking so regal or commanding.

The man she called Jefe stood, still smirking, as if waiting for the situation to play out. Helen wasn't sure what to expect from him, taking a few hesitant steps back. Aerina moved to stand before her.

"No, we stand together," Helen murmured, pushing to her friend's side. She wasn't about to hide behind others. She was going to fight. Fight for what she wanted.

March began gasping, her breathing labored. "What is happening!" she shrieked again. Her panicked gaze went first to Jefe, then to the vehicles still idling behind her. "Jessica, get out here! I need help."

The door burst open from an armored car and Vick's

sister came rushing forward, crouching beside her mother. "What is it, Mother? What did they do to you?"

"I don't know; help me, help me!" March's mouth gaped for air, panic clear in her wide eyes.

"What have you done?!" Jessica screamed, facing the Albans. Her gaze barely paused over the body of her own brother, slouched in front of the Bronco, and her little sister, held in the punishing grip of the scarred man.

Helen's sorrow became rage, and she finally answered. "She's dying, of course. Did you think we would hand over our Technology? She has ingested poison; a form of histotoxic hypoxia."

March began retching violently, interrupting Helen's dispassionate explanation. Jessica gasped, holding her mother's head up, wiping the older woman's face with her shirt. The smell of vomit and fecal matter carried on the wind, and Helen tried to inhale through her mouth.

"Her body is losing control, and eventually, she'll suffocate as oxygen is no longer distributed throughout her body."

"You monsters!" Jessica screamed, hugging her mother's heaving body to her soiled chest. Helen couldn't even appreciate the irony of that statement, feeling sick watching the older woman die before them. She gained no pleasure from the macabre scene, feeling bile rising up in her own throat.

March began gasping and gurgling, her limbs nearly paralyzed as the toxins spread throughout her body. Finally she slumped in her daughter's arms, either dead or unconscious.

"No!" Jessica began screaming, rising from her mother's body, her eyes mad. Helen felt nothing but pity for the young woman, spending a lifetime being abused, tied to a sociopath who broke her mind and used her.

Glancing around wildly, Jessica brought up a weapon, her target obvious.

Helen.

The next moments seemed to happen in slow motion. Helen knew she couldn't outrun the blast, closing her eyes, her hands instinctively covering the small life inside her.

Aerina grabbed at Helen to pull her back, away from the weapon's line of fire. She felt a hand on her shoulder just as a loud boom echoed in the canyon.

Silence followed.

Helen opened her eyes, shocked to find herself unharmed. Looking down, she checked herself for a sign of injury, sure the other woman must have hit her at such a close distance.

Finding nothing, she looked up, seeing Jessica flat out on the ground, a gory wound marking her forehead.

Helen looked around, still uncertain who had fired the blast and saved her.

"Vick," she heard Aerina murmur, and she turned quickly towards the body in the dust. Vick was still slumped against the front fender of the Blazer, but in his hand was the smoking antique gun Chelsea had discarded earlier. The second of six shots was now embedded in Jessica's forehead.

Helen stared in disbelief as Vick met her gaze, his beloved hazel eyes gleaming.

Ignoring the enemy army, Helen rushed forward, dropping to her knees in the dust.

"I saw him shoot you!" she cried, her hand going to the bloody hole in his t-shirt. Gently she ripped the hole larger to better inspect the wound.

"The bastard just nicked me. I blacked out when I hit my head on the truck fender, but other than a possible concussion and this flesh wound, I'm fine."

His breath hissed in through his teeth as she prodded the wound. "But that does sting a little."

"Now what?" The army leader's voice rang out, interrupting their moment. Helen looked up from Vick's wound, remembering the army of mercenary Texicans stretching before them.

The sound of an approaching engine echoed through the canyon. It took a moment for her to realize it was not another vehicle on the ground, but a jet approaching.

An Alban jet.

Her eyes met Aerina's. Her friend's "oh shit" expression told her it must be Marcus.

"Ah, the real cavalry. I did wonder why they would send two young women to face an army alone." Jefe held his weapon loosely at his side, and the army behind him remained silent, waiting.

The jet settled in the canyon, dust swirling to briefly restrict view of the hatch that opened. And then Marcus was disembarking.

He was dressed in the black of the Reapers, his weapon vest bulging with extra firepower. It was his eyes, however, that caught her attention. They were the eyes of death. His stark features were empty of emotion, and he stood, still and ready, as he scanned the scene before him.

"A little late to the party, Marcus," Vick called out, defusing some of the tension. "Helen here has already taken care of the crazy old bitch. Now we just need to decide what to do about the army she left behind."

The scarred man, Jefe, limped forward, favoring the leg Chelsea had shot.

"The question on everyone's mind, hmm? I suppose I could carry out my contract, but Ms. March only paid me for half. Now, she cannot pay me, yes?" The man shook his head as if disappointed. "So I will offer you a deal. Pay me what was promised, and I shall see to your protection until this plague Ms. March bragged about has gone. Then my men and I, we shall return to Texico to await our next customer."

Marcus was silent for a long moment, then nodded once.

"You have a deal."

The leader of the army smiled, limping forward to shake hands with Marcus. Instead of releasing his hold on Chelsea, he tucked his weapon in his pants to shake hands.

"If we're all friends now, don't you think you can release me?" Chelsea asked, trying to twist her arm free. Jefe held her fast.

"No, abeja. You and I have business to discuss of our own."

"You can't take my sister, Rey," Vick called out, rising to his feet with Helen's assistance. Her eyebrows shot up. Vick knew this man?

"I go by just Jefe now, Jefe Militaire if necessary."

"Warlord, eh? How original." Vick walked over carefully, his hand on the wound in his side.

"Half the battle is reputation, amigo. You know this. And I am afraid I cannot let my little abeja shoot me without consequence. Reputation again. It is all we mercenaries have."

"Marcus here is already going to pay you a fortune. Isn't that compensation enough for a dent in your massive ego?"

"Money is business. This ... this is personal. Were she a man, I would have just killed her. But she is a beautiful abeja, so I must think of something more appropriate. It would be such a waste to destroy something so interesting." Jefe ran a long finger down Chelsea's cheek. She didn't pull away, but grabbed his hand to stop the movement.

Vick's face darkened, and Helen began to worry about the tenuous truce falling apart. Surprisingly, it was Chelsea who intervened.

"I think we can all guess where this is going," Chelsea said. "If you can agree to quit calling me honeybee, I'll agree to be subjected to whatever punishment you've got in mind. It can't be much worse than what *that* doled out over the years," she said, indicating the body of her mother.

"Then we have a bargain?" Jefe asked softly.

"Yes, although why you insist on whining about such a paltry wound is a little embarrassing, really."

Jefe smiled, the expression twisting his features. Helen contained a shiver. Chelsea seemed unfazed, meeting the man's amber-colored eyes unflinchingly.

Vick turned to his sister. "Chels, you don't — "

"It's fine," she interrupted. "I owe you for letting that bitch coerce me into setting you up. Besides, I don't need you to start playing big brother now after twelve years of playing dead. I can take care of myself. Worry about your pregnant girlfriend, here." Chelsea looked over Helen before dismissing her. "Lead on, captor," she instructed Jefe.

Jefe smiled at the group, his golden gaze settling on Helen for a moment. She resisted the urge to look away. "Poison? Not so original, and such a woman's weapon. Ironic that it took down such a formidable opponent as Madame March. I will have to remember to be careful if you ever serve me tea." His amused gaze flicked to Vick, who looked on the exchange with narrowed eyes.

Vick watched as Chelsea walked away, the limping warlord close to her side.

"What just happened? I think that concussion must have confused me more than I thought."

"I think your sister was trying to help, in her own way," Helen murmured. Pity mingled with admiration as she watched the other girl walk towards an uncertain future, shoulders squared and head high. "And I think she's going to be fine."

They both watched as Jefe solicitously offered to help Chelsea up into his large all-terrain truck. Vick's sister pushed away the warlord's hand, hauling herself in.

"I think you're right," Vick agreed, nodding to Jefe as the mercenary saluted them before climbing in behind Chelsea.

Marcus and Aerina joined them, the tension between the two palpable. They all watched the army slowly turning to disperse. Jay excited the jet, a hand cannon still gripped in his hands. He was frowning at their younger sister as she slowly disappeared from sight.

"So they're going to hang around? Not sure if that makes me feel better or worse," Vick said.

"He said they'll make camp nearby, and I'm sure he's expecting me to deliver payment promptly. Is he trustworthy?"

Vick nodded in answer to Marcus' question.

"Yes. I'd trust him with my life. He's saved it a couple times, including today. He's got a reputation for never failing, and never turning on a customer. Like he said, reputation is everything in that business."

"I suppose I'd better pay the man then. Can I subtract your sister from what I owe?"

Aerina moved to swat Marcus' arm, but withdrew her hand when she glimpsed his face. The embers of fury were banked, but still apparent in his dark eyes. "Not funny. That poor girl." She looked at Vick accusingly. "I cannot believe you just let him take her."

Jay joined them, his expression dark. "You let him take Chels? I know she set you up, but she's still our sister. And she saved your life."

"Calm down. I know Damien Rey. I spent a lot of time with him growing up. Our father and his mother … were in a relationship. He's a businessman first. He wouldn't hurt Chels; not knowing how close our ties are to Alba and the potential goldmine Alba could be for his business. And I've never seen him act that way. I think he might kind of like her."

"I did get the sense that there was something between those two." Helen stared at the cloud of dust following the disappearing army. Then her gaze went reluctantly to the two bodies they'd left behind. "What should we do with them? We could give them some kind of burial—"

"Leave them for the vultures," Vick interrupted brusquely, not even looking at the remains of his mother and sister. "It's what they would have done to us."

"I'll take care of them," Jay said quietly.

"I'll help." Marcus returned to the vehicle, digging in the back and returning with a pickaxe and shovel.

"If you're all here, who's running Alba?" Vick deliberately turned his back, his arm still around Helen's shoulder as if he needed her support to stand.

"Ramus." Marcus handed the shovel to Jay, shouldering the pickaxe. "He's overseeing the search for a traitor."

"Another?" Vick looked over at Jay.

Jay looked up from his digging to glare at his brother. "I was a spy. Not a traitor. And I've already been cleared; thanks for your vote of confidence."

"Do you have it handled?"

"We will." Marcus' voice promised retribution. Helen shivered, not envying the traitor when he or she were found.

"Then I suppose I'm no longer needed," Vick said. "The vaccine should soon get the illness under control, and the city will be back to normal."

"As normal as it can be with the Patrician population nearly decimated," Aerina retorted.

"It might be a good time to rethink our structure and policies." Helen looked up at Vick as she responded absently. He seemed anxious to leave. She frowned, wondering what had him so uneasy now that the action had ended.

Did his mother's death affect him more than he was letting on? Or did he just want to escape Alba. And her.

He finally turned to Helen, his eyes darting to Aerina and then back to her. Aerina took the hint, heading back to the vehicle.

"Yes?" Helen asked after a long moment ticked by in silence.

"I need to get back to Vicksburg; I'm sure there's a lot to take care of after my prolonged absence."

Helen nodded, waiting. When he didn't continue, his hand stroking the scar beneath his beard, she said, "Are you alright, about your … mother?"

Vick's hand tightened briefly on her shoulder. "The only regret I have is that I wasn't the one to end her."

"Sorry. You appeared a little busy at the time. I didn't

think you'd mind if I took over." Helen's dry tone hid the lingering whispers of horror she'd felt when Vick had been lying prone in the dust, presumably dead.

"You risked a lot to come here." His tone was accusatory; his hazel eyes dark with some deep emotion she couldn't identify.

"Aerina understood why I had to come. And I'm pretty certain Marcus will have a thing or two to say about it."

"How could you be sure the antidote and poison wouldn't affect the baby?" He was looking at the mound of her stomach where her hand instinctively rested.

"The antidote to cyanide poisoning has been around for decades; since the old world, in fact. It was the safest choice we had. I wasn't about the let you come here alone."

"I work best alone."

"Can't you just admit you needed us today?" Helen's voice was even, masking the emotional turmoil still raging, and the adrenaline wreaking havoc on her body.

"I needed you today."

Helen let out a shaky breath at the words she'd wanted to hear. That he needed her. But now that he'd said them, she realized it wasn't enough. She studied his dust-streaked features, his gruff exterior and guarded eyes revealing little of his thoughts.

"Is there a doctor that can look at your injury?" She turned the topic, noticing the red stain on his side was slowly spreading.

"I can take care of it myself. I just need some antiseptic and a bandage."

"Why don't I look at it." It was more of a command than a question. Helen led him over to the open door of his Bronco, digging in the dash compartment Vick called a glove box for the first aid kit she knew he carried there. Gently pushing him onto the front seat, she lifted his shirt to reveal the seeping wound. She tried to ignore the sight of his tanned skin and well-honed muscles, focusing on the injury

He was right; it was just a nick. The bullet had scraped along his side, removing a layer of skin and muscle but doing little damage to any organs. The scarred man was quite the marksman, if this was what he intended.

Carefully cleaning the wound and applying a bandage, Helen surreptitiously breathed in Vick's scent. He smelled of dust, gun powder, and the musky scent that was his alone.

She was going to miss him desperately when he was gone. Even after the arguments and misunderstandings, he had become a steady presence in the uncertain and changing world around her.

More than that, she admitted. He'd easily gotten beneath the careful walls she'd built, revealing the vulnerable woman she'd tried so hard to keep concealed.

But she had apparently not affected him in the same way. He still wanted to escape to his refuge; to continue hiding from the world and running from his past.

Vick sat motionless as she completed the ministrations, his eyes burning on her downcast head. What was he thinking? Was he going to miss her, or was he relieved to be free of the responsibilities thrust upon him in Alba?

"There," she stated, lowering his shirt slowly.

"Helen..." he began, but stopped. She waited, breath held, for him to say something. To say what she wanted to hear. "Thanks," he finished, and her heart sank.

She nodded, keeping her gaze downcast as she packed away the unused items into the first aid kit. She couldn't stand for him to see the disappointment and sorrow she was certain were clear on her face.

I don't want him asking because he thinks I want him to. I need to know he wants me — needs me — as much as I want him.

"I suppose this is goodbye then," she said finally when she'd gotten herself under control. She smiled, holding out her hand to shake his.

Vick looked at her hand before taking it and using it to pull her close, wrapping his thick arms around her. Helen remained still, then melted helplessly into the hug, holding onto him tightly like the lifeline he had become.

Don't cry. Don't you dare cry.

His lips brushed lightly across her forehead, her eyelids, and found her lips. He marauded her mouth for a long moment. She moaned softly in response, desire and a more painful emotion mingling. And then he pulled away, kissing her nose before setting her gently back.

"Goodbye, little one," he murmured, and Helen realized he was talking to her baby as his hand softly brushed her rounded stomach.

"If you need me, Marcus can reach me. Anytime," he told her as he slid into the driver's seat of the Bronco. Helen nodded, taking another few steps back.

The Bronco roared to life and he turned it around, driving away swiftly, his hand saluting out the window her last glimpse of him as he disappeared from the canyon.

Helen turned, walking blindly back to Marcus' vehicle. She was almost there when emotion overtook her, sobs wracking her body.

Arms went around her, and she leaned into Aerina's familiar hug.

Aerina said nothing, just holding her while she cried herself out.

"You saved Vick, Helen. You saved Vick, and you saved Alba." Aerina finally said softly as Helen's sobs subsided. "Just as you said you would."

I'm going to fight for what I want. She remembered the words she'd told Aerina and Marcus that morning when they'd realized Vick had gone.

But had she? Had she fought for Vick? They'd saved Alba, but Vick was still gone.

Perhaps she still had some fighting to do.

Chapter 22

"He was brave and bold, taking on a mighty enemy to save our city and preserve peace for future generations. His name shall be honored always." -Epitaph for Stephen Augustus Rhodes

The jet was silent on the return trip, each lost in their own thoughts. Marcus had refused to allow Aerina and Helen to take the all-terrain vehicle back on their own, and for once Aerina hadn't argued. Marcus was still furious with Aerina, not looking at or speaking to his subdued partner.

Helen watched the horizon where Vick had disappeared, regret a bitter taste on her tongue. Exhaustion weighed on her heavily.

A muted roar and flash of light brought her from her laments, and all passengers stared in horror at the sight outside the jet's windows.

Their city was burning.

An explosion had come from the top Terrace of Alba, and was now burning brightly in the early evening.

"Is it the Capitol?" Aerina asked in horror.

"The Training Grounds," Marcus responded, his voice devoid of emotion.

Helen looked at him. He had to be sick, she thought. Everyone he worked with, trained with, grown up with … everyone in that building had to be gone.

"Lina," Jay muttered hoarsely, his eyes fixed on the orange flames seething about the hillside. "I left Lina in the Training Grounds. I told her to stay. I thought she'd be safe … ah god!" his voice ended in torment, and he turned away, ripping harnesses from the jet's walls, smashing supplies and gear in a fit of anguish.

"Maybe she wasn't there. Maybe she left." Helen heard her own words from a distance, but as she watched the inferno lighting up the evening, she doubted their truth. How could anyone survive that?

The anti-fire systems in place began to slowly shut down the flames as they neared, and the pilot set the jet down in the closest open area, the University sports fields.

"We'll go and help fight the blaze; see if there are any survivors," Marcus said. The others nodded, following him across the fields towards the Capitol.

Helen was unprepared for the new sight awaiting them.

A small army waited on the steps and in the courtyard of the Capitol, their weapons trained on their small group.

A lone figure detached from the crowd of Armati soldiers, his elegantly lean form back lit by the setting sun.

Anthony Delacroix, Aerina's father.

"What is going on?" Marcus demanded when Anthony drew closer.

Anthony raised his arm, a signal for the soldiers to hold their fire, Helen supposed. Her arms moved over the slight mound of stomach, the pointless motion only serving to draw Anthony's attention to her.

"Helen, what are you doing with this group?" Anthony looked disappointed, his bright blue eyes, the same as Aerina's, darkening with sorrow.

"I'm trying to save Alba," Helen responded, meeting the older man's gaze unflinchingly.

"As am I. Saving her from the savages trying to take over our once-great city." His eyes moved to Marcus, resentment replacing the regret. "And protecting the Technology that it has been my duty to preserve since my father passed it down to me, as was the duty of his father before him."

"Everyone who knew anything about that Technology was in the building you burned, you lunatic," Jay snarled. His whole body was shaking with rage as he fought to control himself. Helen wouldn't be surprised if the large man lunged forward and ripped out the Senator's throat before the soldiers standing at ready even had a chance to fire.

Anthony must have had a similar thought, for he took a small step backwards. He shook his head, a smile flitting around his thin lips. "No, that isn't true at all. The real secret of Alba is right here." He held up a rectangular device, almost like an old world calculator.

"You're about as melodramatic as an old world film," Helen snapped. "Enough of the histrionics. Just tell us what you have there and what you plan to do with it."

"Ah Helen, always the logical one. It is a shame you threw your lot in with the losing side. You would have made one excellent Senator." Anthony shook his head regretfully. "Nevertheless, I'll acquiesce. It is the least I can do. This little device is a family heirloom, passed down from Cecilia herself to a single descendent in each generation." Anthony looked over at Aerina. "You, daughter, were going to be its next caretaker. You see, those vials you cherished so greatly, and worked so hard to recover, were only an archaic form of the final product created by Cecilia and her team."

"What is the final product?" Marcus asked. He remained unmoving, his dark eyes never leaving Anthony's face. The older Senator shifted slightly as if the intense gaze were discomfiting, even with the armed Armati behind him, ready to fire.

"You all have it. Each citizen, here and in the Empire, is embedded with a Technology chip."

"The ID chip," Aerina murmured.

"Yes," Anthony nodded approvingly. "Our engineers have been creating the Technology themselves for years without realizing it. Each chip only needs to be activated, and the individual wearing it will have all the capabilities of our dear deceased Lina. Only with more power over what they send and receive. A firewall, if you will."

Jay twitched again at the mention of Lina, his features twisted in a grimace Helen found difficult to look at. His face was so like Vick's and the agony so apparent on the bold features.

"Now what?" Marcus asked. "Why act now?"

"The same reason Julius tried to have you killed, Trent. You've taken on too much power. And your control is threatening the ideals of our nation; the very basis Cecilia built Alba on. We can't have peace with a warrior running our nation, now can we?"

"Don't be foolish, Father," Aerina spoke up. "We only have peace because of people like Marcus. Peace comes as the result of war, not in spite of it. How long do you think Alba will stand against the rebuilding world once the Virmortus are gone?"

"We won't need the Virmortus, the *Reapers*," he practically spat the word, "once I retake the Consulship and complete the alliance with the World Council."

"World Council?" Helen could feel the skepticism etched on her face.

"Yes, my dear, a Council that has existed since the downfall of our society. We've remained underground, communicating only occasionally in secret. This Council, with the aid of the Technology, will be able to rebuild the global economy that existed a century earlier."

"So is this the part where, now that you've revealed your scheme, you kill us all?" Helen's heart pounded in her chest, blood rushing in her ears, making her lightheaded with fear.

"I'd prefer not to kill you all. Just Trent. And the Confederate, of course. If you pledge your public support for our new government, I will be happy to let everyone else live a long, full life."

"How convenient that everyone who would oppose your Consulship is now dead. Anyone who would uphold the law, like Senator Caius." Helen couldn't stop the rush of bitterness.

"None of this was convenient. Just necessary."

Anthony motioned to the large group behind him. "Do you think it is easy to decimate the population of Alba? Do you think I want to see my own daughter, my only remaining child, gunned down?"

"You planted the virus." Helen stared at Aerina's father, the man she'd cared for and respected her entire life, as if she didn't recognize him. Because she didn't. The monster standing before her was not the caring father and wise Senator she'd always looked up to. "I thought it strange President March didn't claim the deaths. I thought she was being political. But she really wasn't responsible. It was you."

"Unfortunately," Anthony began with a sigh, "I needed Alba weak, before we could make her strong again. When people are sick and afraid, it is very easy to sway their opinions and become the better alternative. Aerina, you were the first to be infected, although your symptoms were mild because I had you vaccinated. At the time, I was still hoping to pass my knowledge on to you. I still believed you would turn your life around."

"You son of a bitch," Aerina breathed. "Mother is *dead* because of your virus. Because of your stupid political maneuverings. You killed her!" Her voice continued to rise, thick with tears. Marcus grabbed her as she lunged forward, pulling her gently back.

Anthony took another quick step back, watching Aerina sadly. *He's genuinely sorry to be on opposing sides with her*, Helen thought in surprise. *He cares for her.*

She looked over at Marcus, wondering if he saw the same thing.

Of course he did.

"I suppose you won't need these, then." Helen set down the case of remaining poison vials she'd taken from President March's lifeless fingers.

"The Technology vials? No. They were saved only as a precaution. No one has even been in the vault room since Cecilia had it built. No one except that Neanderthal." He loved Aerina, but he obviously hated Marcus.

Aerina met Helen's gaze, and an unspoken message passed between them. Bending slowly, she picked up a vial from the case, turning it between her slender hands. The syringe gun was still tucked neatly in the case, and she loaded it slowly.

Anthony frowned at Aerina. "What are you doing? That Technology is worthless. You have something more powerful already embedded."

Aerina shook her head. "You're wrong, Father. I've removed my chip and had it destroyed. This might be my only chance to experience the Technology. Marcus wouldn't allow me to be injected, but now ... I can see what it's like. I can become powerful."

"Nonsense, dear. I can merely have a new chip created for you. We create new chips every day in the labs."

Aerina took another small step forward, still looking at the vial. "No, I don't think I ever want another chip."

"Don't be silly. That Technology is ancient compared to what we have now. Once I activate your chip, you'll see how truly amazing it is."

A tear trailed down Aerina's cheek, followed quickly by another. She lunged forward, the needle piercing her father's forearm as he instinctively blocked her.

"Hold your fire!" he called desperately, shielding Aerina's form with his own body. The Armati waiting some distance behind him shifted, looking uncertain. "I'm fine. It is just the Technology." His breath hissed. "That stings. No wonder Cecilia upgraded it."

Aerina stood before her father, tears streaming unchecked now. Helen felt her own eyes prickle, blinking quickly to clear them.

"No, Father. It isn't just the Technology. It's the poison we used to kill President March."

Anthony's eyes widened as he looked to Marcus, then to Helen, and finally back to his daughter.

"Aerina...?" He seemed disbelieving that his own daughter would inject him. They all waited tensely to see if he would order their deaths, but instead of anger, sadness and panic overtook him.

"Quickly Aerina, I need you to take this." Anthony handed Aerina the rectangular box in his hand. "It contains the code to unlock the Technology in the chips. To access the code—"

Aerina covered her father's mouth with a gentle hand. "Perhaps it is best if the secret dies with you, Father."

"No!" He began to breathe more quickly, either in panic or as the poison began its deadly journey through his body. "The Council will be expecting it. They'll destroy Alba searching for it."

"Get the code, Aerina," Marcus ordered.

"It is your DNA. It needs your Delacroix DNA," he choked, sinking slowly to his knees. Aerina crouched down with him, her arm around his shoulder. "Don't fire!" he called hoarsely to the anxious Armati hovering behind him.

"Trent must die, dear," he told Aerina. "He is too dangerous to run Alba. I've ordered the soldiers to kill him, and they will."

Aerina said nothing, just crying silent tears.

Helen looked away from the heart-breaking scene, her stomach twisting with the sounds of retching coming from behind her. It wouldn't be long now.

Jay, she noticed, had distanced himself from their group. He'd done it slowly, but was now nearly ten feet away from Marcus.

The sun was about to dip below the horizon, long shadows stretching across the field from the Capitol. As she watched the Armati shift uncomfortably, distracted by Aerina and Senator Delacroix, Jay was suddenly moving forward, pulling an object from his shirt and launching it towards the group of Armati.

At the same time, Marcus dove towards Aerina where

she crouched with her father, covering her with his bulk.

"Duck, Helen!" he roared a moment before a fiery blast shook the field.

Instinctively Helen collapsed into a ball on the ground, shielding her face and stomach from the scorching heat that blew past her, feeling as if every hair was singed.

Screams of agony came from the soldiers as fire spread through the group, the few on the outside alighting and burning more slowly than the center of the crowd that had been killed immediately.

Helen kept her face covered after daring one look, the sight too much to keep down the bile threatening all day. The bit of lunch she'd consumed hours earlier found its way into the grass. She crawled away, keeping her back to the dangerous heat behind her.

Alba was burning. Everything seemed to be afire.

From the haze that was beginning to settle on her senses, Helen saw Marcus shouting at Aerina, pulling her away from the fire. Aerina stubbornly clung to her dying father's arm, not willing to leave him as his body slowly began shutting down from the poison.

Sluggishly she turned her head to see Jay still standing, his face red in the reflection of the blaze. His jaw was clenched, tears streaming down his face, from sorrow or the heat, she wasn't sure. For a moment, she thought he would throw himself into the blaze, but then he turned and headed towards the Training Grounds.

As chaos reigned around her, she gave up on her fight with consciousness.

*   *   *

Aerina saw Helen fall. "Help her!" she called to the men, her arms still around her dying father. Marcus paused to check Helen, his hand on her friend's neck to search for a pulse.

This is all your fault.

The old guilt rose, overwhelming her. The onslaught of

emotion was a physical weight on her shoulders, making her arms ache as she met her father's bright blue eyes, the same color as her own.

She was surprised to find, instead of the expected accusation, a gleam of respect, and perhaps love.

"I'm sorry," she choked, ignoring the madness around them.

"You made your decision, daughter. I can't fault you. I made my decision. Just remember—" He choked, his breathing becoming more labored. "Just remember that sometimes duty must come before love."

His chest heaved as he breathed but was unable to get air to his lungs, his eyes wide with panic. Suddenly Marcus was beside her, pressing his hands on her father's neck. The older man lost consciousness, his eyes going back into his head and his lids fluttering closed.

Aerina's breath shuddered in, and she clung to her father's body for another long moment.

Marcus rose, turning to head in the direction of the fiery Training Grounds.

"Aerina."

She turned to look at him, his towering figure hazy as moisture continued to pool in her eyes.

"I want you to know … I chose love over duty."

Aerina smiled through her tears.

"So did I."

Marcus returned to drop a hard kiss on her forehead before sprinting after Jay.

The Training Grounds lit up the darkening evening. The fire burned strong, but the blaze wasn't as ferocious now as it had been initially. The anti-fire system was slowly bringing it under control.

Marcus and Jay alighted from the e-car they'd commandeered from the University, moving towards the crowd gathered to help.

Nemo approached them quickly.

"How did so many people escape the fire?" Marcus asked, his eyes on Jay as the other man went searching the survivors for Lina.

"We had warning. Someone hit the evac alarm; they must have found a bomb."

Marcus still watched Jay. The Confederate's long legs took him through the lot quickly. No sign of Lina.

Then Jay turned towards the entrance of the burning structure; towards the heart of the inferno.

His first instinct was to let the other man take his chances. Then he considered if Lina *had* survived, which was likely considering how many people made it out, he'd never be allowed a moment of peace if he let the dumbass Confederate die in the fire.

"Goddammit." He took off after Jay, tackling the equally large man uncomfortably close to the heat of the blaze. He barely felt the burn of gravel through his black suit, using Jay as a cushion to avoid the worst of the impact.

Jay hit the ground hard but didn't hesitate, turning on him, the madness of grief giving him added strength. Only Marcus' lifetime of training and quick reflexes saved him from a blow to the throat. He took the sharp jab to his collarbone instead. Ignoring the pain, he retaliated with a blow to Jay's head meant to disorient. Jay managed to duck, taking the hit to his forehead instead. Marcus felt something give in his knuckle as he dodged another hit.

The battle was fierce but brief. Marcus sensed the moment the fight left Jay. His opponent lay on the rocky ground, pressing the palms of his hands hard against his eyes, letting out a strangled cry.

Marcus sat in the dust beside the grieving man, the flames reddening their faces eerily, and had the uncomfortable urge to offer comfort.

"Quit blubbering. Have you sent someone to her house to see if she's there?"

Jay looked over from where he also sat in the gravel, his eyes bloodshot, expression haggard.

"I've called her at least a hundred times. I told her to stay in the Grounds because I'd thought she'd be safest. I assumed the target would be the Capitol, maybe the labs..." He again pressed his hands against his head, clenched in fists, working to regain his control. "I never should have left her. I should have—"

The muted chiming of a Com device filtered through the crackles of the flames and shouts of the firefighters.

Jay dove for the device that had flung from his pocket during their brief struggle.

Lina's concerned face appeared. Marcus stood, glancing away to give the flustered man some privacy.

"Where the hell are you?!"

"Me? I'm home. I took some melatonin to help me sleep. The emergency alert sirens woke me and I saw the fire at the Capitol. Where are *you*? Are you alright?"

"Don't leave. Don't move. Stay where you are. I'll be right there." Jay disconnected, turning towards Marcus.

"I'm just going to—"

"Get out of here," Marcus told him. Jay was already sprinting towards the e-car as Marcus turned back to look for Ramus.

Once the blaze was out, he dreaded what came next. Accounting for the missing.

Time passed quickly as he worked beside Virmortus and Patricians to control the blaze and get medical attention to the injured.

Aerina and the Senator of Health were working to calm the people, broadcasting positive updates every half hour. Marcus was thankful he could focus on search and recovery, rather than the headache of politics.

The fire had abated enough that he, along with a few others, could suit up and enter the Grounds with oxygen masks to continue the grim search for bodies.

A heavy metal beam covered the hallway to his office, and he heaved, grunting with effort. Suddenly, a second pair of hands gripped the heated beam, lifting with him. It moved with a protesting screech. Marcus glanced to the side, looking again when he recognized the bearded face behind the mask.

"Vick? What the hell are you doing here?"

He could see the other man grin through the mask. "I heard you were having a bonfire. I didn't want to miss the marshmallow roast."

Marcus shook his head, his mouth quirking. Only Vick could make a joke at a time like this.

The two men were silent after that, only communicating to remove debris and call for help in removing a body as they made their way through the devastation that was the Training Grounds.

A few survivors remained, sealed inside fire-doors built for that very purpose.

The bunkhouse was destroyed, as most of the bombs had been planted there. The lower garage, Tech Room, and Marcus' office had also seen considerable damage. But the more secure areas, like the interrogation rooms and holding cells, as well as the labs, were all safe.

Vick entered Marcus' blackened office, standing beside him to look on the melted, warped screen that used to be the Network Grid, tracking the citizens of the city through their ID chips.

The chips that supposedly contained a newer version of Alba's secret Technology.

Not so secret anymore, Marcus thought ruefully. It seemed the world knew more about it than he.

But he was going to change all that.

"We've cleared the entire Grounds, Marcus, and the sun is coming up. Aerina's been bugging me to send you home."

Marcus looked over at his friend; the man he'd attempted to kill nearly a decade ago but spared on an unusual whim. He never would have thought the Confederate-turned-outpost mayor would become one of the few men in the world he trusted.

"I just need to debrief with Ramus, then I'll head home for some rest."

Vick nodded. "I'm going to check in with a friend before I head out. I'll see you before I leave."

Marcus raised one brow. "You're just going to leave her again?"

Vick slid his mask up, wiping sweat off his forehead with a filthy hand, leaving a streak of dirt. "She belongs here. And I don't. It's as simple as that."

"Sometimes you need to choose love over responsibility."

Vick's jaw dropped as Marcus turned away to look for Ramus. He'd helped his friend as much as he could. If the man was too much of an idiot to hold onto what he wanted as much as he obviously wanted Helen, there was nothing more Marcus could do for him.

Chapter 23

Vick stood before Helen's house. Now that he was here, he felt oddly hesitant to enter. He was filthy, exhausted, and not in the best of moods after dealing with uncovering the dead all night after traveling four hours to be here.

On his drive back to Vicksburg, he couldn't shake the feeling that he had unfinished business in Alba. Turning towards the city, he'd seen the night ablaze before he'd even reached the gates. Terror had filled him, intensifying when he couldn't reach anyone on their holoreaders.

Finally, Aerina had answered, filling him in on what had happened, assuring him that everyone, including Helen, was fine. She'd also cleared him at the gate, allowing him to enter the city.

He'd wanted to check on Helen first, but Aerina had told him she was with her friend, who had collapsed from exhaustion after the Capitol explosion. He'd gone to help Marcus, instead.

But he couldn't stay away any longer. His conscience told him to just leave; to not bother Helen any longer. She deserved to have her life return to normal; to find her place among her peers. With an outsider like him hanging around, she'd never have the respect she deserved.

Yet he couldn't leave without seeing her, at least once, just to be sure she was alright.

Before he could talk himself out of it, he took the front steps in one leap, banging on the door.

A long moment passed, and then the door opened, revealing her delicate features pulled into a perplexed frown. She had obviously still been sleeping, clothed only in a long, white T-shirt.

His.

The sight hit him like a blow in the chest, part tenderness and part pure desire.

Her expression had changed to one of shock, and then she was pulling him in.

"Are you hurt?" she asked, looking over his filthy, blackened form.

"No, just dirty." He stood in the foyer that had been his home for the last month, feeling out-of-place for the first time.

"Are you ... ok? Aerina told me you blacked out last night."

Helen was already waving away his concern. "I'm fine. Just hadn't eaten anything all day and it caught up with me. That and the shock of finding Senator Delacroix had infected everyone intentionally to wrest power of Alba from Marcus..." She shook her head, obviously still in disbelief.

Silence stretched between them as Vick studied her familiar features, a vise gripping his heart as he searched for something to say. Her face was still overly-thin from her illness, stretching taut over her high cheek bones and gently curved jaw. Her dark brows contrasted with her pale hair and skin, which had taken on a little more color since her illness passed.

Desire still throbbed hotly as he stared at her standing only in his T-shirt, and he clenched his hands into fists to avoid reaching for her.

"I just wanted to check on you. I should probably go," he said, but neither moved.

"You can get cleaned up here, if you'd like. I'm sure I can dig up a T-shirt and jeans," she offered.

Vick hesitated. If he stayed, he wasn't sure if he would be able to leave...

"Never mind. I'm sure you have a lot to do—" she began quickly as if embarrassed to have made the offer.

"No," he interrupted. "That sounds perfect."

"You know the way." She motioned towards the bath,

and he finally uprooted himself enough to head down the hall.

Helen watched him go, her own emotions in turmoil. Seeing his familiar face at the door had caused those erratic butterflies to re-emerge for another wild fling in her stomach. She felt almost breathless, like some pitiful pre-teen getting a glimpse of their first crush.

In her room, she gathered up the few items of clothing he'd left behind only a few days earlier, bringing them to her face to breathe in the unique masculine scent that was Vick. It seemed an eternity since they'd spent those quiet evenings together in her home, working as a team to get through the chaos of the world outside.

They'd made a good team, Vick with his endless optimism and her calm pragmatism. But that didn't mean he wanted something more.

You'll never know if you don't ask, her inner voice taunted.

Setting the clothes on the hall chair, she listened to the sound of the shower running, turning to the kitchen to make tea. Anything to take her mind off the naked man in her villa.

The muted sound of running water stopped, and her straining ears caught the faint rustling as she imagined him drying off.

The door to the bath opened, and he caught her staring. She couldn't look away. The towel wrapped around his waist revealed a tan, broad chest marked with scars and his latest trophy, the bullet wound from the Texican warlord. Light hair tapered down his navel, disappearing below the edge of the towel that seemed to hang on his lean hips, waiting for him to move to drop to the floor.

Her breathing was coming quickly and the heat in her cheeks matched the throbbing warmth growing at her core.

Neither of them moved. His hair was slicked back, stopping just at the base of his neck, and droplets of water glistened in his short beard. His hazel eyes gleamed nearly jade, and she knew his own desire matched hers.

She was out of her chair and walking towards him before she'd even made the conscious decision to do it. He met her halfway, not wasting a moment to claim her mouth with his.

Their tongues met in the oldest of dances, his hands reaching down to grab the hem of his t-shirt that hung nearly to her knees, breaking contact with her mouth for a moment to haul it over her head.

Then he was again marauding the softness of her lips, his callused hands running over her skin, from her shoulders to her hips, then gripping her bottom tightly, their forms melded together.

His towel hadn't survived the assault from her own hands, falling forgotten to the floor.

"We're not doing this against the fucking wall again," he muttered, scooping her up and carrying her into her bedroom.

Setting her gently on the bed, he pulled her to the edge, kissing the inside of her pale thighs.

Her hands fluttered nervously around his damp head. "Vick, I've never... I don't..."

His tawny head raised, his eyebrows up. "No one has ever—"

"I've never allowed anyone," she interrupted him quickly, a strange shyness mingling with the raging desire.

"Well sweetheart, allow me." His head lowered, and before she could decide if she was going to pull him in or push him away, his mouth was on the tiny nub that ached for his touch, making the decision for her.

She gasped, her back arching at the feeling of his hot tongue caressing her clit. He kissed her gently, his lips moving slowly across her sex. She raised her hips to increase the pressure, needing more.

Her hands ran through his hair at the delicious torture, trying to pull him even closer. He laughed softly before giving in to her unspoken demands, pressing his mouth harder against her, gently inserting a finger inside, caressing both simultaneously.

"Vick, please, please..." she begged, not certain what she was begging for. He increased the speed, and the pressure inside continued to build until pleasure burst in a cascade, inundating her entire body with the aftershocks of the orgasm that shook her. As Vick drank the last of the tremors, he made his way slowly up her body, kissing a slow path until he reached her mouth.

His mouth settled on hers at the same time she felt his erection pressing against her, easily entering her primed heat. She felt her inner muscles stretching to accommodate him, the ache of desire intensifying as he began to move slowly at first and then increasingly faster. His squared jaw was clenched as he fought for control, the muscles in his arms bunched as he leaned forward on the bed, holding his weight off her.

She wrapped her legs around his waist, trying to pull him deeper, arching to meet each thrust. She'd thought nothing could match the orgasm from moments earlier, but the tension was again growing, and she pulled him closer, gripping his forearms and unknowingly leaving crescents from her nails.

He bent forward, his damp hair brushing her chest as the heat of his mouth surrounded her overly-sensitive breast. She heard small gasps of pleasure, which she realized distantly were her own. A siren could have gone off in her room— Nothing mattered but finding the ultimate release that was so close...

His teeth gently scraped her nipple and then he tugged, the sensation pushing her over the edge.

She cried out, gripping his hair, as her muscles tightened rhythmically around him with her release. His own eyes closed and he threw his head back, letting out a guttural cry with his own climax, her entire body shaking with the force of his thrusts.

As the aftershocks faded, an intense languidness overcame her. Vick scooped up her boneless body, rolling onto the bed with her atop him. She rested her head on his hard chest, the light whirls of hair tickling her nose. Her arm brushed a damp bandage, and she gasped.

"Your injury. I'm sorry, I forgot—"

"So did I. It's fine."

He stroked her hair back, his blunt fingers moving gently over her brows, down her cheeks, and over her parted lips.

His gaze was intent as it moved over her features, as if memorizing her. She opened her mouth to ask what he was looking for, but he touched his hand to her lips.

"Shh. Rest. We'll talk later."

Helen nodded, laying her head back on his chest, the gentle ministrations of his hands on her back lulling her into a dreamless slumber, feeling secure for the first time in days.

*   *   *

The bright light of early evening shone directly on Helen's face as she awoke from a deep sleep. Memories of that morning rushed back, and she turned to Vick with a smile.

The other pillow was empty. Only the indentation from his tawny head told her that morning had been more than just a dream.

Angrily scrubbing away the prickle of tears from her eyes, Helen sat up, scanning the room to be sure of what she already knew.

He had been here, but now he was gone.

Forcing herself out of bed, she walked mindlessly down the hall to the kitchen. As she reached for a mug to make tea, she saw the picture propped against the cupboard.

It was a photo of a young woman with dark hair and eyes, smiling with obvious affection at the person taking the photo.

Turning the picture over, she read the simple words on the back. *Thanks for giving me joy.*

Her eyes flooded with tears as she remembered their conversation weeks earlier. *I hope someday you can look on your relationship with Nina with joy instead of regret,* she'd told him.

She looked back at the photo again, blurry through her

tears.

"Your chance was stolen from you. I won't throw away my own chance at love out of foolish fear." She gently tucked the picture back into the glass panes of the cupboard where she could see it.

Renewed energy flowed through her as she made tea. She finally knew what she wanted again. And it felt good to have purpose.

Thanks for giving me joy.

Chapter 24

"Never give up; never quit fighting. Death is the only surrender." -Virmortus Training Manual

Sunlight streamed down, heating up the early morning. Vick studied the manual on his holoreader again before diving back into the broken Energy Tower that had stopped producing electricity at about 3 A.M. that morning.

"I thought these new ones were supposed to be better," he muttered to himself, inspecting the coils again for any sign of the problem.

The month that had passed since his return to Vicksburg had been long and admittedly boring. No angry mobs to face, no quarantine plans to enforce. No burned out buildings to search through.

No Helen.

He thought about her often. Too often. He wondered if she was eating right, how big her bump was growing, and worried that she was probably over-working herself creating the vaccine and helping restore the Capitol.

He hoped she was happy. Happier than he was.

Maybe if you hadn't been such a damn coward, she'd be here now.

He shook his head at the thought. He couldn't ask her to leave Alba. It had always been her home. It was her future, and the future of her baby.

He'd thought it best if they each returned to their own homes, but Vicksburg had seemed empty without her. His large stone house on the hill was lonely. He missed their evening conversation; the tea she brewed him with a shot of whiskey. Her lemony scent invaded his dreams.

He'd decided to see her; to see if they could have a chance. Today had been the big day.

Then the Energy Tower broke.

He was the town's handyman, and so he'd headed over to the town hall that housed the unit to repair it. And now, several hours later, he was still stuck inside the unit, unable to determine the problem. He'd traded his standard t-shirt and jeans for a suit he'd dug out of his closet. The coat had been discarded, his sleeves rolled up, and grease stains streaked its once-crisp white shirt.

"Probably gave me a goddamn defective one," he muttered again, tightening a few of the loose bolts on the outside of the unit. He could bring it back to Alba with him, but that meant his people would be without power for a few days.

They won't be my people for much longer, he reminded himself. But giving up on Helen was harder to swallow than leaving his town behind.

He had to at least give it one last shot. If she turned him down, he wouldn't have to lay awake at night wondering.

Qui asi sea.

Fuck that. His father's phrase didn't fix anything. Maybe if his father hadn't been so accepting of his lot in life, things wouldn't have turned out so messed up.

He wasn't going to give up so easily. Even if she turned him down, they had something between them worth a little time and effort. If necessary, he'd move to Alba and become part of her life slowly; convince her to give him—them—a chance.

His holoreader began insistently dinging, interrupting his thoughts. It was the warning from the sentry on duty that a vehicle was approaching.

"Now what?" He dropped his tools, closing the unit to keep kids from playing with the potentially dangerous contents, and turned towards the north tower.

News from Alba? He sprinted towards the guard post, quickly ascending the wooden ladder.

"Hey Vick," the young man said in excitement. "A

vehicle is approaching from the north. I think it's from Alba."

Vick adjusted the zoom on his Alba sunglasses using the ocular controls. The vehicle was definitely Alban, and he was fairly certain he knew the driver.

Jay.

He groaned. "Just what I need; a family reunion. Did that bastard get kicked out of Alba already?"

"What did you say?" the kid manning the tower asked in confusion.

"Nothing," Vick responded, slapping his shoulder. "You did great, Liam. And you are correct, it is an Alban visitor. Let 'em in. I'll meet them at the main house."

"Yes, sir!" Liam responded. It was his first week manning the walls himself, and admitting a visitor would be the highlight.

Besides the single visit from Rey — excuse him, Jefe — they had few visitors here recently. The presence of Jefe's small army camped twenty miles out kept any travelers and vagrants at bay. Chelsea hadn't been with Jefe when he visited, but the warlord had assured Vick that his sister was happy and healthy. *At least the second; I'm working on the first,* he'd said.

Vick walked back to the main house to await his brother's arrival. He could find out more details than the brief messages from Marcus about the disease.

And he could ask about Helen.

He felt a quick stab of fear. Was Jay coming to tell him something was wrong? Perhaps her baby —

Calm down, you idiot. Marcus would have sent you a message. He knows you wanted to stay updated.

The new Com Towers and extended range holoreaders made is much easier to keep in touch with Alba. Less than a year ago, the only way to get a message to and from Alba was the old-fashioned way — through a messenger.

Now, he could send and receive messages, although the connection was too sporadic to hold an actual call.

A few minutes later, he saw the large Alban all-terrain vehicle rolling up the dirt drive towards his house. Vick remained perched on the top of the stone steps until the truck rolled to a stop.

Unlike the open all-terrain vehicle Marcus normally took, this one was completely enclosed, nicknamed a tank for its armored coating and built-in EMW.

Jay hopped down, going around to open the passenger door for Lina, who climbed down more carefully.

"What brings you here?" Vick asked, walking forward to shake his brother's hand and give Lina an engulfing hug.

Jay pointed his thumb at the tank behind him. "Got the first of Jefe's payment. Energy Towers."

"I might need to take a look at one of those before you head out. I assume this was just a courtesy visit?"

"We stopped here to drop someone off," Lina spoke up, exchanging glances with Jay.

Vick narrowed his eyes. What was this?

Before he could form a question, the back door to the tank opened, and Jay stepped back to help another person down.

Helen descended slowly from the tank, her knees feeling weak, her heart racing. She gripped Jay's hand, afraid her legs would give out and she'd collapse to the ground in a heap.

What if he was unhappy to see her? What if he really wasn't interested in anything beyond a passing friendship?

Fight for what you want.

Stepping to the ground, she unconsciously straightened her ribbed blouse that was designed to fit around her enlarged abdomen.

Vick's eyes went over her slowly, and she imagined what he saw: her coiffed hair loosened, the tendrils dangling around her face and neck; her cheeks flushed with nerves and the heat, the breasts she'd never really known she'd had doubled in size, and the even larger mound of her stomach where her child lay.

She couldn't read his thoughts; his hazel eyes were devoid of emotion.

"You cut your hair!" she blurted out in surprise. He looked younger, his tawny hair cropped, his beard gone. The clean lines of his face were revealed, along with the thick scar running along his jawline. He looked so much like Jay, they could have passed for twins.

Vick grinned, the expression not quite reaching his eyes, as his hand went up to stroke the missing beard.

"Yeah, just yesterday, actually. Still haven't gotten used to it."

"Why?" Helen felt as if there had to be some significance. He'd worn his scruff with such pride. Why was he trying to change now?

Vick's eyes slid to Jay and Lina. Jay held up his hands. "We'll head inside and help ourselves to some refreshments. Come on, *bella diosa*, I know Vick has some fine wine hidden in that old wine cellar."

Helen heard Lina complaining about the endearment as the two disappeared inside, but her eyes remained on Vick's smooth-shaven jaw. She was afraid to meet his eyes; afraid of what answers she might find there.

"Walk with me?"

Helen nodded, falling into step beside him. They walked around the house, and down the hillside towards the old grape fields where untended vines still climbed into towering trees and leafy shrubs.

After a few stumbles, Vick slid her arm through his as they walked.

Finally he stopped, turning to face her. "Helen, I'm thinking of moving to Alba."

Helen was shocked, her mind trying to work out how best to deliver her own announcement. He watched her as if waiting for her response.

"I don't think that is a good idea," she finally said, not

able to imagine Vick enjoying life as an Alban resident. Not even after the changes Marcus was going to be making. She knew her response must have been wrong, because Vick's face became shuttered for a moment before the gleam came to his eyes, and a wide grin slid across his newly-shaven face.

"Yeah, well, I need a change. I think Alba would be a good change in pace for me."

"Cutting off all your hair wasn't enough of a change?" she asked dryly.

He pushed on as if she hadn't spoken. "The responsibility of running Alba was good for me; forced me to be a better man. I liked it. I—"

Helen snorted delicately at that. "You hated the responsibility. You were counting the days until you could escape back to Vicksburg."

Vick was becoming more agitated. He dropped her hand, running his hands through his non-existent hair before letting them fall to his sides in frustration.

"I could learn to like it. It—"

"You'd never like it; not even if you had a lifetime to learn it."

"Goddamnit, Helen, is that what you really think of me? Some lazy, irresponsible outsider who'll never amount to anything?" Vick spun away, pacing a few steps away before turning back, his face tight with anger.

Helen held back a smile. This was the real Vick she'd been looking for. Taking a step forward, she placed her hands on his jawline, the stubble already beginning to regrow.

"I think you are a man who takes on whatever responsibilities are necessary, whether he likes it or not. A man who cares about the people around him, even when he feels like an outsider. A man who is careful about commitments, because his word is worth his life. A man I respect, and the man I fell in love with. The man who gave me joy."

Vick was silent, and Helen was surprised to see his eyes

become watery. He blinked quickly, muttering something about the dust. He looked away, rubbing the back of his hand over his eyes quickly before turning to face her again.

"Say that again."

"I respect you."

"Dammit, Helen—"

"Alright, you big softie, I love you, although I reserve the right to blame this all on pregnancy emotions." Helen laughed as Vick stepped close, fitting himself around her swollen form, lowering his forehead until it touched hers.

"Damn but I love you. I haven't been able to think straight for wanting you; I can't sleep without you in the same house, not knowing if you're safe, if you're eating right... That's why I want to come to Alba. I need to be close to you."

Helen felt tears of her own pricking behind her eyes. Emotions were such a waste of time ... but these emotions ... they felt good.

Euphoria spread as she kissed him gently. "I don't want you to come to Alba."

"Why the hell not?"

"You'd be miserable, and I would be miserable. I was coming here to inform you that I've decided to move in. Here."

Vick's eyebrows raised. "I like a woman who knows what she wants. But what will you do here? You'll be mindless with boredom in a week."

"I hear Vicksburg could use a Medella."

A smile spread across Vick's face. "We sure can. There are a few portions of my anatomy that could use a little of your close attention."

Helen smiled in return, shaking her head. Still the same Vick she'd fallen in love with.

It felt good to admit.

She loved him, whatever that word meant. What she had with Vick was trust, reliability, respect, and some crazy mixture of passion and laughter.

Whatever it was, she wanted it. She wanted it for her, and she wanted it for her baby. She didn't care where she had to move to find it.

And, if she were honest, she was looking forward to the challenge of starting a clinic here in Vicksburg. Perhaps she could travel and help other outposts set up their own clinics; begin training some youths in healing and medicine.

"Stop plotting and kiss me," Vick commanded as his mouth closed over hers. All thoughts vanished beneath the onslaught of passion, his hands moving with gentle desperation beneath her clothing, her own hands less gentle in their attempt to touch the hard planes and grooves beneath his t-shirt.

"I love your pregnant body; so perfectly rounded." His hand found her enlarged breast, pinching the nipple gently. Helen laughed softly as he pulled her carefully down into his lap on the soft grass in the overgrown vineyard, his back against a large tree.

"I'm glad one of us does," she said as she awkwardly tried to position herself. With a quick movement, he effortlessly flipped her around so her back was against his hard chest, her legs sprawled on either side of his muscular thighs.

His hands smoothed down her ripe body, finding the center of her heat, messaging her with gentle strokes.

Her head fell back against his chest. "Vick..." she sighed, love and desire mingling to create a heady drug, intoxicating her.

As Vick continued to work magic with his hands and mouth, a ray of sun streamed down through the trees above. It felt as if heaven itself were giving its approval.

She was right where she belonged.

Epilogue

"When history writes our story, I hope they know it isn't a love story. But it *is* a story about love." – Vicktor March

"Can I carry her out?"

Helen looked over her shoulder at Lina and laughed.

"Of course, but I need to change her first. This little lady did something in her pants very unladylike."

Lina wrinkled her nose as she got a whiff of what Helen referred to. A few minutes later, Baby Stephanie was changed and ready to greet their guests properly.

Helen watched as Lina carefully took Stephanie in her arms, her heart bursting with love so big, it was almost painful. The protective emotion that had begun to blossom when Stephanie was still growing in her womb was now in full bloom, eclipsing everything else in Helen's life.

The friends had gathered at Vick and Helen's house in Vicksburg to celebrate Alba's biggest holiday, Peace Day.

The odd group of friends—Jay, Lina, Marcus, Aerina, Vick, Helen, and Baby Stephanie—all gathered around the large wooden dining table for the feast Helen had prepared. Without a Dispensare, she was proud to boast to everyone.

Vick stood, raising a glass. "I guess I'll make a little speech. Just seems appropriate." He ignored Marcus' quirked brow and Jay's scoffing laugh. "I used to think family was about being dysfunctional. Now I know it is." The group laughed, Aerina rolling her eyes. Vick's expression grew unusually serious. "But I also know it is about love. Love isn't happily-ever-after. It's dealing with shit together. It's knowing someone's got your back. It's trust. It's remembering." Vick looked over at Helen, holding Baby Stephanie in her arms. Her eyes misted and she blinked quickly, taking his hand.

"To love. Not some sappy ideal, but the in-the-trenches, not-giving-up kind. When history writes our story, I hope they know it isn't a love story. But it *is* a story about love. To us. To family."

He raised his glass, and the others followed suit, toasting to one another. Silence lingered around the table but for the baby's babbling.

"That was beautiful," Lina finally said, wiping at the copious amount of tears streaming down her face. Several sighs were followed by tissues being passed her way.

"I guess I wasn't the only March born with a smooth tongue," Jay teased. Aerina slapped his arm, beating Lina to it.

"We've got an announcement," Aerina said.

"You're pregnant?!" Helen asked in excitement.

"Um, no," Aerina answered, warily eyeing the baby who was beginning to fuss. "We're not quite ready for that. But we did submit marriage papers. We are now officially Mr. and Mrs. Trent."

A round of congratulations, hugs, and back-slapping ensued, which Marcus accepted with his normal lack of expression.

Stephanie began to fuss, and Helen rose to feed her.

"I'll help you," Vick said, quickly standing to pull her chair back. Helen sighed as she walked towards the nursery, Vick on her heels. To say he was an overprotective father was a bit of understatement. He was so excited to be part of everything, Helen didn't have the heart to tell him that his hovering was driving her mad.

"What are you going to do, hold the nipple for her?" she asked wryly as she settled into the rocking chair Vick had made.

"I wouldn't turn that down if you're offering."

Helen laughed in spite of herself.

"Go take care of our guests. Let her nurse in peace."

Vick bent down to kiss the soft blonde hair sticking out from his daughter's head. He stole a gentle kiss at the top of her mother's breast, earning him a light whack.

"Alright, I'm going." But still he paused, watching the scene. Helen shook her head, smiling slightly. He might not be Stephanie's biological father, but he was the best father a child could ask for.

And the best husband. The past eight months had been the best of her life. How such wonder had come from such sorrow amazed her every day. She was determined not to take any of their time for granted.

"I love you," she said, including both Vick and the baby in the statement.

"I love you, too," he returned, bending to kiss her lips.

As the day faded to night, the strange mix of friends and family found in one another what all of mankind searches for: A place to belong.

Did you enjoy the Secret of Alba series? Don't forget to leave a review! Indie authors like me depend on reviews to spread the word about our books. Thanks!

Like exclusives deals and news?

You can join my mailing list to find out first about promotions and new releases.
http://www.lindseywinsemius.com/

Don't want this series to end?

Tell me what story you'd like to read next! Check out my Reader Exclusives!
http://www.lindseywinsemius.com/reader-exclusives

Find out what I'm working on now!

Get an exclusive glimpse of my upcoming Contemporary Romantic Suspense *Just to Keep You*.
http://www.lindseywinsemius.com/just-to-keep-you